The Joke

Milan Kundera

THE JOKE

TRANSLATED BY DAVID HAMBLYN
AND OLIVER STALLYBRASS

Coward-McCann, Inc.
New York

The Joke

I
Ludvik

$\mathcal{H}$ERE I was—back in my hometown after all these years. Quite indifferently, I stood in the familiar main square—flat and ugly beyond redemption from its military past as a bastion against Magyars and Turks—mentally comparing it to a huge parade ground, and the guildhall spire above the rooftops to a soldier in some antique helmet.

Why had I come? Certainly not from sentiment. I hadn't lived here for fifteen years, I had very few remaining friends or acquaintances (and prefer to ignore even these), and my mother is buried among strangers, in a grave I do not tend. I suddenly realized that I was *not* indifferent, that I positively hated the south Moravian town in which I had grown up; and that this hatred had been the irresistible reason for my choosing it, when the chance arose, for the prosaic and cynical mission that I could perfectly well have fulfilled in Prague.

I gave the unlovely square a final scornful glance and turned my back on it, walking down the street to the hotel where I had booked a room for the night. The room proved unprepossessing: a bed up against the wall, in the middle a small table with one chair, by the bed an ostentatious mahogany bedside table with a mirror, and a tiny cracked washbasin by the door. I put my briefcase down on the table and opened the window. It looked out over a yard onto some houses displaying their bare grubby backs to the hotel. I closed the window, drew the curtains, and went over to the washbasin with its two taps marked with red and blue. I tried them and cold water trickled from both. I looked at the table. It was just about adequate, and a bottle with two glasses would have gone quite well on it, but there was only one chair in the room. I drew the table up to the bed and tried to sit at it, but the table was too high and the bed too low. The latter, moreover, apart from making a rotten chair, sank so much under me that its performance as a bed at once became equally suspect. I leaned my fists on it; then I lay down on it, carefully raising my feet in the air so that my boots wouldn't dirty the coverlet and quilt. The bed sagged so much that I lay as if in a hammock or a narrow grave. It was impossible to imagine anyone else lying in that bed with me.

I sat down on the chair, stared at the threadbare curtains, and began to think. Then steps and voices sounded in the passage. It was a man and a woman, whose every word I heard. They were talking about some Peter who'd run away from home and Aunt Clara who was a fool and had spoiled the boy. Then a door opened, and the conversation continued in the room next door. I could hear the woman sighing (yes, one could even hear her sighing!) and the man resolving to give Clara a good talking-to.

I made my decision. I stood up, washed my hands again in the washbasin, wiped them on the towel, and walked out of the hotel, without even knowing where I was heading. All I knew was that unless I wanted this unsuitable hotel room to jeopardize the entire object of my long and laborious journey, then I must, however repugnant the idea, find someone here to whom I could go with a confidential request. I passed in rapid review all the faces I remembered from my youth, rejecting each in turn through my aversion for the business—which the nature of my request would necessitate—of attempting to bridge the long years of separation. Then I recalled that there was probably one man living here, a newcomer for whom I had once been instrumental in finding a position, who would, if I

knew him at all, be only too glad to repay one favor with another. He was an eccentric, scrupulously moral yet strangely
unsettled and feckless, whose wife, as far as I knew, had di-
vorced him years ago because of his living anywhere and everywhere except with her and their son. Then with a shock I
wondered whether he might have remarried, for that would
have complicated my request, and I hurried on toward the hospital.

The local hospital is a complex of buildings and pavilions
straggling over a large expanse of garden. I entered an un-
sightly shed by the gates and asked the porter to connect me
with the virology department. He pushed the telephone over
to my side of the table and said, "O-two." I dialed O2 and
learned that Dr. Kostka had left only a few seconds before and
was on his way to the exit. I sat down on a bench by the gates
and in a few minutes I saw him. He was walking along deep in
thought, tall and thin, ugly in an agreeable sort of way, and
quite unmistakable. I got up and walked right up to him, as if
wishing to collide; he looked at me in annoyance, then suddenly recognized me and thrust out his hand.

I explained that I'd arrived less than an hour before on some
unimportant business which would keep me here for two days,
and he expressed gratified surprise that my first move had been
to come and see him. I suddenly felt guilty at not having done
so for his own sake and because the question I was now asking
him (I boldly inquired whether he had married again) was
inspired by calculation, not by genuine interest. He told me,
to my satisfaction, that he was still by himself and regretted
that he had only an hour now before returning to the hospital
and in the evening he had to make a bus journey out of town.
"Don't you live here?" I asked in dismay. He assured me that
he did and that he had a studio apartment in a new block but
that " a man doesn't feel right on his own." It turned out that
Kostka had a fiancée in another town twelve miles away, a
schoolteacher with a two-room apartment of her own. "Will
you be moving in with her eventually?" I asked. He said it

would be hard to find a position in the other town as interest-ing as the one I had helped him get, and his fiancée would have difficulty finding a job here. I began, quite sincerely, to curse the ineptness of our bureaucracy, which cannot even help a man and woman to live together. "Calm down, Ludvik," he said indulgently. "It's not quite as intolerable as all that. The trip does cost me a little money and time, but my solitude remains untouched, and I remain free."

"Why do you need freedom so much?" I asked him.

"Why do *you?*" he countered.

"I'm a lady's man," I replied.

"I don't need freedom for women, I want it for myself," he said, and went on, "I'll tell you what—come over to my place for a while until I have to leave." I could have wished for noth-ing better.

We left the hospital and soon came to a new housing pro-ject, its blocks slanting disharmoniously upward one after an-other from an unleveled dusty terrain (without lawns or path-ways or a road) on the town's edge. The elevator was out of or-der, so we climbed the narrow stairway to the third floor. As we crossed the vestibule of Kostka's room I felt highly satisfied. In the corner stood a wide comfortable day-bed covered with a red patterned blanket; besides the daybed his room had a table, easy chair, large bookcase, phonograph, and radio.

"Looking at this attractive studio of yours makes me won-der," I said, "what you're doing tomorrow afternoon and eve-ning."

"Unfortunately," he apologized, "I have to work late to-morrow and won't be back till around seven. Have you got a free evening?"

"I may well have the evening free," I replied, "but I won-der if you could lend me your place just for the afternoon?"

My question surprised him, but he replied at once, as if eager to show his willingness to help, "I'd be very glad to share it with you." And he went on, as if deliberately not trying to guess my purpose, "If you have trouble finding accommodation you can always sleep here tonight. I won't be back till tomorrow morning, and even then I'll be going straight to the hospital."

"No, there's really no need. I've booked at the hotel. The thing is, the hotel room's not very nice, and tomorrow afternoon I need some pleasant surroundings. Not just for myself, you understand."

"Of course," said Kostka, with an air of conspiracy. "That's what I guessed." After a while he added, "I'm glad to have the chance of doing you a favor. That is, if it really is a favor."

Kostka made coffee, and we sat and talked for a while. I tried the daybed and discovered with delight that it didn't sag or even creak. Then Kostka announced that he must be getting back to the hospital, and gave me a quick initiation into some of the mysteries of the household: the bath faucets had to be tightened well, hot water in defiance of all conventions flowed from the tap marked C, the socket for the radio was hidden under the daybed, and there was an almost full bottle of vodka in the cupboard. Then he gave me a ring with two keys and showed me which was for the outside door and which for his studio. During a lifetime of sleeping on various beds and sitting at various tables I've developed a special cult of keys, and I slipped Kostka's into my pocket with quiet glee.

As we left, Kostka hoped his place would bring me luck.

"Yes," I said, "it will help me do a splendid demolition job."

"What's splendid about demolishing things?" he asked, and I laughed inwardly, recognizing in this question the Kostka I had first met fifteen years ago. I liked him, but at the same time he amused me, and I replied, "I know you're a quiet toiler on God's eternal building site and don't like hearing about demolition, but I'm not one of God's masons. Mind you, if God's masons built real walls, I doubt if our demolitions could harm them. But instead of walls all I can see everywhere is theater curtains, and the demolition of curtains is merely justice."

We were exactly where we had parted ways last time, some nine years before. We hadn't changed, we were as different as

ever, and of course it was this very difference that endeared
Kostka to me and made me love these arguments, which gave
me the chance for another clarification of who *I* was and how *I*
thought. So as to leave me in no doubt he replied, "What you've
just said sounds fine. But tell me: if you're such a skeptic, how
can you be so sure of telling a curtain from a wall? Have you
never doubted that the illusions you ridicule *are* only illusions? What if you're wrong? What if they're real values that
you're busy demolishing? The disparaged value and the de-
bunked illusion have the same miserable substance, they resemble each other, and there's nothing easier than confusing
them."

I accompanied Kostka back through the town to the hospital,
playing with the keys in my pocket. I was happy to be with my
old friend, ready as he was at all times to attempt my conver-
sion, even now on our way across the bumpy surface of the new
project. Of course he knew that tomorrow we had the whole
evening in front of us, and after a while he turned from philo-
sophizing to more mundane matters, making sure once more
that I'd wait for him at his place until seven tomorrow (he had
only the one set of keys) and asking me if there was really
nothing else I needed. I put my hand up to my face and said
only a visit to the barber's, for I was disagreeably stubbly.
"Excellent," said Kostka. "I'll arrange for you to have a personal shave."

I accepted his patronage and let him take me to a small barbershop with three revolving chairs towering before three
mirrors, two of them occupied by men with heads bent forward and faces covered with soap. Two women in white coats
were leaning over them. Kostka approached one of them and
whispered something. The woman wiped her razor on a cloth
and called something to the back of the shop; out came a girl
in a white coat who took charge of the abandoned gentleman,
while the woman Kostka had spoken to motioned me to sit
down in the third chair. I shook hands with Kostka as he left,

and I sat down, leaning my head back on the leather headrest and letting my eyes wander over the blotchy white ceiling.

As I felt the barber's wet slippery fingers smearing soap on my face, it occurred to me what a strange and ridiculous thing it was to have some unknown woman who meant nothing to me, and to whom I meant nothing, gently caressing me. I pretended —for my mind never stops playing games even in moments of repose—that I was an unarmed victim who'd just been surrendered to the mercies of this woman, and imagined her hands lovingly holding my head, turning it and fondling it, as if they had no interest in the body apart from the head, and that the sharp razor now waiting on a nearby table would merely consummate that independence.

Then the touch ceased and I heard the woman step back; now, no doubt, she was taking the razor in her hand. I told myself that I must see how she looked, this woman holding my head, this tender assassin. I lowered my eyes from the ceiling to the mirror, and as I did so the game I was playing became uncannily real. I seemed to recognize the woman who was leaning over me in the mirror.

With one hand she held the lobe of my ear while the other was carefully scraping soap off my face. I gazed at her, and the likeness, so dreadfully certain a moment before, began slowly to dissolve and disappear. Then she leaned over the washbasin, flicked the ball of foam off the razor with two fingers, stood up, and gently turned the chair around. For an instant our eyes met, and again I knew it was she. Admittedly the face was different, rather as if it belonged to an older sister, grayed and faded, slightly sunken. But it was fifteen years since I'd seen her last. During that period, time had masked her real face, but luckily the mask had two holes through which her old eyes could look at me once more, and they were just as I remembered them.

Then the trail became confused again. A new customer came into the shop, sat down behind me, and began talking about the fine summer we were having and the swimming pool which was being built outside the town. The woman shaving me answered him. I paid more attention to her voice than to the words, which were of little significance, and I was sure that it wasn't a voice I recognized. It sounded matter-of-fact, careless, unconcerned, almost rude—the voice of a stranger.

Now she was rinsing my face, pressing her palms into it so that, in spite of the voice, I again began to believe that this was she, that after fifteen years I could once more feel her hands on my face, stroking me long and tenderly, for I had completely forgotten that she was not in fact caressing me. Meanwhile her stranger's voice was directed to the talkative customer, but I didn't want to believe the voice; I wanted to believe the hands, to recognize her by the hands. By the measure of tenderness in her touch I tried to determine whether she'd recognized me.

Then she took a towel and dried my face. The customer was laughing loudly at one of his own jokes, and I noticed that the woman wasn't laughing; she'd probably stopped listening to him. This disturbed me—it seemed to prove that she was secretly upset. I resolved to say something to her as soon as I got up from the chair. She removed the cloth from my neck. I stood up. I took some change from my pocket. I waited for our eyes to meet again so that I could call her by name (the other man was still going on about something), but she kept her head turned unconcernedly away and took the money so briskly that I felt as though I were hallucinating and could not find the courage to speak.

I left the shop strangely shaken. All I knew was that I knew nothing and that it was a sign of callousness to be uncertain of recognizing a face which I'd once loved so dearly.

Of course it was not difficult to get at the truth. I hurried to the hotel—on the way I saw my old friend Jaroslav, first fiddle in the local cymbalo, or dulcimer, band, but avoided his eyes as if fleeing from his intrusive noisy music—and telephoned Kostka. He was still at the hospital.

"That woman barber you left me with—could her name by any chance be Lucie Sebetka?"

"She goes under a different name now, but that's her, all right. How do you know her?" asked Kostka.

"It was ages ago," I replied.

I didn't even go in to dinner. I walked out of the hotel in the gathering dusk and began wandering around again.

II
Helena

*T*ONIGHT I'm going to bed early. I don't know if I'll get any sleep, but I'm going early anyway. Pavel left for Bratislava this afternoon, I'm off to Brno tomorrow by plane and the rest of the way by bus. Zdenicka will be here on her own for two days, but she won't mind that. She doesn't like our company much, or rather my company. She adores her father. Pavel is the first man in her life, and he knows how to handle her, as he always did women, as he did me—and still does. Only this week he was his old self again, stroked my face and promised to look me up in south Moravia on his way back from Bratislava. He said we had a lot of things to talk over. Perhaps he's seen it was no good the way things were going and wants them to be the way they were before. But why now, now that I've met Ludvik? It's depressing me, but I mustn't let it, I mustn't. *Let sadness not be linked with my name*—those words of Julius Fucik's are my motto, and I don't care if they *are* out of date now. Maybe I'm silly, but the ones who say I am are no better. They've got their slogans, "absurdity," "alienation," and the rest, and I don't see why I should trade in my silliness for theirs. I don't want to split my life in two; I want it to be one life, one from beginning to end, and that's why I'm so crazy about Ludvik, because I don't have to alter my ideals and tastes when I'm with him. He's ordinary, straightforward, cheerful, says what he means, and these are the things I love, the things I've always loved.

I'm not ashamed of the way I've always been. Until I was eighteen all I knew was being cooped up in a convent, two years in a TB sanatorium, another two years catching up on the schooling I'd missed. I didn't even go dancing; all I knew was the tidy apartment of a tidy Pilsen family and endless schoolwork. Life passed me by. Then in '49 I went up to Prague, and all of a sudden it was like a miracle, I was so happy. I'll never forget it. And that's why I can never erase Pavel from my heart, even though I don't love him, even though he hurt me so much, I just can't. Pavel is my youth, Prague, the university, and most of all the Fucik Song and Dance Ensemble. Nowadays no one knows what all that meant to us. That's where I met Pavel; he sang tenor and I sang alto. We did hundreds of concerts and shows, and I fell so much in love with Moravian folk songs that even though I was Pilsen born and bred I used to think of myself as a Moravian girl, and they became the leitmotiv of my life. And I hear them every time my sun comes out, and I can hear them now, these last few days.

As for how I got to know Pavel, I can hardly bring myself to tell anyone now. It was like something out of a school reader. It was the anniversary of the liberation and there was a big demonstration in Old Town Square. Our ensemble was there, we were always together, a little handful of people among the tens of thousands, and up on the rostrum there were politicians, speeches, applause, and then Togliatti came to the microphone and made a short speech in Italian, and the audience responded as usual by shouting, clapping, and stamping their feet. Pavel was standing right next to me in that enormous crowd, and I heard him shout something different, looked at his lips moving, and realized he was singing, or rather shouting, a song. He wanted people to hear him and join him in singing an Italian revolutionary song that was in our repertoire and very popular at the time. That was Pavel all over. Not content with merely attacking one's reason, he wanted to strike at people's feelings as well. I thought it was marvelous to be greeting an Italian workers' leader in a Prague square with an Italian revolutionary song, and I longed for Togliatti to be moved, just as I had. So I joined in with Pavel as loud as I could, and more and more people followed us until our whole ensemble was singing it. Gradually other voices joined in with us, people began to understand what was going on, and the song slowly wound its way out of the pandemonium on the square like a butterfly out of an enormous clamoring chrysalis. At last the butterfly, the song, or at least the last few bars, reached the rostrum and we gazed up eagerly at the Italian's face under his graying hair. We were happy when we thought we saw him respond to our singing with a movement of his hand, and I was even sure, although I couldn't possibly have seen from that distance, that I saw tears in his eyes.

And in the midst of that excitement and emotion, somehow, I don't know how, I suddenly gripped Pavel's hand, and Pavel squeezed mine, and we stayed holding hands until the end of the demonstration and didn't let go even afterward. The crowds broke up and we spent several hours strolling together through a Prague decked with flowers.

Seven years later, when Zdenicka was five, he told me, and I shall never forget it, that "we didn't marry for love, we married for Party discipline." I know it was only said in the heat of an argument, I know it was a lie, I know Pavel married me for love and it was only afterward that he changed. But even so it was a terrible thing to say, because he was the one who was always arguing that love today was different from what it used to be, that it wasn't an escape from people but a support in the battle, and indeed that was the way it was for us. At midday we didn't even have time for lunch—all we ate were two dry rolls in the Youth League secretariat, and then we might not see each other again all day. I'd wait for Pavel to come home around midnight from his endless meetings. In my spare time I typed the reports he had to read at all sorts of conferences and political instruction classes. He attached immense importance

to them. Only I know how much store he set by their success.
A hundred times he'd repeat in these speeches that the new
man was different from the old in having abolished the distinction between his private and his public life. And now, years
later, he suddenly complains that the Comrades in those days
wouldn't leave his private life in peace.

We went around together for almost two years and I was
getting a little impatient. There's nothing odd about that. No
woman can be content forever with friendship. But Pavel was.
He'd got used to its convenient lack of ties. All men are basically
selfish, and it's up to the woman to stand up for herself and her
mission as a woman. Unfortunately Pavel didn't appreciate
this. The Comrades in the ensemble did though, especially some
of my girlfriends, and they put their heads together and finally
summoned Pavel before a committee. I still don't know what
they said to him, we've never discussed it, but I imagine they
made things pretty awkward for him. Morals were very strict in
those days—exaggeratedly so—but I daresay it's better to exaggerate morality than immorality, as they do today. Pavel kept
out of my way for a long time and I thought I'd ruined everything. I was terribly depressed. I wanted to kill myself.

But then he came to me, and my knees were trembling, and
he asked me to forgive him and gave me a locket with a picture
of the Kremlin on it. It was his most treasured possession and I
never take it off, for it means a lot more to me than a keepsake.
I cried with happiness, and two weeks later we were married.
The entire ensemble was at the wedding, and the singing and
dancing went on for almost twenty-four hours. And I told Pavel
that if we betrayed each other we'd be betraying all the people
who celebrated the wedding with us, betraying the demonstration in Old Town Square, betraying Togliatti. Today it makes
me laugh to think of all the things we ultimately *did* betray . . .

Let me see, what shall I wear tomorrow? I think the pink

sweater and the plastic trenchcoat—they suit my figure best. I'm not the slimmest woman in the world nowadays, but maybe I've a different sort of attraction in return for my wrinkles, something the young girls don't have, the charm of experience. I know that's what Jindra sees in me, poor boy, and I can still see his disappointed look when he heard I was flying off the next morning and he'd be going by himself. He's happy when he can be with me and demonstrate his nineteen-year-old maturity. He'd do eighty with me along, I'm sure, just to impress me. He's a plain-looking boy but an excellent mechanic and driver. Editors like having him out in the field on minor reporting jobs. Anyway, why not? It's nice to know there's someone around who likes me—these last few years I haven't been too popular at the radio station. They say I'm a nuisance, a fanatic, a dogmatist, a Party bloodhound, and I don't know what else, but I don't see why I should feel ashamed of loving the Party and sacrificing all my spare time to it. What else have I got left? Pavel has other women, I never bother to check on them anymore, my daughter adores only her father, my work has been exactly the same for the last ten empty years: reports, interviews, programs about targets being met, cowsheds, and milkmaids.

It's only the Party that's never done me any harm, nor I it, not even in '56 when almost everyone wanted to desert it, when it all came out about Stalin, and people went crazy and dropped everything and said our papers told lies, our nationalized shops were useless, our culture was in decline, the collective farms should never have been set up, the Soviet Union was a slave state. And the worst thing was that even the Communists used to say these things at their own meetings— even Pavel, and they clapped him all the same. Pavel was always being applauded, ever since he was a child. He was an only child, his mother took his photo to bed with her, her wonder child. Now he can't live without applause, it's his narcotic, and so he was glad to have the chance to pull at people's heartstrings

again, and he spoke about those dreadful executions with such
feeling that people all but wept. I felt how much he enjoyed
being indignant, and I hated him.

Luckily the Party rapped the hysterical ones over the knuck-
les and they calmed down. Pavel cooled off too; his post as university lecturer in Marxism was far too soft for him to risk it.
But something remained in the air, a germ of apathy, mistrust,
misgiving, a germ that went on quietly and secretly multiplying. I didn't know how to counter it and I clung more tightly
to the Party than ever, and now it's as if the Party was a human
being, more female than male, a wise woman to confide in, at a
time when I have nothing to say to anyone, and not just to Pavel
—the others don't like me either. That became obvious enough
when one of our editors, a married man, was having an affair
with a young girl on the technical staff, irresponsible and cynical, and his desperate wife turned to our committee for help.
We spent hours discussing the case and interviewing the wife,
the girl, and various witnesses from her department. We tried
to see every point of view and be fair. The editor received a
Party reprimand, the girl was admonished, and they had to
promise to split up. They only did it to keep us quiet and went
on seeing each other. But we soon found out about it, and I took
the hard line and proposed that the editor be expelled for deliberately deceiving and misleading the Party. After all, what
kind of a Communist is it that would lie to the Party? I hate
lies. But my proposal wasn't accepted, and the editor escaped
with another reprimand while the girl had to leave the company.

They really got back at me for that, making me out to be a
monster. They led a regular smear campaign against me, pry-
ing into my private life. Naturally this was my Achilles' heel,
because no woman can live without emotion, otherwise she
wouldn't be a woman. Why deny it? Since I didn't have love at
home I'd looked for it elsewhere, and even so had looked in
vain. They attacked me at a public meeting and called me a
hypocrite, trying to pillory other people for disrupting mar-

riage, trying to expel and dismiss and destroy, when I myself was unfaithful to my husband at every opportunity. That was how they put it in public, but behind my back they said even more vicious things. They said I was a nun in public and a whore in private. As if they were incapable of understanding that it was my unhappy marriage that made me strict toward others, not from hatred of them, but from love—from love of love, love for their homes, for their children, because I wanted to help them, and because I too have a child and a home and am afraid for them.

But then again, maybe they're right, maybe I really am just a malicious old woman, a horrid commissar sticking my nose into things that are none of my business. But that's what I'm like and I can only act as I feel. Now it's too late to change. I've always believed that people are one and indivisible and that only the petty bourgeois is hypocritically divided between his public and private self. That was my credo, and I've always acted on it.

And if they say I'm spiteful, then I readily admit that I hate these young girls with the cruelty of youth, without an ounce of compassion for older women. They'll be thirty one day, and thirty-five and forty. And don't let anyone say that she loved him. What does *she* know about love? She'll sleep with any man on the first night; she's got no inhibitions, no sense of shame. I feel insulted to the core when anyone compares me with girls like that just because I as a married woman have had affairs with other men. I've always looked for love, and if I made a mistake and didn't find it I turned elsewhere, even though I knew how simple it would be to forget my girlish dreams of love, forget them and cross the frontier into the land of strange, disquieting freedom, where everything is permitted, where men and women turn into beasts.

And I know too that if I crossed that border I'd cease to be myself, I'd become somebody else—I don't know who—and I'm terrified of it, that dreadful change, and that's why I keep looking for love, a love I could embrace just as I am, with my old dreams and ideals, because I don't want my life split in two,

I want to keep it one from beginning to end. And that's why I was so fascinated when I met you, Ludvik, oh, Ludvik . . .

It was really funny the way I first walked into his office. He didn't make much impression on me and I got right down to business. I told him what I needed to know and how I saw the feature taking shape. But when he started to talk to me I suddenly found myself confused and tongue-tied, and when he saw my embarrassment he turned the conversation to general topics, asked whether I was married, whether I had any children, where I went for my holidays. And he said I looked young and pretty. He wanted to help me get over my shyness and that was nice of him. I've known egotists galore who aren't a tenth as clever as he is. Pavel would have talked entirely about himself. But it was really funny the way I spent a whole hour with him and knew no more about his institute at the end than I did at the beginning. Back home I threw something together but it just wouldn't come right. Perhaps I was glad it didn't—at least I had an excuse to telephone him and ask him if he'd care to read over what I'd written. We met in a coffeehouse and my unfortunate feature was only four pages long. He read it, smiled gallantly and said it was excellent, and made it clear from the start that I interested him as a woman and not as a journalist, and I didn't know whether to feel pleased or offended at this, but he was nice to me and we seemed to get on. He wasn't a wishy-washy intellectual. He had a full life behind him, had even worked down in the mines, and I told him that those were the people I liked, people whose lives were right out of Gorky. But what shook me most was that he was from south Moravia, had even played in a cymbalo band. I couldn't believe my ears. I recognized the leitmotiv of my own life, saw my vanished youth as clearly as yesterday, and felt my heart going out to Ludvik.

He asked me what I did all day and I told him and he said— I can still hear his voice, half joking, half sympathetic—"My dear lady, that is no kind of life." And then he said it must be changed, I must start living differently, spending more time on the joys of life. I told him I had nothing against that, joy had always been my creed and there's nothing I loathe more than all that fashionable ennui, and he said my creed doesn't matter, since those who profess joy are often the saddest people of all. I felt like shouting, "You're right! Oh, you're so right!" and then abruptly he said he'd call for me the next day at four o'clock outside the radio building and we'd take a trip together into the country. I protested that I was a married woman, that I couldn't just go off into the woods with a strange man, and Ludvik answered jokingly that he wasn't a man, only a scientist. But how miserable he looked as he said it! Seeing him that way made me all hot with joy that he wanted me and wanted me all the more because I was married, because it set us further apart, and men are always crazy for the unattainable. Eagerly I drank in all the sadness in his face and I knew in that instant that he was in love with me.

The next day the Vltava murmured on one side of us and the forest rose sheer on the other and it was all utterly romantic. I love things to be romantic and I behaved like a silly girl, not like the mother of a twelve-year-old daughter. I laughed, I danced in the grass, I took him by the hand and made him run with me, and we stopped and my heart was beating, and we were standing close together, and Ludvik bent down slightly and kissed me gently, and I pulled away from him and took him by the hand and we ran on again. I have a little trouble with my heart. It beats madly after the slightest exertion—I only need to run up a flight of stairs. So I slowed down a little and gradually my breathing quieted and I began humming the first two bars of my favorite song, and when I felt he was with me I began singing it out loud, and I felt all the years, cares, worries, thousands of gray scales falling off me. And later we sat in a little inn at Zbraslav and ate bread and sausage, and everything was so simple and ordinary, with a surly landlord and a stained cloth, and yet such a lovely adventure. I said to Ludvik, "Do you know I'm going to south Moravia for three days to do a feature on the Ride of the Kings?" He asked me where exactly, and when I told him he said that was where he was born, and it was such a coincidence that it took my breath away. He said, "I'll take some time off and come with you."

I was alarmed when I thought of Pavel and that little spark of fresh hope he'd kindled in me. I'm not cynical about my marriage and I'm ready to do anything to protect it, for Zdenicka's sake, or, more truthfully, for my own sake, for the sake of everything that ever was, the memory of my youth. But I didn't have the strength to say no to Ludvik, I just didn't have the strength. And now the die is cast. Zdenicka is asleep and I'm frightened. Ludvik is already in Moravia, where tomorrow he'll be waiting for me when my bus arrives.

III
Ludvik

*Y*ES, I began wandering around again. I stopped on the bridge across the Morava and gazed downstream. What a repulsive river the Morava is—brown as if it runs mud rather than water—and how dismal its banks look: a street of five single-story houses, each standing on its own, eccentric and forlorn. Two of them have angels and small scenes carved in stucco, which needless to say are chipped and cracked. Then the street of orphan houses peters out, and there are only steel electricity pylons, grass with a few straggling geese, then fields, fields without horizons, fields stretching to nowhere, fields in which the liquid mud of the Morava is lost to sight.

Towns are well known for their ability to produce mirror images of each other, and this view, which I'd known since childhood, suddenly reminded me of Ostrava, that mining town full of deserted houses and dirty streets leading nowhere, like a huge, cheap rooming house. I had been decoyed; I stood there on the bridge like a man exposed to machine-gun fire. I couldn't bear to look at that woebegone street with its five solitary houses because I couldn't bear to think about Ostrava. So I turned around and looked upstream.

Along the bank there was a path, flanked on one side by a thick row of poplars to form a narrow promenade, from which the bank dropped down to a surface overgrown with grass and weeds. Across the river, on the opposite bank, were scattered the stores, workshops, and yards of several small factories. On the other side of the path was first a sprawling garbage dump, then again open fields punctuated by steel pylons. I realized that the ghostly atmosphere of the landscape symbolized everything that I hadn't wanted to recall after my encounter with Lucie. It was as if suppressed memories were being projected onto everything I saw, onto the desolation of the fields and yards and storehouses, onto the murk of the river, and onto that pervasive chill which gave a painful unity to the whole scene. There was no escaping the memories. They surrounded me.

The events leading to my first major disaster—and through this harsh agency to Lucie—would be easy enough to relate ironically, the cause of it all being my fatal predilection for stupid jokes and Marketa's fatal inability to understand them. Marketa was serious in all things (and thus in perfect harmony with the spirit of the age), and credulous in most, as well. This is not a euphemistic way of suggesting that she was stupid. On the contrary, she was gifted and bright and in any case young enough, as a first-year student of nineteen, for her naïve trustfulness to number among her charms rather than her defects, particularly as it was accompanied by an undeniable physical attractiveness. In the department we all liked Marketa and we all more or less made a pass at her, which didn't stop some of us, at least, from making gentle and unmalicious fun of her at the same time.

Of course fun cut little ice with Marketa, and even less with the spirit of the age. It was the first year after February, 1948; the new life had begun, a completely different life, whose features, as I remember them, were rigidly serious—though the seriousness took the surprising form not of a frown but of a smile. Yes, those years proclaimed that they were the most radiant of all years, and anyone who failed to rejoice was immediately suspected of lamenting the victory of the working class or, equally sinful, of being *individualistically* submerged in his own inner sorrows.

I had few inner sorrows at that time; moreover, I had a considerable sense of fun. Yet it can't be said that I was accepted without reservations by that radiant age. My jokes weren't serious enough, and the joyousness of the time didn't take kindly to irony or practical jokes. It was, as I have said, a very serious kind of joy, proudly entitling itself "the historic optimism of a victorious class," an ascetic and ceremonial joy— Joy, you might say, with a capital J.

I remember how in those days the entire department was organized into so-called study circles, which met fairly frequently for mutual public criticism and self-criticism, and to work out an assessment of each of its members. At that period, like any other Communist, I had plenty of responsibility (I held an important post in the League of University Students) and, as I was also a good student, it was hardly likely that these evaluations would affect me adversely. But the public testimonials to my efficiency, my correct attitude to the State, my work and my knowledge of Marxism, were usually followed by a single qualification—my lingering "traces of individualism." This needn't have been dangerous, as it was customary to include some critical remark in even the most enthusiastic tributes—to castigate "lack of interest in revolutionary theory," or "coldness in dealing with people" or "lack of alertness and vigilance" or even "an incorrect attitude to women." But whenever these were not the only factors involved, when a further note of reservation was sounded, or when one was involved in some sort of conflict or under suspicion or attack, "traces of individualism" or "an incorrect attitude to women" could become the seeds of one's destruction. And every one of us—yes, every single one of us—carried such a seed around with him in the form of his Party card.

Sometimes, more in fun than from any real concern, I'd defend myself against the charge of individualism and ask my colleagues for proof. Their evidence was hardly concrete. They would say, "It's the way you behave."

"How do I behave?" I'd ask.

"You always have that strange smile."

"So what? I enjoy life."

"No, you smile as if you were thinking to yourself."

When the Comrades classified my conduct and smile as intellectual—those days another notorious pejorative—I actually came to believe them, since it was beyond the limits of my audacity to imagine that all the others could be wrong, that the Revolution itself and the spirit of the age could be wrong, or that I, a mere individual, could be right. I began to discipline my smiling and presently to feel a tiny crack opening up between the person I was and the person the spirit of the age required me to be.

But which of them was really me? To be completely honest, I was the man with several faces.

And I acquired more and more of them. About a month before the vacation I began to get friendly with Marketa, and like any young man of twenty, I tried to impress her by donning a mask. I pretended to be more mature and experienced than I was. I assumed an air of aloofness, of detachment, of wearing an additional layer of skin, invisible and impenetrable. I thought, quite correctly, that humor would reinforce my aloofness, and even though I had always been one for a laugh, the banter I carried on with Marketa was particularly forced, affected, and tedious.

But which was the real me? I repeat: I was the man with many faces.

At meetings I was earnest, enthusiastic, and convinced. Among my closest friends I was teasingly provocative. With Marketa I was cynical and fitfully scintillating, and when I was alone, and thinking of Marketa, I was as helplessly excited as a schoolboy.

Was this last face the only real one?

No. All were real. I did not, as hypocrites do, have one real face and various false ones. I had several faces only because I was young and did not know who I was or who I wanted to be. But the difference between all these faces frightened me; none of them seemed to fit properly, and I changed from one to the other clumsily and haphazardly.

To ease the weight of my embarrassment and awkwardness I showed off in front of Marketa, disagreeing with her at every opportunity or just poking fun at her opinions. She was, as I've said, a girl of trusting simplicity who could never look *behind* anything and saw only the thing itself. Thus she had a remarkable understanding of botany but frequently failed to see the point of a joke. Similarly, though she allowed herself to be carried along by all the enthusiasms of the time, when confronted with some political action carried out on the principle of the end justifying the means, she would be as bewildered as when told a joke. From this the Comrades concluded that she needed to fortify her enthusiasm with knowledge of the strategy and tactics of the revolutionary movement, and they resolved that during the vacation she should take part in a fourteen-day course of Party instruction.

This didn't suit me at all, as I'd intended being alone with Marketa in Prague for part of the vacation in order to put our relationship, which up to then had consisted of walks, talks, and a few kisses, on a more definite footing. I had only those two weeks—I had to spend the next four on an agricultural work party and the last two of the vacation with my mother in Moravia—and I reacted with painful jealousy when Marketa, far from sharing my annoyance about the course, told me she was looking forward to it.

From the course, which took place in some castle in central Bohemia, she sent me a characteristic letter, full of earnest agreement with everything happening to her. She liked it all, even the early morning exercise period, the speeches, the discussions, the songs. She described the "healthy atmosphere" which prevailed there, diligently adding her opinion that the revolution in the West would not be long in coming.

As far as that goes, I agreed with everything Marketa said. I even believed in a speedy revolution in western Europe. There was one thing, however, I did not agree with: that she should

be so happy and contented when I was missing her so much. So
I bought a postcard and, to hurt, shock, and confuse her, wrote:

Optimism is the opium of the people! The healthy
atmosphere stinks! Long live Trotsky!

Ludvik

Marketa answered my provocative postcard with a brief
lettercard bearing a few trite words and made no reply to my
many other letters. I was somewhere in Sumava, raking hay
with a student work party, and Marketa's silence left me in very
low spirits. I wrote to her almost every day, letters full of a
pleading, mournful infatuation. Couldn't we, I begged her, at
least see something of each other during the last two weeks of
the vacation? I was willing to give up my trip home, forgo seeing my poor deserted mother, do anything to see Marketa, not
merely because I liked her but because she was the only woman
on my horizon, and being a boy without a girl was an unbearable state of affairs. But Marketa didn't answer.

I couldn't understand what was going on. I arrived in Prague
in August and managed to catch her at home. We went for our
usual walk along the Vltava; Marketa told me that nothing had
changed between us and acted accordingly—but with that un-
wavering *sameness* (sameness of kiss, sameness of conversation,
sameness of smile) which I found so depressing. When I asked
her for a date the next day, she told me to phone her and we'd
arrange things then.

I did phone her; an unfamiliar woman's voice told me Marketa had left Prague.

I was unhappy as only a womanless young man of twenty can
be—a young man, that is, who is rather shy, who has brushed
with physical love on only a few occasions, and then fleetingly
and clumsily, but whose mind is constantly preoccupied with it.
The days were unbearably long and useless. I couldn't read. I
couldn't work. I went to the movies three times a day, to one
performance after another, just to kill time and to drown the

owl's screech that kept issuing from somewhere inside me. I, whom Marketa regarded, thanks to my own laborious attempts at showing off, as a man almost totally blasé about women, didn't even have the courage to speak to the girls in the street, girls whose beautiful legs pierced me to the marrow.

And so I was heartily glad when September came at last, and with it the university term; also, a few days earlier, my work in the League of Students, where I had a room of my own and plenty to do. However, on the second day a telephone call summoned me to the Party secretariat. From that moment on, I remember everything in complete detail. It was a sunny day, and as I left the League of Students building I felt the low spirits which had haunted me all the vacation slowly dissolving. It's fortunate that one's private passions are matched by a passion for public work. I was glad that this passion was drawing me into its embrace again, and I walked toward the secretariat with an agreeable feeling of curiosity. I rang the bell and the door was opened by the committee chairman, a tall thin-faced youth with fair hair and ice-blue eyes. I gave him the standard greeting, "Honor to Labor," but instead of responding he said, "Back there—they're waiting for you." In the last room at the very back of the secretariat I found three members of the Party University Committee waiting. They told me to take a seat. As I sat down I could sense something ominous in the air. The three Comrades, with whom I was on terms of the utmost familiarity, had all become suddenly distant. True, they used the familiar form of address (as is the rule among Comrades), but this was an official and menacing brand of familiarity.

I sat in front of those three students and they asked me the first question: Did I know Marketa? I said I did. Had I written to her? I had. Did I remember what I had written? I said I didn't, but as I did so the postcard with its provocative text popped up in front of my eyes and I began to have some idea of what this was about. "Can't you remember?" they asked me. I said I couldn't. "And what did Marketa write to you?" I shrugged my shoulders, as if to imply that she'd written about intimate matters which I couldn't possibly discuss there. "Didn't she write anything about the course?" they asked.

"Yes, she did," I said.

"What did she say?"

"That she liked it."

"And?"

"And she wrote that the speeches and the staff were good."

"Did she tell you there was a healthy atmosphere prevailing in the course?"

"Yes," I said, "I believe she did write something like that."

"Did she tell you she was discovering the power of optimism?" they continued.

I said she had.

"And what do *you* think of optimism?" they asked.

"Optimism? What am I expected to think of it?"

"Do you consider yourself an optimist?" they persisted.

"Yes," I said with some diffidence. "I like a little fun. I'm a man who likes having a good time," I added, trying to lighten the increasingly grim tone.

"The lover of life can be a nihilist as well," said one of them. "He may even enjoy a laugh at the expense of those who suffer. He can be a cynic as well," he went on. "Do you think Socialism can be built without optimism?" asked another of them.

"No," I said.

"Then you're opposed to Socialism being built in this country," said the third.

"What do you mean?" I said angrily.

"Because for you optimism is the opium of the people." They were on the attack.

"What do you mean, opium of the people?" I was still on the defensive.

"Don't try and dodge the issue—that's what you wrote. Marx called religion the opium of the people, but you think our optimism is opium! That's what you wrote to Marketa. I should like to hear what our workers would have to say, those dedicated workers busy overfulfilling the plans, if they were to learn that their optimism is opium." Another one had taken it up. And the third added, "For a Trotskyite constructive optimism is always opium. And you are a Trotskyite."

"For heaven's sake, where did you get that idea?" I asked.

"Did you write it or didn't you?"

"I may have written something of the kind as a joke. Anyway it was two months ago and I don't remember."

"We can remind you," they said and read my postcard aloud: "Optimism is the opium of the people! The healthy atmosphere stinks! Long live Trotsky! Ludvik."

The words sounded so awful in the little room belonging to the political secretariat that I was afraid of them and felt they had a destructive power against which I was helpless. "Comrades, it was meant as a joke," I said, knowing no one could possibly believe me.

"Do you consider it funny?" one of the Comrades asked the other two. Both shook their heads.

"You'd have to know Marketa," I said.

"We do," they replied.

"Well, then," I said, "Marketa takes everything seriously, and we've always made fun of her and tried to shock her."

"Interesting," said one of the Comrades. "We wouldn't have thought from your other letters that you didn't take Marketa seriously."

"Do you mean you've read all my letters to Marketa?"

"So it's because Marketa takes everything seriously," said the second one, "that you make fun of her. But tell us, what is it that she takes seriously? The Party, optimism, duty, wouldn't you say? And all those things she takes seriously are one big joke to you."

"Look, Comrades," I said, "I don't even remember writing it, I dashed it off, just a couple of sentences, as a joke, without thinking. If I'd had some sinister motive I wouldn't have sent it to a Party school!"

"It's immaterial how you wrote it. Whether you wrote it

quickly or slowly, on your knee or on a table, you could only have written what you felt. Perhaps if you'd thought more about it you wouldn't have written it. As it is, you wrote without any dissimulation. As it is, we know whom we're dealing with. We know at least that you're two-faced, one face for the Party and one for the rest." I felt I'd completely run out of arguments. I went on repeating the same things over and over again—that it was all a joke, that the words were meaningless, that it was just the way I felt at the time, and so on. I made no impression on them whatever. They said I'd expressed my sentiments on an open postcard and that anyone could have read them, that the words had an *objective* content and that they were not accompanied by any explanatory notes on my mood at the time. Then they asked me how much Trotsky I had read. I told them none at all. They asked who had lent me the books. I said no one—I had read *no Trotsky*. They asked me to name the Trotskyites I had meetings with. I said I didn't know any. They told me they were relieving me as of that moment of my post in the League of Students and demanded the keys to my room. These were in my pocket and I handed them over. Then they told me that my case as a Party matter would be decided by my branch at the natural science faculty. They stood up and looked right through me. I said, "Honor to Labor," and left.

Then I remembered that I had a lot of my own things in my room in the League offices. I've never been very tidy, and my desk drawer contained my socks as well as various private papers, while nestling among the official documents in the closet was a plum cake my mother had sent me. I had just given up my key, but the porter on the ground floor knew me and gave me the master key, which used to hang with a lot of other keys on a wooden board. I unlocked the door and sat down at the desk. Opening one drawer after another, I removed all my things. I worked slowly and with concentration, because I was trying in those few moments of relative peace and quiet to understand what had happened to me and to decide what I had better do.

It wasn't long before the door opened, and in came the same three Comrades from the secretariat. This time they could hardly be described as looking cold or reserved. This time their voices were loud and excited, particularly the shortest one, the committee personnel officer, who snapped at me: How had I got in? What right did I have there? Did I want him to have the police take me away? And what was I doing ransacking the desk? I told him I had come for my plum cake and my socks. He told me I had no right whatever to come here even if I had a whole closet full of socks. Then he went to the desk and scrutinized paper after paper, notebook after notebook. They were in fact my own private belongings, which he finally allowed me to pack in my suitcase while he watched. I put the socks in as well, crumpled and dirty, and the cake which was lying in the closet on a sheet of waxed paper covered with crumbs. They watched my every move. I left the room with my bag, and as I did so the personnel officer told me not to show my face there again.

As soon as I got out of range of the men from the district and the invincible logic of their interrogation, it appeared to me that I was innocent, that there was nothing evil in what I'd written or said, and that I ought to go and see someone who was well acquainted with Marketa, someone whom I could confide in and who would understand that the whole business was absurd. I looked up one of the students from our department, a Communist, and when I told him the whole story he said the district was too bigoted and humorless but that he, knowing Marketa, had a clear idea of what it was all about. In any case I should go and see Zemanek, who was to be this year's Party chairman of our department and who knew both me and Marketa very well.

I had no idea that Zemanek was to be department chairman and it struck me as excellent news, as I knew him very well indeed and was confident, moreover, that he'd be entirely sympathetic on account of my southern Moravian origins. For Zemanek, though Prague born and bred, loved singing Moravian songs, which at that time were extremely popular. While I, as the only genuine Moravian Slovak in the college, was constantly being invited, at meetings, celebrations, or on the First of May to take up my clarinet and join two or three other amateurs in an imitation Moravian band. Zemanek, handsome and stage-struck, would march with us and, dressed in a borrowed folk costume, would dance in the procession and wave his arms in the air and sing. Though he'd never been near Moravian Slovakia in his life, Zemanek loved acting the village swain, and I couldn't help liking someone who so obviously adored the music of my homeland.

And Zemanek knew Marketa, which was another advantage. The three of us often found ourselves together at student functions. On one occasion I'd invented some nonsense about tribes of dwarfs living in Sumava, illustrating it with quotations from an alleged scientific study. Marketa was astonished that she'd never heard of them. I said it wasn't surprising: bourgeois science had deliberately suppressed their existence, as the capitalists had bought and sold them as slaves.

"But someone ought to write about it!" cried Marketa. "Why isn't there anything written about it? It would make a very strong case against the capitalists!"

"Perhaps we don't write about it," I pronounced thoughtfully, "because the whole subject is rather delicate. The dwarfs had an extraordinary capacity for the act of love, and that was why they were so much sought after and why our Republic secretly exported them for fat sums of foreign currency, particularly to France, where they were engaged by aging capitalist women as servants—though naturally destined for another use altogether."

The others stifled their laughter, and some of them, Zemanek in particular, joined in and confirmed my account of the dwarfs. When Marketa asked what they actually looked like, I remember Zemanek with a serious expression telling her that Professor Cechura, whom Marketa and all her classmates had the occasional honor of seeing behind his professorial desk, was of dwarfish stock, possibly on both sides, certainly on one. Zemanek had apparently been told by one of the lecturers how he had once spent a holiday in the same hotel as Mr. and Mrs. Cechura, who between them were not quite nine feet in height. One morning he'd entered their room without realizing they were still asleep, and was horrified to find them lying in the same bed, not side by side but one below the other, Cechura huddled in the lower half of the bed and Mrs. Cechura in the upper.

Yes, I confirmed, this proved beyond doubt that both Cechura and his wife were Sumava dwarfs by origin, because sleeping head to toe was the atavistic custom of all the dwarfs in that region, and in earlier days they would never build their huts on circular or square plots but always on extended rectangles, since not only husband and wife but entire clans were accustomed to sleep in a long chain, one below the other.

Recalling this little piece of nonsense on that black day, I experienced a faint glimmer of hope. Knowing my sense of humor and knowing Marketa, Zemanek would understand that the postcard was merely a joke aimed at provoking a girl whom we all admired and, perhaps for that very reason, liked to belittle. And so at the first opportunity I gave him an account of my misfortune. Zemanek listened attentively, then frowned and said he would see what he could do.

Meanwhile I lived in a state of suspended animation, attending lectures as before and waiting. I was hauled before numerous party commissions which were attempting to establish whether or not I belonged to a Trotskyite group. I tried to prove that I had no real idea even of what Trotskyism was. I met head-on the glances of all those examining my case and tried to read belief into them. Sometimes I succeeded, and then I'd carry the look with me for a long time, trying patiently to kindle a spark of hope from it.

Marketa continued to avoid me. I realized that this was on account of my postcard, and I was too proud and sensitive to feel like seeking her out. One day, however, she stopped me in a corridor and said, "I'd like to talk to you about something."

And so we went out together for the first time in months. It was already autumn, and we were both wearing long trench-coats, really long ones reaching below the knee, in the fashion of those inelegant days. There was a thin mist, and the trees on the embankment were leafless and black. Maketa told me how it had all happened. While she was still attending the course, the Comrades running it had suddenly summoned her and asked her if she'd received any mail there. When she said she had, they asked where from. She said she'd had letters from her mother. No one else? Oh, another student, she said. Could she tell them the name? She gave my name. And what did Comrade Jahn write? She shrugged her shoulders, not wanting to recite the words on my card. Had she written to him as well? She said she had. What had she written? Nothing much, she said, just about the course and things like that. Was she enjoying the course? Yes, she loved it. And had she told him that in her let-ter? Yes, she had. And what had he replied? Marketa had hesi-tated. "He's a little odd, you'd have to know him," she said. "We do know him," they replied, "and we would like to know what he wrote. Can you show us this card?"

"You mustn't be angry with me," said Marketa, "but I had to show them the card."

"You don't need to apologize," I told her. "They knew all about it before they saw you—or they wouldn't have called you in."

"I'm not apologizing," she protested, "and I'm not ashamed of having given them the card. You mustn't make it sound like that. You're a Party member, and the Party has a right to know who you are and what you think." And then she told me she'd been horrified by what I'd written; after all, everyone knew that Trotsky was the archenemy of everything we were fighting for and everything we lived for.

What could I say to Marketa? I asked her to tell me what else had happened.

Marketa said they read the card and were shocked. They asked her opinion of it. She told them it was disgraceful. They

asked her why she hadn't brought it in herself to show them.
She shrugged her shoulders. They asked her whether she knew
what vigilance meant. She looked down. They asked her
whether she knew how many enemies the Party had. Yes, she
knew, but she didn't believe that Comrade Jahn. . . . They
asked her if she knew me well and what I was like. She said I
was strange sometimes—I was a staunch Communist but occasionally I would come out with things a Communist oughtn't
to say. They asked her for examples. She said she couldn't remember any specific instances, but that for me nothing was sacred. They said my postcard had made that abundantly clear.
She told them that she often had arguments with me, and that
I talked in one way at meetings and in another way with her. At
meetings I was enthusiasm itself, whereas with her I would
mock and disparage everything. They asked her whether she
thought a man like me should be a member of the Party. She
shrugged her shoulders. They asked her whether the Party
could encourage the development of Socialism if its members
went around proclaiming that optimism was the opium of the
people. She replied that a Party like that would never build
Socialism. All right, they said, that would do. For the time being she was to tell me nothing about the interview, because
they wanted to see what else I would write. She told them she
never wanted to see me again. They said that this would be a
mistake and that on the contrary she was to write to me, so that
they could find out more about me.

"And so after that you showed them all my letters?" I asked,
blushing furiously at the recollection of my romantic effusions.

"What else could I have done?" said Marketa. "But I simply
couldn't go on writing to you after that, just to set a trap for you.
I wrote you one more card and called it a day. I didn't want to
see you because I wasn't supposed to tell you anything, and I
was afraid you'd ask me questions and I wouldn't be able to
lie to you, because I don't like telling lies."

I asked Marketa what had inspired her to see me today.

She told me that Comrade Zemanek was responsible. He had

met her after the vacation in the corridor of the college building and had taken her into the little room where the natural
sciences department Party branch had its secretariat. He said
he'd heard about a postcard I'd sent her containing anti-Party
sentiments and asked her for the exact words. She told him. He
asked her what she thought of them. She said she condemned
them. He told her she was right to do so and asked if she was
still going around with me. She was embarrassed and answered
evasively. He told her that the department had received very
favorable reports about her from the summer school and that
the Party branch thought highly of her; that he didn't want to
interfere in her private life but that in his opinion a person
is judged by the company he keeps and it wouldn't be exactly
an advantage for her to choose me.

This had apparently weighed heavily on Marketa's mind for
weeks afterward. She hadn't in fact seen me for several months,
and Zemanek's suggestion was therefore quite superfluous. Indeed, the very cruelty and moral inadmissibility of suggesting
to someone that she should desert her boyfriend just because
he'd made a mistake made her wonder whether she'd been unfair when she stopped seeing me in the first place. She consulted
the Comrade who'd been in charge of the vacation course on
whether the injunction of silence about the events surrounding
the postcard still held, and on learning that there was no longer
any reason for secrecy she had stopped me and asked to speak
to me.

She then confided in me all the things that had been worrying her. She agreed that she'd behaved badly in deciding not to
see me anymore; no man is completely damned, whatever his
mistakes. She recalled the Soviet film *Honest Justice,* at that
time very popular in Party circles, in which a Soviet medical
scientist places his discovery at the disposal of another country
before his own—an action smelling of "cosmopolitanism" and
treason. Marketa was visibly moved as she made her main point,
the way the film ended: though the scientist is finally condemned
by the honest justice of his colleagues, his wife does not desert

him but tries to infuse her strength into him and help him to atone for his great wrong.

"So you've decided not to leave me," I said.

"Yes," said Marketa and took me by the hand.

"But, Marketa, do you really think I've done something seriously wrong?"

"Yes, I think you have."

"Do you think I still have the right to remain in the Party, or not?"

"I think not, Ludvik."

I knew that if I'd been willing to enter into the spirit of the play which Marketa was living out, I would have succeeded where months ago I'd failed. Impelled as she was by the pathos of her chosen role of the redeeming woman, she would doubtless have given herself to me, body and soul. But this would of course have been on one condition: that her evangelism should be fully gratified by the object of redemption—in other words, myself—conceding its own profound guilt. And that was the one thing I couldn't do.

I didn't give in to Marketa, I refused her, and so I lost her. Did I then feel myself blameless? Certainly I kept assuring myself of the stupidity of the whole affair, but even as I did so I started seeing those three sentences on the postcard through the eyes of the men who'd interrogated me; I began to feel outraged by the words, and to fear that behind the façade of my humor there did in fact lurk something serious and sinister, that I'd never really been one with the body of the Party, never been a true proletarian revolutionary, but had "gone over to the revolutionaries" on the basis of a mere personal decision.

Looking back on my state of mind at that time, I'm reminded of the enormous analogous power of Christianity to persuade the believer of his own fundamental and unceasing sinfulness. I stood, we all stood, before the revolution and its Party with our heads continually lowered. And so, as I gradually came to accept the idea that my message, however jokingly intended, was still reason for guilt, a reel of critical self-denunciation wound itself through my head. I told myself that those words of mine were no mere accident but exemplified all too clearly the "traces of individualism" and "intellectual tendencies" for which the Comrades had formerly reproached me; that I'd taken to preening myself too much on my education, my undergraduate status, and my future as a member of the intelligentsia; and that my father, an ordinary workingman who'd died during the war in a concentration camp, would have found it hard to understand my cynicism. I examined myself mercilessly on every possible score and even became reconciled to the necessity for some act of contrition. One thing, however, I did resist, and that was my expulsion from the Party and consequent branding as its enemy. To live as the branded enemy of a set of ideals I'd chosen as a boy, and to which I'd remained so close, seemed to me a desperate kind of existence.

Such was the self-criticism—at the same time a kind of whimpering self-justification—which I recited a hundred times to myself, at least ten times before various committees and commissions, and finally at the decisive plenary session of our departmental organization, when Zemanek delivered his brilliant and unforgettable opening address on me and my errors, and proposed on behalf of the committee that I be excluded from the Party. The discussion that followed my public self-denunciation went against me. No one supported me, and finally the meeting—there were about a hundred people present, including my teachers and my most intimate friends—decided by a unanimous show of hands to approve not only my expulsion from the Party but—and this I hadn't expected—my enforced departure from the university.

That same night I got on a train and went home, but home brought me no comfort, because for several days I couldn't work up the courage to tell my mother what had happened—my mother, who took such a proud interest in my studies. Then on the second day Jaroslav, a school friend who'd played in the same folk ensemble, came over and was delighted to find me at home. It seemed he was to be married in two days and wanted me to stand up for him as "witness" according to the traditional local wedding rites. I couldn't refuse an old friend, and so I found myself celebrating my downfall with the festivities of a wedding.

Jaroslav was in all things a dyed-in-the-wool local patriot and Moravian folklore expert. He was the enthusiastic leader of a thriving song and dance ensemble—and he even put his own wedding to the service of his enthusiasm, cramming it with old popular rites: national costume, a cymbalo band, a "giver" pronouncing florid speeches, the carrying of the bride over the threshold, songs, and an entire day of ceremonies which, of course, he'd reconstructed more from books than from any living memory. But one curious thing caught my attention. My friend Jaroslav, while retaining every possible old custom, was, it seemed, sufficiently mindful of his career and obedient to atheistic slogans to give the church a wide berth, although a "traditional" wedding without priest or God's blessing was unthinkable. Similarly he had the "giver" utter all the popular ceremonial speeches but carefully omit any Biblical motifs, although it was precisely these which constituted the principal imagery of the traditional ritual.

My low spirits prevented me from joining in the drunken wedding party, and when Jaroslav asked me, as a sentimental reminder of old times, to take up my clarinet and sit in with the other players, I refused. I remembered the last two May Days, when Zemanek danced along beside me in national costume, gesturing gaily and singing; and the whole business of high-pitched folk squealing suddenly made me feel sick to the very soul . . .

By forfeiting my right to study, I forfeited also my right to defer national service. To fill in the period of waiting for the autumn draft I did two long stints with a labor gang, first on road repairs somewhere near Gottwaldov, and at the end of the summer on seasonal work with Fruta, the fruit processing plant. Finally autumn came, and one morning, after a sleepless night

on the train, I made my way to the barracks in a grim and unfamiliar suburb of Ostrava.

I stood in the barracks square along with other young men
drafted to the same regiment. We were complete strangers, the
only human bond between us being our uncertain future. Some
maintained we were in the "black" division, others denied this,
others didn't even know what it meant. I knew all right, and
these surmises filled me with horror.

Then the sergeant came for us and led us away into one of
the blocks. We poured along the passageway and into a large
room with enormous posters and slogans, photographs and
primitive drawings, all over the walls. On the end wall was
pinned up a large inscription, WE ARE BUILDING SOCIALISM, cut
out of red paper, and under this inscription was a chair with a
wizened little old man standing beside it. The sergeant pointed
at one of us, who then had to sit on the chair. The old man tied
a white sheet around his neck, put his hand in a bag which was
leaning against the chair leg, drew out an electric haircutter,
and plunged it into the lad's hair.

The barber's chair inaugurated a production belt designed
to turn us into soldiers: from the chair on which we forfeited
our hair we were hustled into another room, where we had to
strip, pack our clothes into a paper bag, tie this with a string,
and hand it in at a window. Then, naked and shorn, we proceeded along the corridor to the next room, where we were issued nightshirts; in our nightshirts we made our way through
another door, where we received our heavy boots; in boots and
nightshirts we marched across the square to another block, where
we were given shirts, pants, socks, belts, and battle dress (there
were ominous black facings on the tunics . . .); finally we
reached the last block, where an NCO read out our names, divided us into companies, and assigned us rooms and bunks in
the barracks.

Thus, with remarkable speed, each of us was stripped of his
own will and became something externally resembling an object (dumped, disposed, dispatched, consigned) and internally

something like a man (suffering, irritated, apprehensive). That same day we were ordered on parade, then to supper, then to our bunks. In the morning we were wakened and taken out to the mines; at the pithead we were assigned to production gangs by companies and issued tools—drill, shovel, safety lamp —which none of us knew how to use. Then the cage carried us below the ground.

When we surfaced again with aching bodies the waiting NCO's assembled us and marched us to the barracks for dinner. After dinner there was drill, and after drill kit cleaning, political instruction, and compulsory singing. Our every human activity was replaced by the impersonal, prescribed functions we carried out. For private life we had a twenty-bunk room. And so it went on from day to day.

The depersonalization which had overwhelmed us appeared in those first days to be utterly opaque. After a time it slowly began to grow clearer, and in that twilight of depersonalization the men's humanity began to show. I have to admit that I was one of the last to accommodate his vision to the altered light.

This was because my entire being refused to accept its fate. The soldiers with their black facings among whom I found myself were drilled in only the most perfunctory way, they had no weapons, and they worked in the mines. They were paid for their work—and indeed paid better than other troops—but for me this was a very poor consolation. We consisted entirely of those whom the young Socialist Republic was unwilling to entrust with arms because it regarded them as its enemies. Obviously this led to rougher treatment and the threat of our military service stretching on longer than the normal compulsory two years. But what horrified me more than anything was finding myself in the midst of men I considered my own mortal enemies as well as the State's and knowing that I'd been assigned to them, definitively and irrevocably, by my own Comrades. I spent the early period in the black, or penal, division as a stubborn recluse. I didn't want to get used to my enemies, I didn't want to become acclimatized. Thus on those alternate Saturdays when, as a privilege rather than a right, the soldiers surged out in gangs to the bars and after the girls, I preferred to be left on my own. I would lie down on my bunk in the hut, trying to read or even to study (for certain branches of mathematics all one needs is pencil and paper) and drawing nourishment from my nonconformity. I took the view that I had only one job to do there: to continue the fight for my political honor, for my right not to be regarded as an enemy, for my right to be somewhere else.

I paid several visits to the company's political officer and tried to convince him that my presence in the penal corps was all a mistake, that I'd been excluded from the Party for intellectualism and cynicism but not as an enemy of Socialism. For the umpteenth time I recounted the ridiculous story of the postcard. I am bound in all fairness to say that the political officer heard me out patiently and showed a somewhat unexpected understanding of my desire for justice. Indeed, he made some inquiries about my case "higher up" (an indeterminate and invisible place). Finally, however, he summoned me and said with unconcealed resentment, "Why try to fool me? I've discovered you're a Trotskyite."

It took me about two weeks to become accustomed to the hard labor down in the mines, holding the heavy drill whose vibrations I felt pulsating through my body even in my sleep. But I worked with a sort of diligent fury; I wanted to produce exceptional outputs, and soon I began to have some success.

Except that no one saw this as an expression of my conscientiousness. For we were paid piece rates, so that many of the others, whatever their political opinions, worked with considerable verve in order at least to wrest something worthwhile from those otherwise wasted years.

Even though everyone regarded us as violent enemies of the regime, all the forms of public life that are customary in Socialist collectives were maintained in the barracks; we, the enemies of the regime, were given ten-minute physical training sessions under the eye of the political officer, we had political pep talks every day, we had to monitor the bulletin boards, on which we pasted photographs of Socialist statesmen and painted slogans about the radiant tomorrow. At first I volunteered almost demonstratively for these tasks. But no one saw any evidence of conscientiousness in this either; all the others volunteered as well when they needed to be noticed by the commanding officer and granted an evening's leave. None of the men saw this political work for what it was, only as an empty tribute which had to be rendered up to those in power.

Among the NCO's into whose tender mercies we were delivered was a dark-haired Slovak sergeant who was distinguished from the others by his mildness and complete lack of sadism. He was popular among us, though there were some who said maliciously that his kindheartedness sprang only from his stupidity. The NCO's, of course, carried arms, and from time to time they went off for shooting practice. Once the dark sergeant came back from a shooting practice covered with the glory of having placed first in marksmanship. A number of us were loud in our congratulations—half good-natured, half mocking—but the sergeant merely blushed.

Later that day, finding myself alone with him, I asked him, just for something to say, "How do you manage to be such a good shot?"

The sergeant gave me a quizzical glance and said, "It's a special gimmick I have. I pretend the tin target's an imperialist. And I get so angry that I hit the bull's-eye."

I was about to ask him how he imagined this imperialist as looking, but he stopped me dead by saying, seriously and thoughtfully, "I don't know why you all congratulate me. If there was a war on I'd be shooting at you."

Such a remark, coming from this good-natured fellow, who never even shouted at us—and was later transferred for it—showed me that the bonds connecting me with the Party and my Comrades had been broken beyond repair.

Yes. Every tie was cut: my studies, my work for the Movement, my friendships, love and the quest for love, everything that had made life meaningful.

To be in the army at that time and have a wife or fiancée at home was a very harsh fate indeed. Not only did your imagination stand permanently and uselessly on guard over her unguardable existence, but you were in a state of constant anticipation about her occasional visits, mixed with fear lest on the appointed day the company commander should refuse leave, and she should come to the camp gates in vain. With a humor as black as their epaulettes, the men used to tell stories of officers lying in wait for these frustrated wives and reaping the fruit of desires which rightly belonged to the privates confined in their barracks.

And yet for those with a wife or girl at home there was a thread stretching across the abyss, a desperately thin and fragile thread perhaps, but still a thread. I had no such thread. I'd broken off all relations with Marketa, and the only letters I received came from my mother. . . . But wasn't this a sort of thread? No, it was not; home, the parental home, is not a thread. The letters received from parents are messages sent from a stronghold from which one is continually receding, and serve only to make you conscious of your alienation.

Slowly I grew used to the idea that my life had lost its continuity, and that it only remained for me to commit my spirit to its inescapable destiny. Gradually my eyes grew accustomed to the dim light of reality, and I began to notice the people around me; later than the others, but luckily not so late as to be estranged from them altogether.

The first to emerge from the murk was Honza from Brno, who had been assigned to the penal division for assaulting a policeman. He'd thrashed him as an old schoolmate with whom he'd had an argument, but the court didn't see it that way. Honza had served six months in jail and then come straight to us. He was a skilled fitter but was openly unconcerned about whether he would ever return to his craft, or what he would do.

He had no ties, and his indifference to the future was the true source of his impudent and carefree independence.

The only one who could measure up to Honza in this rare sense of freedom was Bedrich, the most eccentric inmate of our twenty-bunk room. Bedrich had come to us two months after the regular September draft, having originally enlisted in an infantry regiment, where he'd stubbornly refused, on strict religious grounds, to be issued with a rifle. The authorities did not know quite what to do with him, especially after intercepting letters he'd addressed to Truman and Stalin with an impassioned appeal to both statesmen to disband their armies in the name of Socialist brotherhood. In their confusion they even permitted him, for a while, to go on drill parade, where he was the only man without a weapon and executed the commands to slope and order arms perfectly but with empty hands. He also took part in the early political sessions and joined eagerly in the discussions, inveighing against the imperialist warmonger. But when, on his own, he made a poster calling for total and universal disarmament and hung it in the barracks, he was court-martialed for mutiny. The court, however, was so nonplussed by his pacifist harangue that they had him examined by a psychiatrist and after further temporizing withdrew their charge and transferred him to our group. Bedrich was delighted. This was the remarkable thing about him: he was the only man there who'd deliberately earned his black epaulettes and took pleasure in having them. That was why he felt free—though in his case, unlike Honza's, independence took the form not of insolence but of quiet obedience and contented industry.

The others were all much more weighed down by their cares and sorrows. There was the thirty-year-old Hungarian, Varga from Slovakia, who, oblivious of national prejudices, had fought during the war in several armies and been captured several times by both sides. There was the red-haired Petran, whose brother had escaped across the border, shooting a frontier guard as he did so. There was the simpleminded Josef, a rich peasant's son who was so accustomed to blue horizons and soaring skylarks that the infernal labyrinth of shafts and galleries oppressed him with a suffocating terror. There was Stana, a twenty-year-old madcap from Prague's East End, on whom the local council had passed a savage sentence for his getting drunk in a May Day procession and *deliberately* urinating on the edge of the pavement in full view of the cheering citizens. There was Pavel Pekny, a law student, who at the time of the coup had demonstrated against the Communists with a handful of his fellow students; he soon discovered I belonged to the same camp as those who'd subsequently kicked him out of the university, and he was the only one who made evident his malicious satisfaction that I'd ended up in the same boat.

Of them all the one I liked best was Honza. I remember one of our first conversations together; it was during a short break in a pit gallery where we found ourselves side by side. Honza slapped me on the knee and said, "Hey, you, are you deaf and dumb or something?"

I was indeed at that time deaf and dumb, or rather permanently withdrawn into my shell, and I found it difficult, when we got talking, to explain to Honza, in words which immediately struck me as unpleasantly affected and artificial, how I came to be there and what a mistake it was. He said, "Do you think any of us ought to be here, you fool?" I wanted to explain my position again, but as I searched for more convincing words Honza swallowed his last crust of bread and said slowly, "If you were as tall as you're crazy, the sun would burn a hole through your skull." These words, with their urban brand of mockery, made me feel suddenly ashamed of fretting over my lost privileges—I whose convictions had been based on hatred of privilege and self-indulgence.

In time Honza and I became close friends. He respected me for my skill and speed at mental arithmetic, a talent which on several paydays prevented us from being shortchanged. On one occasion he called me an idiot for spending my free evenings in camp and dragged me out with the rest of the gang. I remem-

ber that outing vividly. There were quite a few of us, about
eight in all, including Varga the Hungarian and Stana the May
Day urinator. There were also, both from another company,
Ambrose, who was forty and had been there four years already,
and Cenek, a failed industrial art student who had been posted
to the penal division for persistently doing cubist paintings at
college and now sought to ingratiate himself by doing huge
charcoal drawings of Hussite warriors with mace and flail all
over the barracks rooms.

Our choice was strictly circumscribed: the center of Ostrava
was out of bounds, and many other places too. We got as far as
the next suburb and struck it lucky, for there was a dance in
progress at a former drill hall, to which none of our restrictions
applied. We paid the nominal entrance fee and surged in. The
hall contained plenty of tables and chairs but only a small group
of people—about ten girls and perhaps thirty men, half of them
soldiers from the artillery barracks nearby.

The moment the gunners saw us they came alert, and we
could feel them eyeing us and counting heads. We sat at a long
empty table and ordered a bottle of vodka, but an ugly-looking
waitress announced sternly that she wasn't permitted to serve
alcoholic drinks. Honza then ordered eight lemonades, collected a banknote from each of us, left the hall, and presently
returned with three bottles of rum. In topping up our glasses
of lemonade under the table we employed the utmost circum-
spection, knowing full well that the artillerymen were watching us and that they were perfectly capable of reporting us for
illegal consumption of liquor. The armed forces all detested
us. On the one hand, brought up on the spy stories of the day,
they viewed us as suspicious elements, criminals, assassins,
monsters ever ready to murder their sleeping families in their
beds; while on the other, and perhaps more seriously, they envied us for having so much more money to spend than they
themselves could afford.

That was the curious thing about our position. We knew only
toil and sweat, we had our heads shaved clean every two weeks

to keep our hair from giving us any unseemly self-confidence, we were the disinherited of the earth, with nothing in our lives to look forward to; but we had money. We were not millionaires, but in those few hours of freedom two nights a month, and in those few permitted places, we could behave like millionaires and compensate for the chronic frustration of the rest of our endless days.

Up on the platform an indifferent dance band alternated between polkas and waltzes. A few couples whirled around the floor, while we coolly eyed the girls and sipped our lemonade laced with rum, which assured us of a certain immune superiority to the others in the hall. We felt marvelous. I experienced an intoxicating conviviality, a sense of companionship I hadn't experienced since the last time I played with Jaroslav and the boys in the cymbalo band. All the while Honza had been devising a scheme to whisk as many girls as possible away from the gunners. His ploy was admirably simple, and we lost no time putting it into effect. Cenek, that extrovert comedian, took the lead, and to our delight carried out the plan brilliantly. Having invited a dark, heavily made-up girl for a dance and then brought her over to our table, he had a rum lemonade poured for himself and one for her, saying to her significantly, "Let's drink to it then!" The girl nodded and they clinked glasses. At that moment a young artillery corporal sauntered up and said to Cenek in as offhand a tone as he could manage, "All right if I . . ." "Go on, friend, have a waltz if you want one," said Cenek. While the girl and her corporal were skipping to the inane rhythm of the polka, Honza was phoning for a taxi, and as soon as it arrived Cenek went over and stood by the exit. His girl finished the dance, told the corporal she was going to the ladies'—and the next moment we heard the taxi speeding away.

Old Ambrose from B Company was the next to achieve success, finding himself an older girl whose miserable appearance didn't deter four gunners from vainly circulating around her. Ten minutes later Ambrose rode off with his girl and with

Varga (who, it seemed, was diffident about his own chances) to rendezvous with Cenek in a bar at the other end of town. Soon two more of our number had managed to get a girl between them, which left just three of us: Stana, Honza, and myself. By now the gunners were looking at us more and more ominously as they began to realize the connection between our diminished number and the disappearance of three women right from under their noses.

We tried to look innocent but we could feel the growing tension. "One more taxi now for an honorable retreat," I said, looking wistfully at a blonde I'd managed to dance with earlier on. I'd hoped during the next dance to pluck up the courage to lure her away, but the gunners had mounted such a guard on her that I was unable to get near her. "It's no good," said Honza, getting up to phone. As he walked across the hall, the gunners all got up from their tables and closed in on him. There was a fight brewing, and Stana and I had no choice but to get up and force our way through to our threatened companion. The crowd of gunners was standing around Honza in menacing silence, broken presently by the appearance of a soldier who was far from sober—he too probably had a bottle under the table. This character launched into a sermon about how his father had been unemployed in the First Republic and how he wasn't going to stand by while these bourgeois with their black bands lorded it over them, no, he wasn't going to stand for it, so his friends had better watch out in case he socked that one (meaning Honza) right in the jaw. Honza kept quiet and at the first pause in the trooper's speech asked civilly what the Comrades of the artillery wanted from him. "We want you to get out on the double," one of them said, and Honza explained that that was just what we were doing and that if only they'd let him go he could phone for a taxi. When he said this it looked as if the trooper was going to have a fit. "Damn it to hell," he shouted in a high-pitched voice. "Damn it to hell, here's us slogging away and not able to get out, working our fingers to the bone and no money for it, and these capitalists, these saboteurs, these bastards, are traveling by taxi! Taxi—they're not leaving here in a taxi, not if I have to strangle them with my bare hands!"

The others all joined in. A number of civilians crowded around the soldiers, including the drill hall staff, who were anxious to avoid an incident. Suddenly I caught sight of my blonde; she'd got up from the table where she'd been abandoned and was now on her way to the toilet, entirely indifferent to the fracas. As inconspicuously as possible I detached myself from the group and followed her into the hallway where the coatroom and toilets were, and a solitary coatroom attendant. I'd been thrown in at the deep end and had to learn to swim. Shy or not, I plunged my hand in my pocket, brought out a few crumpled notes, and said, "Why don't you come with us? We'll have a better time than you can in here." She looked at the notes and shrugged her shoulders. I said I'd wait for her outside and she nodded, slipped into the ladies' room, and emerged a moment later with her coat on. She smiled at me and announced that she could tell right away that I was different from the rest. This delighted me, and I took her arm and led her across the street and around the corner, where we waited for Honza and Stana to come out. The blonde asked me if I was a student, which I confirmed. She then told me that she'd just had some money stolen from her in the factory coatroom, that it was the firm's money and that she was desperate they might sue her for it: could I lend her some? I reached in my pocket and gave her the crumpled notes.

We didn't have long to wait before our two friends emerged with their caps and coats on. I whistled to them, but as I did so three other soldiers, coatless and capless, came rushing out of the hall and dashed up to them. I heard their angry voices, and though the words were lost I could guess their meaning: they were looking for my blonde. Then one of them took a swing at Honza and the fight was on. Stana had one of the gunners on him while Honza had the other two. They had almost forced him to the ground when I arrived and laid into one of them. The gunners had assumed they'd have the advantage in numbers, and as soon as the balance was restored they lost their confidence. Finally, when one of them folded under Stana's fist and sank to the ground moaning, we took advantage of the confusion and beat a hasty retreat.

The blonde was waiting obediently for us around the corner. When my friends saw her they went wild with joy. They swore I was the greatest, and for the first time in ages I felt genuinely and hilariously happy. Honza produced a full bottle of rum from under his coat—how he'd managed to keep it intact during the fight is beyond me—and swung it over his head. Our only problem was that we had nowhere to go. We'd been thrown out of the one neighboring establishment that wasn't off limits; our indignant rivals had denied us our taxi and might at any moment threaten our existence with a fresh assault.

We set off hurriedly down a narrow alley between houses for a short distance, until there was only a wall on one side and a fence on the other. A ladder loomed up against the fence, and close to it some sort of grass-cutting machine with a tin seat. "A throne," I said, and Honza sat the blonde down on the seat, which was about three feet off the ground. We passed the bottle from hand to hand, and all four of us drank freely. The blonde soon became voluble and started on Honza: "Could you lend me some money?" The magnanimous Honza slipped her some notes, and soon the girl had her coat turned back, her skirt drawn up, and her underpants down. She took my hand and pulled me toward her, but I broke away. Without hesitating Stana resolutely grabbed her and thrust into her. Their embrace lasted for barely twenty seconds, after which I wanted to give precedence to Honza, partly because I enjoyed playing host, partly because I was still scared. This time, however, the blonde was more determined and pulled me against her hard, and when, aroused by her touch, I was quite ready to oblige her, she whispered softly in my ear, "I only came because of you, silly." Then she started to moan so convincingly that I suddenly imagined this was really a nice girl who was in love with me and whom I loved. She went on murmuring and sighing, and it

wasn't until I heard Honza making an obscene joke behind me
that I discovered this wasn't the nice girl I wanted to be in love
with. I broke away from her without climaxing, so violently
that the blonde was almost frightened and said, "What's the
matter with you?" but Honza was already on her and the moaning began again.

That night we got back to camp around two in the morning.
At half past four we had to be up for the voluntary Sunday shift,
for which our commanding officer received a bonus and we our
bi-weekly Saturday passes. We were sleepy, the alcohol was
still inside us, and although we resembled wraiths as we moved
about the gloom of the gallery I enjoyed reliving in my imagination the evening we'd just spent.

The Saturday two weeks later was not so good. Honza had
had his leave canceled over some incident, and I went out with
two young men from another company whom I knew only
slightly. We headed straight for a woman who because of her
monstrous height was known as the Candelabrum. The compulsion to put their brief and infrequent free periods to use at any
price caused the men to go for an available woman rather than
an attractive one. In time, by comparing notes, a pool was
formed of those females who, however hideous, were at least
more or less definitely available for general use.

The Candelabrum belonged to this pool. Not that I minded
this. In fact, when the other two started joking interminably
about her abnormal height and about us having to find a brick
to stick under our feet when the time came, in a curious way I
found myself actually enjoying their coarseness and finding
that it even intensified my own lust—for any woman, the more
depersonalized, the more soulless, the better, and best if she
was just *any* woman.

But even though I'd had plenty to drink, the fierceness of my
lust subsided fast enough when I actually laid eyes on the Candelabrum. Neither Honza nor Stana—or anyone I liked—was
there, and everything seemed vile and pointless. The next day
I was terribly hung over and, worse, seized with a sense of dis-

gust that encompassed even the events of my last pass, and I swore I would never again desire either the girl on the grass-cutter seat or the drunken Candelabrum. I suddenly felt intensely sorry for myself. Sorry because I saw quite clearly that this depressing state of affairs had become the norm for my present life—that those two sad and empty Saturday nights had precisely defined the range of my opportunities, had drawn precisely the horizon of the love life I could expect from now on. And I felt afraid—afraid of this bleak horizon, afraid of my destiny itself. I felt my soul begin to contract, to flinch away from all this, and realized with horror that there was no place it could escape.

This same depression was experienced, with varying degrees of intensity, by nearly all of us. Bedrich, of the peace manifestos, resisted it by a contemplative withdrawal into the depths of his being where his mystic God evidently resided—the erotic counterpart of this pious inwardness being the masturbation which he practiced with ritual regularity. The others exhibited a much greater degree of self-deception, balancing their cynical whoring expeditions against romanticism of the most sentimental kind. Some had a love at home whose memory they burnished industriously until it shone with the greatest brilliance; others would secretly persuade themselves that the girl they'd picked up drunk in a bar cherished sacred feelings toward them. Stana had two visits from a girl in Prague whom he'd known before he was called up, and whom he'd certainly not taken very seriously at the time. Suddenly he was head over heels in love and with characteristic impetuosity set the date. He maintained that he was only doing this for the two days' marriage leave, but I knew this was merely a cynical façade. I remember exactly when Stana went off to Prague for the weekend to get married, because his wedding day became a day of great significance for me also.

I had been given leave for the day, and still feeling low after that last free evening which I had squandered on the Candelabrum, I avoided my messmates and went out on my own. On impulse I boarded an ancient narrow-gauge streetcar linking the outer suburbs of Ostrava and let it carry me away. Just as impulsively, I got off and set out on a long walk through the endless Ostrava backwoods with their factories and fields, meadows and garbage dumps, copses and slag heaps, tenement blocks and farmhouses, all thrown together in a weird kind of harmony. I was strangely attracted and at the same time disturbed by all these incongruities, which I saw not only as the common denominator of the entire region but as a striking image of my own fate, my own exile in this city. I didn't belong here, any more than the weeping willow and the ivy-covered cottage I'd just passed did, or the jumble of houses and alleyways that led nowhere, or the monstrous developments of squat prefabs defacing a region once pleasantly rural. And I realized that it was precisely because I didn't belong that I was fated to be here, in this appalling city which clasped in its ruthless embrace everything alien to it.

Then I found myself outside a one-story building with a sign MOVIE HOUSE fastened vertically down one corner. I speculated idly on why it had no name; I looked at it closely, but there was no other sign anywhere on the building, which incidentally looked singularly unlike a theater. Between it and the next building an alley led to a yard and a low-lying extension of the building, with glass cases on the walls for movie ads and stills. I went up to these but once again was unable to discover the name of the theater. Looking around, I saw behind a wire fence a little girl in a neighboring backyard, and asked her what the place was called. She looked at me in surprise and said she didn't know. I grew resigned to this anonymity: in the banishment of Ostrava even the movie houses had no names.

I drifted back to the glass case and noticed for the first time the title of the film announced by the poster and two photographs: *Honest Justice*. This was the Soviet film to whose heroine Marketa had alluded when she'd taken it upon herself to play the role of grand commiserator in my life, the very film whose most severe aspects had been referred to by the Comrades when they instituted proceedings against me. The whole affair had made the film highly distasteful to me, and I had hoped never to hear of it again. And now even here in Ostrava I could not avoid its warning message. Still, if we do not like the warning, we can turn our backs on it. I did just that and headed for the alleyway leading back to the street.

And that was when I first set eyes on Lucie.

She was walking toward me, heading for the backyard of the theater. Why didn't I walk past her and away? Her appearance was perfectly ordinary. Later on, it was this very ordinariness which touched and attracted me, but how was it that she caught my eye and stopped me in my tracks this first time I saw her? Hadn't I seen enough of these Ostrava nonentities out on the streets? What was so extraordinary about her ordinariness? I don't know. I only know that I stood where I was and watched her as she passed. She walked slowly and unhurriedly up to the glass case and stood looking at the stills from *Honest Justice*; then she turned slowly away and passed through the open doors into the lobby.

I believe now that it must have been that singular slowness of Lucie's which captivated me, a slowness suggesting a resigned consciousness that there was nothing to hurry for and that impatience gets you nowhere. Yes, it was probably that melancholy slowness which kept my eyes fixed on the girl as she made her way to the box office, took out some change, bought a ticket, glanced into the auditorium, then turned back and came out into the yard again.

I never once took my eyes off her. She stayed with her back to me, looking out over the yard to where the garden plots began, enclosed by their wooden fences, and the cottages which continued until they were hidden by the outline of a lignite quarry. I shall never forget that yard. I remember every detail: the wire fence with the little girl staring at us from the

steps of the house, the steps themselves, flanked by a low wall
with two empty flowerpots and a gray washtub on top, the
smudgy sun edging down toward the quarry on the horizon.

It was ten minutes to six, which meant that it was ten minutes before the performance was due to begin. Lucie turned
and strolled across the yard and out into the street. I followed
her, and ravaged rural Ostrava was replaced by the city street.
Fifty yards away there was a small square, neatly laid out, with
benches and a little garden, and behind the square a pseudo-
Gothic structure in black brick, with a clock tower. I watched
Lucie sit down on a bench, her slowness never deserting her
for an instant. She even sat down slowly. She did not once look
around her; she didn't even let her eyes wander. She just sat
there, vacant or preoccupied, so that I was able to stroll near
and look her up and down without her even being aware of it.

I hesitate to speak of love at first sight—I am only too well
aware of love's retrospective tendency to turn its own beginnings into myth—but some sort of *second* sight there certainly was: the essence of Lucie's being or, to be precise, the essence of her meaning for me, I sensed and understood in a flash
of intuition like that epiphany in which religious truth is revealed to some men.

I looked at her and took in the clumsy home permanent
crumpling her hair into a shapeless mass of curls; I took in the
wretched brown coat, ragged and too short. I took in her face,
unobtrusively attractive, attractively unobtrusive, and felt that
this girl could supply the calm, simplicity, and modesty that I
needed. It seemed that we were very close in other ways too,
and that, strangers as we were, I need only go up and start
talking to her for her to smile as if she suddenly saw a long-lost
brother standing before her.

Then Lucie raised her head and looked up at the clock tower
—even this movement is fixed in my memory, the movement
of a girl who has no wristwatch and who instinctively sits facing a clock. She got up and walked over to the theater. I wanted
to join her, but suddenly found I lacked not courage so much

as the right words. Instead I followed her as far as the lobby. From there I could see into the auditorium, which was yawning and empty. There is something repellent about an empty auditorium, and Lucie stopped and looked around her with an air of embarrassment. At that moment several people entered the lobby and began surging toward the ticket office. I stepped in front of them and bought a ticket for the terrible film.

Meanwhile the girl had gone in. I followed her to the same row and sat down in the next seat. At that moment there was a squeal of music from a worn record, the lights dimmed, and advertisements appeared on the screen.

Lucie must have realized that it was no accident for a soldier wearing black insignia to have sat right next to her, and she was certainly aware of me the whole time—all the more, perhaps, because I concentrated entirely on her and enjoyed a slightly childish revenge by letting the film so frequently quoted at me by moralists flash past without my paying it the slightest attention.

As the film ended, Lucie got up, lifted the folded brown overcoat from her lap, and put one arm in the sleeve. I quickly put on my cap to hide the clean-shaven skull, and without a word began helping her into the other sleeve. She glanced briefly at me and gave a barely perceptible nod, which I was uncertain whether to interpret as thanks or as a purely instinctive gesture. Then she picked her way out of the row of seats. I quickly put on my green coat and followed her out. We were still inside the auditorium when I spoke to her.

It was as if for those two hours I'd been attuning myself to her wavelength. For once, I was able to start a conversation without a humorous or ironical remark, without my usual compulsion to burden myself with disguises. In fact I was perfectly natural. I asked her where she lived and worked, and whether she went to the movies often. I told her that I worked in the mines, that it was hard work, and that it wasn't often I was able to get out. She said that she worked in a factory and lived in a hostel, that she had to be in by eleven and went to the movies a lot because she didn't care for dancing. I told her I'd be glad to go with her any time she was free. She said she preferred going on her own. I asked her if that was because she felt depressed about life. She said it was. I told her I was in the same boat.

Nothing brings people together so quickly (even if the closeness often proves illusory) as a shared melancholy, a quiet mutual sympathy and understanding—that most simple form of rapport which is yet so rare since it requires you to lay aside cultivated restraint and be yourself. How I managed, suddenly and with no preparation, to do this, I who'd always fumbled blindly behind my masks, I don't know. But I felt it like an unexpected gift or a miraculous liberation.

We told each other the most commonplace things about ourselves as we walked to her hostel. When we reached it we stayed outside for a while. Gentle light from a streetlamp fell on Lucie, and I looked at her brown coat and stroked her, not her cheeks or her hair but the ragged material of this pitiful garment.

I still remember the swaying of the streetlamp and the unpleasantly loud laughter of the young girls who kept passing us and opening the hostel doors. I remember looking up the wall of this building where Lucie lived, a wall gray and bare, with unrecessed windows. Above all I remember Lucie's face, which, unlike the faces of other girls I've known in similar situations, was calm and ingenuous, like the face of a schoolgirl standing by the blackboard and obediently reciting what she knows, seeking neither attention nor praise.

We agreed that I'd send a postcard to let her know when my next leave would be and when we could see each other. We said good night without even kissing and I walked away. After a few steps I turned and saw her standing in the doorway, making no attempt to unlock the door, just standing and watching me. Only then, when I was some way off, did she drop her reserve and allow her eyes, which until then had been rather timid, to fix me in a long stare. Then she lifted her hand like someone who has never waved and doesn't know how, who only knows that it's the proper thing to do at such a moment and is awkwardly attempting to make the gesture. I stopped and waved back. Then I walked on again, stopped again— Lucie was still waving—and in this manner made my slow retreat, until finally I turned the corner and we vanished from each other's sight.

From that evening I was transformed, *reinhabited*. My inner room had suddenly been tidied up and there was someone living there. The clock which for months had been hanging on the wall with its hands motionless had begun to tick. This was significant. Time, which until now had flowed from nothingness to nothingness, without articulation, without measure, had begun once more to dissect itself and measure itself out. I began to live for my passes, and the days between became the rungs of a ladder up which I climbed after Lucie.

Never in my life have I devoted so much silent, concentrated thought to a woman as I did to Lucie. (Though it must be admitted that never have I had so much time for it either.) To no other woman have I ever felt so much gratitude.

Gratitude? For what? First and foremost for releasing me from the bounds of that pathetically limited romantic horizon by which we were all surrounded. The newly married Stana, it's true, was another who'd found a way of breaking the barrier. At home, in Prague, he now had a woman of his own to love and care for; he could sketch to himself the long future of his married life and take pleasure in the knowledge of being loved. But he wasn't to be envied. By marrying, he'd set in motion a destiny over which, the moment he boarded the train and returned to Ostrava, he had lost all influence whatsoever. And so, as the weeks and months went by, more and more disquiet dripped into his initial contentment, more and more helpless anxiety about his life in Prague, a life from which he was cut off and to which he had no access.

In meeting Lucie I too had set my destiny in motion, but I didn't let myself lose sight of it. Our meetings may have been infrequent but at least they were more or less regular, and I knew she was capable of waiting two weeks or more for me and then of meeting me as if we'd parted only yesterday.

But Lucie did not only rescue me from the bitter taste my bleak erotic adventures in Ostrava had left in my mouth. At that time I had finally admitted to myself that I'd lost my fight and wouldn't be allowed to change the black insignia of my corps. I knew it was senseless to alienate myself from people with whom I had to live for two years or more, senseless to be constantly advertising my right to my original career, the privileged nature of which I was only just beginning to grasp. Yet at the same time this realization was a matter of the intellect and the will only, and was powerless to deliver me from my intense regret for my lost destiny. On this inner sorrow Lucie had a miraculous healing effect. It was enough to feel her beside me with the whole warm circumference of her life, a life in which there was no room for questions of cosmopolitanism and internationalism, alertness and vigilance, the definition of the dictatorship of the proletariat, the whole gamut of politics with their strategy, tactics, and "personnel policy."

These were the concerns—so much a part of the age that their jargon will soon become incomprehensible—upon which I'd come to grief, and to which I clung. What had attracted, even infatuated, me about the Communist movement was the feeling, however illusory, of being close to the *helm of history*. In those days we really were making big decisions—not least in the universities, where there were as yet few Communists among the professors, so that in the initial years the Communist students ran the universities almost unaided, making the decisions on academic staffing, on teaching reform, and on the curriculum. The elation we experienced is commonly referred to as the intoxication of power, but with a little good will, I could choose a less severe way of putting it: we were bewitched by history, drunk with having jumped on its back and being able to feel it beneath us. Admittedly, in most cases this did develop into an ugly lust for power, but all the same there was at that time an altogether idealistic illusion that we were inaugurating a human era, an era when man—every man—would be neither outside history nor under its heel, but would direct and create it himself.

I was convinced that outside the radius of that helm of history, to which I made such frequent and heady allusion, there was no life, only vegetation, boredom, banishment, Siberia. And then suddenly, after six months of Siberia, I saw a completely new and unexpected opportunity of life; before me there had opened out the forgotten pastures of ordinary everyday life, previously hidden under the soaring wings of history, and in these pastures stood a poor, unhappy, but very lovable girl—Lucie.

What did Lucie know about those great wings of history? She would hardly have heard of them. She knew nothing of history, she lived under it, but it was alien to her. She knew nothing of the *great problems of the age*. The problems she lived with were trivial and eternal. And suddenly I'd been rescued; it seemed to me that she'd come to me in order to lead me into her gray paradise, and the step which a short while ago had seemed unthinkable, the step by which I was to make my exit from history, was suddenly a cause for relief and rejoicing. Lucie held me shyly by the hand and I allowed myself to be led.

But who in more factual terms was Lucie?

She was nineteen but really much older than that, as women always are when they've had a hard life and been catapulted from childhood to adulthood. She told me that she came from Cheb, that she'd left school at fifteen and became an apprentice. She didn't like talking about her home and would only when I made her. She hadn't been happy there. "They didn't like me," she said. Her mother had married again and her new stepfather drank and treated her badly. Once they'd accused her of concealing some money from them, and they used to beat her. When the situation became intolerable, Lucie took the first opportunity and left for Ostrava, where she'd been for a full year. She had a few girlfriends but preferred being on her own. Her friends went dancing and brought boys back to the hostel. Lucie refused to. She was a serious girl: she preferred going to the movies.

Yes, she actually described herself as "serious" and associated this quality with her regular visits to the films. Best of all she liked war films, of which there were any number showing at that time. This may have been because she found them exciting, but more probably because the great accumulation of suffering they contained made her feel sad, and she thought that this elevated her and confirmed her in the "seriousness" she prized so highly. Once she mentioned to me that she'd seen a "lovely" film; it was Dovzhenko's *Michurin*. And she was quick to tick off its virtues: it gave such a lovely picture of how beautiful nature was; also she'd always loved flowers; and a man who didn't like trees wasn't a nice person at all.

It wouldn't be quite fair to say that Lucie attracted me by the exotic quality of her simplicity. Her simplicity, her fragmentary education, didn't prevent her understanding me—an understanding that consisted not in any experience or knowledge, any skill in debate or capacity for giving advice, but in the anticipation and receptiveness with which she listened to everything I said.

One summer day I'd managed to get out before Lucie had finished work, so I took a book with me, sat down on a garden wall, and started reading. On being drafted, I'd taken three books of poetry with me, which I read over and over again and which brought me comfort: they were poems by Frantisek Halas.

These books played a special part in my life, special because I wasn't a great reader—least of all of poetry—and these were the only books of verse that I'd ever grown fond of. I'd come to them just after my expulsion from the Party, when Halas' name was regaining its notoriety, a leading Party spokesman having accused the recently dead poet of faithlessness, morbidity, existentialism, everything which in those days was considered political anathema. I'd sought out Halas' verse in order to encounter a fellow apostate and discover whether my mentality did in fact resemble his. I also wanted to see whether the sorrow proscribed by his powerful detractor as morbid and harmful would afford me some joy by striking a note to which I could respond. For in my situation I hardly expected to find joy in joy. Before leaving for Ostrava, I'd borrowed all three volumes from a former fellow student, a great lover of literature, and I finally managed to persuade him not to expect them back. And so the verses joined me in exile.

When Lucie found me at the appointed place with a book in my hand, she asked what I was reading. I showed her the open book, and she said in some surprise, "But that's poetry!"

"Do you find it funny for me to be reading poetry?" I asked.

She shrugged her shoulders and said, "No, why should it be?" But I think she did, because in all probability she associated poetry with school readers. We strolled through the strange soot-filled Ostrava summer, that black summer through which, instead of floating white clouds, coal cars shunted along overhead cables. I saw that Lucie was still somehow drawn to the book in my hand. So when we sat down in a little wood just outside Petrvald, I opened the book and asked, "Are you interested in this?" She nodded.

I'd never recited poetry to anyone before and I've never done so since. I have a kind of built-in reserve that prevents me from being too open with people, from revealing my feelings to others, and reading poetry seems to me more than just talking about my feelings; it's as if at the same time I was standing on one leg. There's a certain unnaturalness in the very principle of rhyme and rhythm, and it would cause me great embarrassment to have to apply myself to it other than in solitude.

But Lucie had the miraculous power, which no one else has

ever had, of breaking down this reserve and relieving me of
my burden of shyness. I could permit myself anything in front
of her: candor, emotion, pathos.

So I read:

> *Your body is a lean ear*
> *From which the grain has fallen and will not sprout.*
> *Your body is like a lean ear.*
>
> *Your body is a skein of silk*
> *Written in longing to the last fold.*
> *Your body is like a skein of silk.*
>
> *Your body is a burnt sky*
> *Dreaming watchful in a tissue of death.*
> *Your body is like a burnt sky.*
>
> *Your body is hushed and quiet.*
> *Its tears quiver in my eyelids.*
> *Your body is hushed and quiet.*

I had my arm around Lucie's shoulders, which were protected only by a thin, flower-patterned dress, and I succumbed
to the suggestion that the lines I was reading were all part of
the sorrow of her body, a quiet resigned body condemned to
death. And I read her some more poems, including the one
which to this day evokes a picture of her, and which ends with
the lines:

> *Foolish words I do not believe you I believe silence*
> *Above beauty above everything*
> *The triumph of understanding.*

Suddenly I felt Lucie's shoulders shaking; she was crying.

What had made her cry? The meaning of the words? Or the
nameless sorrow flowering from the melody of the verse and the
timbre of my voice? Had she, perhaps, been exalted by the tri-

umphal elusiveness of the poems and been moved to tears by this very exaltation? Or had the verse simply broken through a mysterious barrier within her?

I do not know. Lucie held me around the neck like a child, with her head pressed against the sweaty cloth of the uniform spanning my chest, and cried unrestrainedly.

How many times in recent years have women of the most varied temperaments reproached me, when I was unable to return their feelings, with being conceited? This is nonsense; I'm not in the least conceited, but, if the truth were known, it does cause me pain to think that ever since I became fully mature I've been unable to establish a real relationship with any woman, that I've never, as they say, loved a woman. I'm not sure that I know the reasons for this failure, whether they lie in some inborn emotional deficiency or are rooted in my life history. I don't mean to sound pathetic, but that's the way it is. Again and again in my reminiscences I return to that hall with its hundred people raising their hands to vote for the destruction of my life. Those hundred people had no idea that one day there would be a 1956 and that conditions would gradually change. They counted on my being an outcast for life. Not for masochistic reasons, but from some malicious streak in my makeup, I've often composed imaginary variations on this theme, speculating, for instance, on what would have happened if it had been moved that instead of being expelled from the Party I should be hanged. I'm sure that in that case, too, they would all have raised their hands, especially had the desirability of my hanging been passionately urged in the opening address. From that time on, each time I've met a new man or woman who might become my friend or lover I have mentally transported him to that assembly hall and asked whether he would have raised his hand. No one has ever passed this test: every one has raised his hand, just as my so-called friends and colleagues—willingly or unwillingly, from conviction or from fear—raised theirs. And take careful note of this: it's a hard thing to live with people who would have sent you to exile or death, it's hard to put your trust in them, and it's hard to love them.

Perhaps it was cruel of me to submit my acquaintances to such severe scrutiny. Some may even say that this procedure of mine had only one purpose: to elevate myself above all others in my moral complacency. But such an accusation of arrogance would not really be justified. I've never myself raised a hand to vote for anyone's destruction, and I've tried for a long time to convince myself at least that if I'd had the opportunity I wouldn't have taken it. But I'm honest enough to laugh at myself for this. Would I have been the only one not to raise his hand? Am I the one just man? Unfortunately, I found no guarantee within myself that I would have been any better. But this consciousness of my own fallibility in no way reconciles me to the same thing in others. I detest with all my heart fraternal feelings based solely on mutual recognition of a similar baseness, and have no desire for this sad sort of brotherhood.

How is it, then, that I was able to love Lucie? Happily my cynical speculation on human nature date from a later period, so that I was still able to accept Lucie eagerly and trustingly as a gift from heaven. This was a happy time for me, possibly my happiest. I was worked to death, beaten, and bullied, but from day to day my joy increased. It's funny really: if the women who resent me today for being conceited and suspect me of regarding everyone else as idiots were to meet Lucie, they'd sneer at *her* as an idiot and fail absolutely to understand how I could have loved her. I was so devoted to her that I couldn't even conceive that we might one day break up; we never talked about it, but I was always quite seriously under the impression that one day I would marry her. And if it ever occurred to me that this was an unequal match, then the inequality attracted rather than repelled me.

For those few happy months I ought to be grateful to my commanding officer as well. The NCO's pushed us around as

much as they could, searched for specks of dust in the folds of
our uniforms, rumpled our bunks if they found the slightest
crease in them; but the officer was a good man. He was getting
on in years and had been transferred to us from an infantry
regiment—a transfer said to have meant a loss of status. So he
too had been in trouble, and, unconsciously perhaps, this may
have predisposed him in our favor. Obviously he wanted us to
keep order, do what had to be done, and put in an occasional
voluntary Sunday shift to give him some political activism to
show his superiors. But he never had us digging holes just to
fill them up again, and he issued our biweekly Saturday passes
without reluctance. I even believe that that summer I managed to get out and see Lucie as often as three times a month.

When I wasn't with her I'd write to her. I sent her innumer-
able letters and cards—and Lucie did not send me one. I
couldn't induce her to write. Perhaps I shouted her into silence with my own letters; perhaps she thought she had nothing to write about, that she made spelling mistakes; perhaps she
was ashamed of the artless handwriting I knew only from the
signature on her identity card. It was not within my power to
communicate that it was precisely her artlessness and igno-
rance that made me so fond of her.

Lucie began by thanking me shyly for my letters but soon
came to long for some way of repaying me for them. And since
she didn't want to write, she chose to give me flowers instead. It
started like this: We were strolling through a little field when
Lucie suddenly bent down for a flower—may I be forgiven for
not knowing its name; it had small violet leaves and a thin stalk
—and handed it to me. This struck me as touching and didn't
bother me at all. But when on our next date she met me with a
whole bunch of them, I began to feel a little embarrassed.

I was twenty-two and avoided like the plague anything that
might cast doubts on my virility or maturity. I felt embarrassed
if I had to walk up the street carrying flowers, and I didn't like
buying them, still less receiving them. In my embarrassment I
suggested to Lucie that flowers are given to women by men, not

vice versa. But when I saw she was nearly in tears, I hastened to add how nice they were and took them from her.

That was only the beginning. From then on, there were flowers waiting for me on every date, and I finally resigned myself to the situation, disarmed by the spontaneity of the gifts and realizing that they meant a lot to Lucie. Perhaps in her inarticulateness she saw in flowers a form of speech—not the rigid symbolism of the ancient flower language, but rather an older, less concrete, more instinctive, form of communication. Perhaps, being on the silent rather than the talkative side, she instinctively longed for a preverbal stage of evolution when people communicated by simple gestures: they pointed out trees with their fingers, they laughed, they touched one another . . .

Whether at that date I'd already grasped, or failed to grasp, the essence of Lucie's flower-giving, I was touched by it and wanted to give her something in return. Lucie's wardrobe amounted to three outfits which she wore in regular alternation, so that our dates followed one another in the rhythm of the three-beat bar. I liked all her clothes, precisely because they were worn and not very tasteful. I liked the brown coat, too short and worn at the cuffs, which I'd caressed before I'd caressed her face. Still, I decided to buy Lucie some clothes, some nice clothes, and plenty of them. I'd stopped throwing my money away in bars, which meant I had ample funds and no desire to save. So one day I took Lucie along to a shop.

At first Lucie thought we were just going for fun, to watch the people streaming up and down the stairs. On the second floor we stopped by a long rack on which women's dresses were hanging in dense array, and when Lucie saw me looking curiously at them, she came nearer and began pointing out the ones she liked. "That's nice," she said, pointing at something with a small pattern of red flowers. There were not actually very many nice dresses, but one or two weren't too bad. I pulled one out and called to the salesman, "Could the young lady try this one on?" Lucie may have wanted to resist but didn't dare in front of a stranger, and so, before she knew what had happened, she found herself behind the curtain.

After a while I lifted the curtain to see how she looked. Although the dress she was trying on was nothing spectacular, I almost stopped dead in my tracks: its modern cut had transformed her. "May I take a look?" asked the salesman standing behind me, and his admiration was obvious. Then he looked at my regimental insignia and asked if I was a political. I nodded. He winked and said, "I might have one or two better-quality things over here—would you like to see them?" and immediately produced a few summer dresses and some smart evening clothes. Lucie tried them on one after the other, and every single one suited her. She looked different in each, while, when it came to the evening gowns, I wouldn't have recognized her in them at all.

Twists and turns in the course of affections are not always the result of dramatic events, but often of matters which at first glance are of no consequence at all. In the development of my affection for Lucie these clothes played such a part. Until then she'd performed every possible role for me—an impressionable child, a source of unqualified affection and comfort, and an escape from myself—everything, that is, except a woman. Our love in the physical sense of the word had not gone beyond a few kisses. And Lucie's were the innocent kisses of a child.

In short I had until then felt affection for Lucie, but not desire. Indeed, I'd become so accustomed to the absence of sensuality in our relationship that I wasn't even conscious of it. Our friendship seemed so perfect that it could never have occurred to me that there was something missing. Everything blended harmoniously: Lucie, her monastically gray clothes, and my monastically innocent relations with her. The moment she put on that first new dress the entire balance was destroyed. Suddenly I saw her as an attractive woman with a good figure and with legs alluringly outlined under the well-cut skirt—a woman whose drab protective coloration melted away in these clothes with their striking colors and subtle lines. I was completely captivated by the revelation of her body.

Lucie lived in the hostel in a room she shared with three other girls. Visitors were permitted only two days a week and even then for no more than three hours, from five until eight. They had to sign in at the desk, hand over their identity cards, and check out as they left. Added to all this, each of Lucie's room-mates had a young man (or more than one), and each of them needed the intimacy of the hostel room for dating purposes, so that there was constant bickering and recrimination over a single minute that one of them might have stolen from the others. All this was so humiliating that I'd never attempted to visit Lucie at the hostel. But I knew that in about a month's time all three of her room-mates had to report for a three-week agricultural work party. I told Lucie I wanted to take advantage of this and see her in her room. She didn't seem at all pleased. Instead she looked almost mournful and said she preferred being with me out of doors. I told her that I longed to be with her somewhere where no one could intrude, where we could concentrate entirely on each other. As a clincher I told her I wanted to see how she lived. Lucie couldn't resist such plausible reasoning, and I remember to this day how excited I was when she finally agreed to my proposal.

I had now been in Ostrava for almost a year, during which the military routine, initially so unbearable, had become habitual and ordinary. It was still hard and unpleasant, but I managed to live with it, to make a few friends, and even to be happy. For me this was a fine summer—the trees were full of soot and yet they still seemed the purest green when I looked at them with eyes just delivered from the darkness of the pit. But, as is so often the case, the germ of sadness was concealed in the midst of joy; the gloomy events of that autumn were conceived in that green-black summer.

It began with Stana. Within weeks of his marriage he began

getting word that his wife was hanging around the bars. He took it badly and wrote her letter after letter, to which he received conciliatory answers. But then, one Saturday early in the summer, he had a visit from his mother; he spent the whole day with her and returned to camp pale and silent. At first he was too ashamed to tell anyone, but the next day he confided in Honza, then in others, until soon we all knew. As soon as Stana realized this, he started talking openly and obsessively about it, saying that his wife was sleeping around and that he intended to wring her neck. He approached the commanding officer to ask for two days' leave, which the CO was loath to grant him, since he was always getting complaints both from the mines and from the barracks about Stana's preoccupation and irritability. Stana then asked for a twenty-four-hour pass, and the CO took pity on him and granted it. Stana left and we never saw him again. What actually happened I know only from hearsay.

Apparently he got to Prague and went after his nineteen-year-old wife, who admitted everything quite readily, perhaps even with relish. He started hitting her and she fought back; he tried to choke her and finally smashed a bottle over her head. The girl fell to the floor and lay there motionless. Stana came to his senses and fled in panic. Somehow or other he managed to get hold of a shack in the Krusny Mountains and lived there in terrified anticipation of being caught and hung for murder. Two months later they found him and put him on trial, not for murder but for desertion. The girl had only been knocked out, and apart from a bump on the head, had suffered not the slightest damage to her health. While he was serving his time she obtained a divorce, and today is the wife of a famous actor in Prague. Stana afterward came to an unhappy end: when his military service was up he stayed on in the mines, where an accident cost him a leg, and the amputation his life.

That woman brought misfortune not only on Stana but on all of us. At least that's what we all assumed, though we can never be certain whether there was any real connection between the scandal surrounding Stana's disappearance and the ministerial inspection commission which shortly afterward visited our barracks. Whether there was or not, our CO was replaced by a young officer, hardly more than twenty-five, with whose coming everything changed.

He looked even younger than he must have been—like a little boy in fact—which made him all the more anxious to acquit himself in the most impressive possible manner. We used to say among ourselves that he rehearsed his speeches in front of the mirror. He wasn't one for shouting; speaking dryly, he let us know with the greatest composure that he regarded us all as criminals. "I know you'd like to see me hanged," this child said to us the first time he addressed us, "but if anyone is going to hang it will be you, not me."

The first clashes were not long in coming. The incident with Cenek has stuck in my memory most, perhaps because we found it so uproariously funny. I can't resist telling it now. During his first year of service Cenek had done a large number of murals which, under the old CO, had always received due recognition. Cenek, as I mentioned before, had a predilection for Hussite warriors and their commander Jan Zizka, but to give pleasure to his messmates he always liked to throw in a few naked women, whom he represented to the CO as symbols of Liberty or the Motherland. The new CO, also eager to make use of Cenek's services, summoned him and requested him to paint something for the room where political instruction classes were held. He took the opportunity of telling him to "leave all those Zizkas alone" and "pay closer attention to modern conditions," and that his picture should depict the Red Army, its alliance with our working class, and its significance for the victory of Socialism in February, 1948. Cenek said, "Will do!" and set to work, spending several afternoons on the floor and using large sheets of paper which he then tacked up all over the end wall of the room. The finished work was a good five feet high and twenty-five feet long, and our first view of it took our breath away. In the middle stood a warmly clad Soviet soldier in battle dress, with a submachine gun slung from his shoulder and a shaggy fur cap over his ears, while all around him were some eight or nine naked women. Two were standing by his side and gazing up at him coquettishly (he had an arm around each and was laughing exuberantly); the rest were eyeing him, stretching out their arms toward him, or just standing there (in one case lying down), showing off their handsome proportions.

We were waiting for the political officer to arrive and had the room to ourselves. Cenek took up a position in front of the mural and began discussing it: "You see this one here on the right of the sergeant? That's Alena, lads. She was the first woman I ever had—she had me when I was sixteen. She was an officer's wife, so this is just the place for her. I painted her the way she looked then. I don't suppose she looks half as good now, and even then she was a bit on the bulky side as you can see here"—pointing—"around the hips. She was a lot better from behind, so I've done another one of her. Over here"—walking to the edge of the mural and pointing at a bare backside— "you see her royal behind just a little oversize, but that's the way we like them. I was a little crazy in those days, and I remember she used to love being beaten on the behind and I didn't know what it was all about. One Easter she kept after me not to forget to bring my whip with me, and when I came she said, 'Beat me, beat me, and you'll get an Easter egg,' so I whipped her with her skirt on, sort of symbolically, and she said, 'What's the point of that? Pull my skirt up,' so I had to pull her skirt up and take her pants down, and I just went on like a damn fool hitting her like before, and she kept shouting, 'Hit me properly, you little monkey!' Anyway, that was all damn stupid, and this one here"—pointing at the woman on the sergeant's left—"that's Lojzka. I had her when I was more grown up. She had small breasts, long legs, and a very pretty face"—pointing at each item as he named it—"and she was in the same year as me. This one's our model from art college. I know her inside out and so do twenty other lads, because she always used to stand in the middle of the classroom while we learned how to paint the human body, but none of us ever touched her. Her mother always used to wait for her in front of the building and take her straight home. So she used to show herself off to us, God bless her, with all due propriety. And this one here, gentlemen, she was a beauty." Cenek pointed at a woman lolling on a sort of stylized dais. "Come up and have a look at her." We did. "See that mark on her stomach? That's where she was burned by a cigarette and they say it was some jealous woman that did it, some woman she went with because, you see, this little lady used to like it both ways. She looked at sex as a steamer trunk that you could get everything in the world into—all of us could get in, and our wives, and our girls, and our children, and our folks back home . . ."

Cenek was evidently approaching the climax of his exposition when the political officer entered the room and told us to sit down. The political officer, who was used to Cenek's pictures, didn't give the new work a glance and began reading aloud from some pamphlet elucidating the differences between Socialist and capitalist armies. Cenek's commentary faded away in our ears and we were just settling down to a quiet nap when the boy commander suddenly appeared in the room. He had obviously come to check up on the lecture, but before he could receive the political officer's report and motion us to sit down again he was transfixed by the mural. He didn't even permit the political officer to carry on with his reading, but pounced on Cenek and asked what was the meaning of this. Cenek leaped to his feet, struck a pose in front of the picture, and began, "Here we have an allegorical representation of the significance of the Red Army for the struggle waged by our nation; here" —pointing at the sergeant—"is represented the Red Army; at his side"—pointing at the officer's wife—"is symbolized the working class, and here on the other side"—pointing at the girl in his class at college—"is the symbol of the month of February. These others"—pointing at the other ladies—"are the symbols of liberty, victory, and equality; and here"—pointing at the officer's wife displaying her behind—"we see the bourgeoisie making its exit from the stage of history."

The CO let Cenek finish his speech, then he announced that the picture was an insult to the Red Army and must be removed immediately, and that Cenek would have to take the consequences. *Sotto voce*, I asked why. The CO heard me and asked if I had any objections. I stood up and said I liked the picture. The CO said he could quite believe this, as it was just the sort of picture masturbators would enjoy. I told him that Myslbek had painted Liberty as a nude woman as well, and Ales had even sketched the river Jizera as *three* nude women. Using nudes allegorically had, I told him, been done by painters throughout the ages.

The boy commander looked at me dubiously and repeated his order that the picture be taken down. Nevertheless, we may have managed to confuse him, because Cenek was never punished. But the CO had in it in for Cenek, and for me too. Cenek was soon up on a charge, and a little later I was on one too.

It happened like this: Our unit was working with picks and shovels in an out-of-the-way part of the camp, under an indolent corporal who didn't bother to watch us too closely. We were leaning on our shovels, talking about women, and failed to notice the boy commander standing nearby, observing us. When he suddenly shouted, "Private Jahn, come here!" I seized my shovel energetically and stood at attention before him. "Is this your idea of work?" he asked. I can't remember how I replied, but I certainly wasn't insolent, because I had no intention of making life in the barracks any harder for myself or of needlessly antagonizing the man who had complete power over me. Whatever I said, his eyes hardened and he stepped quickly up to me, seized my arm and hurled me over his shoulder with an expert jujitsu throw. Then he squatted down beside me and pinned me to the ground. I made no attempt to resist, but just lay there astonished. "Is that enough?" he asked, raising his voice for the others to hear. I said it was. He ordered me to my feet and announced to the assembled unit, "I am giving Private Jahn two days' detention. Not because he was insolent. His insolence, as you saw, I dealt with personally. I am giving him two days for idleness, and I plan to make it hot for the rest of you as well." Then he turned on his heel and stalked off.

At the time my feeling toward him was one of unqualified hatred. I saw him merely as a vindictive, wily s.o.b. Today, however, I see him above all as a man who was young and acting a part. The young can't help acting; they're immature but they're placed in a mature world and have to act as if they *were* mature. So they put on whatever masks and disguises appeal to them and can be made to fit—and they act.

Our commanding officer was such a man. Suddenly he found himself in charge of our unit, required to command a crowd of men he was incapable of understanding. But he knew what to do and had his mask ready-made: the cold-blooded hero of the paperback thriller, the young man of iron nerve who outwits the mob, the man without feelings, cool and collected, with a dry, biting wit and boundless confidence in the might of his own muscles. The more self-conscious he was, the more fanatically he acted his role of the iron superman.

But was this the first time I'd come up against one of these adolescent fakes? At the time of my interrogation about the postcard affair I was only twenty, and my interrogators were at the most a year or two older. They too were adolescents, concealing their immature faces behind the mask they thought most appropriate—the hard, ascetic revolutionary. What about Marketa? Hadn't she simply imitated the girl savior in some banal best seller or grade B film? And what about Zemanek, suddenly imbued with a sentimental morality? Weren't these just masks? And what about myself? Didn't my troubles stem from my having several masks and turning in confusion from one to the other?

Youth is a terrible thing. It's a stage peopled by supposedly innocent children, who stride around on stilts and in the most

varied costumes, pronouncing speeches they've earnestly mem-
orized and only half understand, but which they regard with
fanatical reverence. History too is a terrible thing, because so
often it becomes the playground for adolescents: the youthful
Nero, the youthful Napoleon, the frenzied mobs of children
whose simulated passions and primitive poses are suddenly
transformed into catastrophic reality. When I think of this, the
whole scale of values is reversed in my mind, and I feel a deep
hatred toward youth—coupled, paradoxically, with a measure
of forgiveness for the criminals of history, in whose delinquency
I now see only the terrible irresponsibility of adolescence.

As I recall these youngsters, I think also of Alexej, who appeared one day in our company and was given Stana's orphaned
bunk. Alexej too was attempting to act a part, one which extended beyond the bounds of his ability and experience. He
had something in common with the CO: he too looked younger
than his years, though his boyishness, in contrast with the CO's,
had nothing attractive about it. He was skinny, with myopic
eyes under the thick glass of his spectacles and skin covered with
the pimples of eternal puberty. As a national serviceman he'd
begun by attending a college for infantry officers, but he was
suddenly deprived of his rank and transferred to us. The notorious political trials were brewing, and in Party buildings,
courtrooms, and police stations all over the country hands were
constantly being raised, stripping the accused of trust, honor,
and liberty. And Alexej was the son of a senior Communist official who'd been arrested shortly earlier.

Alexej regarded us much as I'd first regarded my companions, with great reserve. And when the others learned he was a
Party member (his expulsion had not yet come through) they
started to guard their tongues when he was around. As soon as
he discovered that I was a former Party member he opened
up to me, confiding that whatever happened he was determined to pass this supreme test of his life and never betray the
Party. He read me a poem he'd written—apparently his first

literary venture—when he learned he was to be transferred to our regiment. It consisted of exactly four lines:

Comrades, you may put me in the stocks
And spit and throw filth at me.
But, Comrades, I shall remain
Steadfast within your own ranks.

I understood his feelings because I'd felt just the same a year before. But by now I felt it much less painfully: Lucie had guided me back to the everyday world, out of those regions where the Alexejs of this world live in such desperate torment.

While the boy commander was busy establishing his new regime I was beginning to worry about whether I could manage to get some time off before Lucie's room-mates returned from their work party. It was a month since I'd last been allowed out of camp. The CO had taken careful note of my face and name, and in the army that's the worst thing that can happen to you. He lost no chance of letting me know that every hour of my life was dependent on his whim. And concerning leave, the situation was particularly bad. At the outset he'd announced that leave would only be granted once a month, and then only to those who regularly took part in the voluntary Sunday shifts. This being the case, we all took part in them, myself included. But there was no guarantee I'd get a day off, since the merit of working a Sunday shift could easily be offset by a carelessly made bed or some other minor infraction. Arbitrary power, however, manifests itself not only in cruelty but occasionally also in mercy. After several weeks had passed, the boy commander felt inclined to show me some mercy, and at the last moment before Lucie's girlfriends returned I was granted two days' leave.

It was an exciting moment when the nearsighted old concierge signed me in and allowed me to go upstairs to the fourth floor, where I knocked on a door at the far end of a long passage. The door opened, but Lucie stayed hidden behind it, so that all I could see was the room, which can only be described as remarkable. It looked more like a room made ready for some religious celebration. There was a glorious golden bunch of dahlias on the table and two big creepers climbing around the window, and the entire room—the table, the beds, the floor, even the pictures—was festooned with green sprays of asparagus fern, I later discovered, as if Jesus Christ himself was expected to ride in on his donkey.

I pulled Lucie to me and kissed her. She was in the black party dress and high-heeled shoes I'd bought her, and she stood in the midst of that festive greenery like a high priestess.

We closed the door behind us, and it was only then that I recognized the room for what it was, an ordinary hostel room, and realized that under those green garlands were just four iron beds, four chipped bedside tables, a larger table, and three chairs. But nothing could diminish the delight I'd experienced the moment Lucie opened the door. For the first time in a month, I was out of camp for a few hours. But not only that. For the first time in a year I was in a small room again, and this intoxicating intimacy almost overcame me. Whenever I'd been out with Lucie the temporary freedom and spaciousness had helped to reconcile me to the barracks, but the ever-present air circulating around me had kept me chained with an invisible chain to the camp gate with its inscription, WE SERVE THE PEO-PLE, until it seemed there was no place where I could ever for an instant stop "serving the people." For a whole year I hadn't been inside a small private room.

And now all at once there was a completely new situation. For three hours I was absolutely free. I could, for instance, against all military regulations but without fear, throw off not just cap and belt but shirt, trousers, boots, everything, and I could even give them a kick if I felt like it. I could do what I liked, and there was no observation post from which I could be seen doing it. In addition, it was deliciously warm in the room, and the warmth and my new sense of freedom went to my head like alcohol. I seized Lucie, hugged her, kissed her, and carried her over to her green-bedecked bed. I must admit I was unsettled by the green sprays covering the cheap gray blanket. They could hardly be interpreted except as symbols of wedlock; and I fancied that in Lucie's rather touching simplicity I could hear the unconscious strains of time-honored popular custom, and that she wanted to surrender her virginity with due ritual and ceremony.

It was some time before I realized that although Lucie was responding to my kisses and embraces, she was also preserving an element of restraint. Even when her lips were kissing me hungrily they still remained closed; she clung to me with her entire body, but when I put my hand under her skirt to feel her thighs she twisted away from me. I realized that my desire to be carried blindly away with her wasn't reciprocated. And at that moment, scarcely five minutes after I'd entered the room, I remember feeling the tears of disappointment sting my eyes.

We sat down side by side, crushing the unfortunate sprays, and started making forced conversation. When I tried a second time to take Lucie in my arms, she resisted again. I began struggling with her, only to realize that this was no fine amorous contest but a real fight that was turning our affectionate relationship into something ugly. Lucie was resisting furiously, almost desperately, and I soon gave up the battle.

Next I tried to persuade her with words. I turned on all my charm, telling her that I loved her and that loving means giving yourself fully to the other. The argument was no more original than my aims; but if it was unoriginal it was also irrefutable, nor did Lucie try to refute it. Instead she kept silent or merely said, "Don't, please . . . don't, please," or, "Not today," or attempted, with a rather touching lack of skill, to turn the conversation to other topics.

I tried another line. "You can't be one of those girls who lead a man on and then laugh at him—you can't be so cruel and heartless . . ." Then I took her in my arms again and we had another brief struggle, the ugliness of which again filled me with depression. There wasn't a trace of love in it; it was as if Lucie had in that instant forgotten whom she was with, as if I'd been transformed into a total stranger.

Suddenly I thought I understood why Lucie was resisting. God, why hadn't I realized it at once? She was only a child; she'd still be afraid of love. She was a virgin, and she was frightened, frightened of the unknown. I decided I must camouflage my urgency, must be gentle and kind so that the act of love should seem no different from our other caresses, should only *be* one of those caresses. So I stopped insisting and started gently fondling her. For what seemed an age I kissed her and stroked her, insincerely and without pleasure—these preliminaries had become, in Party jargon, a mere *means to an end*—and tried as surreptitiously as possible to get her lying down. At last I managed it. I stroked her breasts, something she'd never resisted, and told her I wanted to be nice to her whole body, because her body was *her* and I wanted to be nice to all of her. I even managed to lift her skirt a little and kiss her four, then eight, inches above the knee. But that was the farthest I got. I tried to lay my head in her lap but she sprang away from me in terror and jumped off the bed. Her face was convulsed by some sort of struggle, an expression I'd never seen on it before.

"Lucie, Lucie, is it the light that makes you embarrassed? Would you like to be in the dark?" I asked, and she clutched at my question like a straw and admitted the light embarrassed her. So I went over to the window and was just going to draw the blinds when she said, "No, don't do it! Don't draw the blinds!"

"Why not?" I asked.

Instead of answering she burst into tears.

Her resistance had aroused no sympathy in me whatever. I considered it senseless, wrong, and unfair; it worried and puzzled me. I asked her if she resisted because she was a virgin, whether she was afraid of the pain. She meekly answered yes to this, and to every question which seemed to offer her a loophole. I told her what a fine thing it was that she was a virgin and that she'd find out everything with me, the man who loved her. "Don't you look forward to being my wife, and everything that goes with it?" Yes, she said, she was looking forward to it. I embraced her again, and again she resisted.

It was with some difficulty that I kept my temper. "Why are you fighting me?"

"Please, next time, I do want it, but please, next time, another time, not today."

"And why not today?"

"Not today."

"But why?"

"Please not today, please."

"When then? You know very well this is our last chance of being alone together—tomorrow your room-mates are coming back. Where else can we be alone together?"

"You'll find somewhere."

"All right, so I might find somewhere. But promise me you'll come with me, because I doubt if it will be as nice a room as this one."

"It doesn't matter, it doesn't matter, it can be wherever you like."

"All right, but promise me that you'll be my girl when we go there, that you won't fight me."

"All right."

"Promise?"

"Yes."

I realized that this promise was the most I'd get out of Lucie that day. It wasn't much but it was something. I suppressed my indignation, and we spent the rest of the time talking. When I left I shook the bits of asparagus fern out of my uniform, stroked Lucie's face, and told her I'd be thinking of nothing else but the next time—and I wasn't lying either.

A few days later the CO had us all lined up at the end of a hard day's work and informed us that an afternoon inspection of our quarters had uncovered certain irregularities. He then

NCO's were completely at a loss, wondering whether to stop
the race, running to and fro to confer, and looking at the CO
out of the corner of their eye. The CO didn't even glance at
them, but stood watching the race with icy calm.

Alexej was one of the last ten. I was curious to see how he'd
behave, and I wasn't mistaken: he wanted to spoil the fun. He
ran ahead with all his might and gained several yards in the
first twenty. But then something peculiar happened. His pace
slowed down and he ceased to gain on the others. At once I
realized that Alexej couldn't spoil the game even if he wanted
to—this sickly young man who'd had to be given lighter work
after only two days with us—he had neither the muscles nor the
wind. This realization turned his sprint into the highlight of
the entire farce. However hard Alexej drove himself, he was
indistinguishable from the boys idling along at the same pace
five yards behind, and the NCO's and the captain must have
been convinced that his brilliant opening and subsequent slack-
off were as much a part of the comedy as Honza's feigned limp-
ing, Matlos' tumbling about, and our ironic cheers. The only
difference between Alexej and the others, running with fists
clenched and making a great display of panting and puffing, was
that Alexej's handicap was real—his efforts to overcome it even
brought real sweat pouring down his face. Halfway across the
track he slowed down even more, until he was overtaken by the
line of clowning runners behind; twenty yards from the end
he stopped running completely and hobbled the rest of the way
with his hand clamped to his groin.

The CO made us all fall in. Then he asked us why we'd been
running so slowly.

"We were tired, Comrade Captain."

He told everyone who was tired to raise his hand. Every hand
went up—except Alexej's. The CO appeared not to notice him.
He said, "I see. In other words, all of you."

"No, sir," came the reply.

"Who wasn't tired?"

Alexej replied, "I wasn't, sir."

"You?" asked the CO, looking at him. "How is it you weren't tired?"

"I am a Communist," answered Alexej, and the whole company hooted with laughter.

"Are you the one who finished last?" asked the CO.

"Yes, sir," said Alexej.

"If you weren't tired then you must have sabotaged the race deliberately. Take fourteen days for attempted mutiny. The rest of you were tired, so you're excused. Since your output in the colliery is insignificant, it's evidently your days off that are tiring you out. In the interests of your own health all leave for this company is canceled for two months."

Before Alexej left for the guardhouse we had a conversation in which he reproached me for not behaving like a Communist and asked me sternly whether I was for Socialism or against it. I told him I was for Socialism but that in this camp the distinction was totally irrelevant; here the only valid difference was between the men who'd lost control over their destinies and those who had not. Alexej wouldn't admit this, maintaining that the line between Socialism and reaction holds everywhere and that our barracks were simply a means to defend ourselves against the enemies of Socialism. I asked him how the boy was defending Socialism against its enemies by sending him, Alexej, to the guardhouse for fourteen days and generally acting as if he wanted to turn the men into Socialism's most confirmed enemies; and Alexej admitted he disliked the CO. But when I told him that if there'd been a dividing line in the barracks between Socialism and reaction then he, Alexej, wouldn't have been here in the first place, he replied sharply that he was here with perfect justice. "My father was arrested for espionage. Do you understand what that means? How can the Party trust me? It's the Party's *duty* not to trust me!"

The good-humored sabotaging of that race strengthened our sense of solidarity and led to considerable activity. Honza organized a sort of miniature council which made a rapid review of the possibilities for going AWOL. In two days it was all arranged: a secret bribery fund was set up, the two corporals in our quarters were suborned, and several strands of wire were cut at a carefully chosen point in the perimeter fence. This spot was right at one end of the camp, where there was only the infirmary and where the nearest cottages were no more than five yards beyond the wire. The closest was occupied by a miner we knew from down in the pit, with whom a speedy agreement was reached whereby he was to leave his back gate unlocked. The escaping soldier would only have to make his way cautiously to the fence, crawl quickly under, and sprint the few yards to the cottage gate. He would then simply walk through the house and emerge from the front door onto the suburban street.

The exit was relatively safe. It was important, however, that it not be abused—if too many men left the barracks on the same day, their absence could easily be spotted. Honza's informal council had therefore to regulate the escapes and determine a schedule.

But before my turn came, the entire enterprise came to grief. The commanding officer made a personal inspection of the quarters one night and discovered three men missing. He turned on the NCO in charge of the room, who hadn't reported the men's absence, and asked, with a knowing air, how much he had got for it. The corporal, dazed by the CO's being apparently in full possession of the facts, made no attempt to deny them. Honza was summoned before the CO, and in the subsequent confrontation the corporal admitted taking money from him.

The CO had us checkmated. The corporal, Honza, and the three men on French leave were all sent for court-martial. I didn't even have time to say good-bye to my best friend, since everything happened during a single morning while we were at work. It wasn't until much later that I learned they'd all been sentenced, Honza to a full year's jail. The CO announced to the assembled company that the ban on leave was extended for an additional two months and that the entire company would come under a correctional training routine. And he asked the authorities for two watchtowers with searchlights to be placed at opposite corners of the camp, and two dog patrols.

The captain's swoop was so sudden and so successful that we all believed Honza's scheme had been betrayed. I wouldn't say that informing was particularly common in our regiment; indeed we were unanimous in despising it, and the great majority refrained from practicing it. But we all knew that it was an ever-present possibility, being the most effective means at our disposal for improving our conditions, getting home on time, receiving good character references, and ensuring ourselves some kind of future—and so we were too ready to suspect others of it.

On this occasion suspicion ripened rapidly and universally into certainty, and fastened smack on Alexej. At the time he still had to serve another two days inside, but he still went to work with us every day, and everyone asserted that he had had ample opportunity, with his well-trained ears, of overhearing Honza's scheme.

On emerging from the guardhouse, poor Alexej found there were even worse things in store for him. The shift foreman, one of us, started allotting him the most grinding jobs. He regularly lost his tools, which he then had to replace out of his pay. He was forced to listen to insinuations and insults and to put up with hundreds of minor inconveniences. On the wooden wall over his bed someone had written with bicycle oil in big black letters: BEWARE OF THE RAT.

A few days after Honza and the others had been led off under escort, I looked into our barracks late one afternoon. It was empty except for Alexej, who was making up his bunk. I asked him why he had to remake it, and he told me the boys rumpled his sheets several times a day. I told him they were all convinced that he'd informed on Honza. He protested almost tearfully that he knew nothing about it and would never inform on anyone.

"Why do you say you wouldn't inform?" I said. "You regard yourself as an ally of the CO. It's only logical that you would give him information."

"I'm *not* the CO's ally. The CO is a saboteur!" he said, with a break in his voice. Then he told me the conclusions he'd reached during his long hours in solitary. The "black" regiments were run by the Party for men it couldn't trust with arms but whom it wished to reeducate. The class enemy, however, was not asleep and wished at all costs to prevent the reeducation process from being successful. It wanted the "black" troops sustained in their violent hatred of Communism, as a reserve force for the counterrevolution. The CO's treatment of the men was an obvious part of this plan. One never knew where the Party might have enemies, and the CO was definitely an enemy agent. Alexej knew his duty and had written a detailed account of the CO's activities.

I was flabbergasted. "You wrote what? And who did you send it to?" He replied that he had sent a complaint about the commander to the Party.

As we left the hut, he asked me if I wasn't afraid of being seen with him by the others. I told him he was a fool for asking and a bigger one if he thought his letter would ever reach its destination. He replied that it was his duty as a Communist to act in all situations in a way he need not be ashamed of. Then he reminded me again that I too was a Communist, even after being expelled from the Party, and that I ought not to behave as I did: "As Communists we are responsible for everything that happens here." I thought this ridiculous and told him that responsibility was unthinkable without freedom. He replied that he felt sufficiently free to act like a Communist, that he must and would prove that he was a Communist. As he said this his jaw was trembling; today, after all these years, I can still recall the incident and am more aware now than I was then that Alexej was not much over twenty, that he was an adolescent, a boy, and that his destiny hung on him like a giant's suit on a dwarf.

Shortly after my conversation with Alexej I was asked by Cenek, just as Alexej had feared, what I'd been talking to "that rat" about. I told him that Alexej might be a fool but he was no rat, and I repeated Alexej's account of his complaining about the commanding officer. Cenek was unimpressed. "I don't know if he's a fool or not," he said, "but a rat he most certainly is. Anyone who can publicly denounce his own dad must be a rat." He was surprised by my not understanding this allusion; apparently the political officer himself had shown them newspapers from a few months back in which a statement by Alexej had been printed. He had denounced his father for "betraying and dirtying the most sacred things his son knew."

That evening the searchlights which had been constructed during the last few days made their first appearance on the watchtowers and illuminated the darkened camp, while a guard with German shepherds patrolled the barbed wire. I suddenly felt terribly lonely: I missed Lucie and knew I wouldn't see her for a good two months. The same evening I wrote her a long letter; I told her that I wouldn't be seeing her for some time, that we weren't allowed out of camp, and that I was sorry she'd denied me what I'd longed for and what would, in memory, have helped me to survive those gloomy weeks.

The day after I mailed this letter we were doing our compulsory afternoon drill, about-turning, forward-marching, and hurling ourselves to the ground. I was following the prescribed movements quite automatically and hardly noticed the corporal's orders or my colleagues marching around and dropping to the ground. I paid no attention to my surroundings: huts on three sides, barbed wire on the fourth, and beyond it the road. Every now and then someone would walk past outside the wire. Occasionally someone would stop—mainly children, alone or with their parents. For me everything on the other side of the wire had become a lifeless backdrop, so many pictures on the wall. That's why I was scarcely even conscious of the wire until someone called softly in that direction, "Hey, girl, what are you looking at?"

Then I saw her. It was Lucie, wearing her old brown over-coat—it occurred to me that when buying clothes in the summer we had forgotten that the summer would end—and the fashionable black high-heeled shoes I'd given her, which clashed ludicrously with the shabby coat. She was standing motionless outside the wire and watching us seriously. The men, more earnestly still, commented on her strange, patient air, packing their remarks with all the sexual desperation of men kept in enforced celibacy. The corporal in charge noticed that the men's attention was wandering and soon realized the cause. He was evidently enraged at his powerlessness to order the girl away from the wire; outside the wire was the land of relative freedom over which his jurisdiction didn't extend. Instead, after warning the men to keep their mouths shut, he stepped up the volume of his voice and the tempo of the drill.

After drill we had to endure an hour of political instruction, and it was only after the lesson, when it was already getting dark, that I was able to slip out and see if Lucie was still waiting by the wire. She was, and I ran over to her.

She told me not to be angry with her, that she loved me and it worried her if she made me unhappy. I said I didn't know when I'd see her again. She told me that it didn't matter and that she'd come here for me. At this point some of the men went past shouting vulgar comments at us, and I asked her whether she wouldn't mind the soldiers shouting at her. She said she wouldn't mind that because she loved me. She handed me a rose through the fence—at that moment a bugle sounded, calling us on parade—and we kissed through a gap in the barbed wire.

After that, Lucie came to the fence almost every day. At each visit I received a bunch of flowers (once during a kit inspection the sergeant threw them on the floor), and on each occasion we exchanged a few utterly stereotyped words, for we had no ideas or information to exchange, and only wanted to reassure each other of the one constantly reiterated truth. At the same time I maintained my flow of almost daily letters. The searchlights on the watchtowers, the barking dogs, the strutting young officer—for all this there was very little room in my mind, which was focused exclusively on Lucie's visits.

In a way I was happy within those barracks with their dog patrols, and down in the mines where I leaned on my shuddering drill. I was happy and confident because in Lucie I possessed a prize not shared by any of my companions or even of the officers: I was loved, publicly and demonstratively loved. Even though Lucie wasn't my companions' idea of the ideal woman, and even though they regarded her way of showing her affection as downright eccentric, it was still a woman's love, and as such it gave rise to wonder, nostalgia, and envy.

The longer we were severed from the world of women, the more we talked about them and about their minutest details. Birthmarks were vividly recalled, and the lines of breasts and backsides were sketched in pencil, with a pickax in the mud, or with fingers in the sand. There were heated arguments about the relative shapeliness of various women's buttocks. Words and murmurings during intercourse were evoked with great precision. All this became more and more garbled and embroidered with constant repetition. Naturally enough, I too came under fire, particularly as they knew what the girl looked like; so I told them about Lucie's nakedness, which I had never seen, and about making love to her, which I had never done— and immediately a precise and detailed picture of her quiet passion rose before my eyes.

What was it like then when I loved her for the first time?

In my narrative I saw this as the quintessence of reality. It happened in her room at the hostel. She took off her clothes in front of me, loyally but with a certain modesty, since she was after all a country girl and I was the first man to see her in the nude. And it was this obedience mingled with shyness which excited me so insanely, and when I went over to her she shrank away and covered her crotch with her hands . . .

Why does she always wear those black high-heeled shoes?

I told them I'd bought them so that she could wear them for
me when she was naked. She was shy about it but did everything
I wanted her to. I always stayed fully dressed as long as possible and she would walk around naked except for those shoes
(how I loved seeing her naked when I was dressed!), and she
would go to the cupboard where she kept the wine and, still in
the nude, would pour some out for me . . .

And so when Lucie came to the wire she was gazed at not
only by myself but by at least a dozen of my companions, all
of whom knew precisely what she was like when she made love,
what she said and how she moaned; and they would make innuendos about how she was still wearing her black high-heeled
shoes and would picture her walking naked around her tiny
room.

The feeling of comradely solidarity which had induced me to
paint such a detailed picture of Lucie's nakedness and her way
of making love had the effect of painfully intensifying my desire for her. I was not in the least indignant at the vile comments with which my companions celebrated Lucie's visits;
on the contrary, they merely brought my blurred impression of
her into sharper focus, and by linking us together gave the picture a terrible seductiveness. When I went over to her at the
wire I felt myself trembling. I was unable to speak for desire
or to understand how I could have gone out with her six months
and not seen the woman in her.

I was willing to give anything for a single night in bed with
Lucie. I don't mean by this that my attitude to her grew more
violent or coarse, or that it lost any of its affection. I would even
say that this was the only time in my life when I felt a total desire for a woman, in which everything was involved: body and
soul, lust and tenderness, loneliness and frenzied vitality, hunger for the vile and hunger for consolation, desire for momentary pleasure and desire for eternal possession.

I had Lucie's promise that next time she wouldn't "put up
a fight" and that she'd see me whenever I wanted, a promise
she'd confirmed many times during our brief conversations

across the wire. All it needed on my side was one bold, perilous stroke.

It was not long before my plans were hatched. Honza's precise escape plan had never been discovered. The wire remained inconspicuously severed, and the arrangement with the miner who lived opposite the barracks merely needed renewing. Escape by day was of course impossible, and even in the dark there were the circling dog patrols and the glare of the lights. But all this was evidently designed more to gratify the CO's love of effect than from any real suspicion of a break on our part. Attempted escape carried a court-martial and was therefore much too risky; and precisely for this reason I told myself that my project had a good chance of succeeding.

It only remained to find a suitable refuge for Lucie and myself, preferably not too far from the camp. The area around the camp was inhabited largely by miners who worked in the same colliery as ourselves, and with one of these, a fifty-year-old widower, I managed to negotiate the use of his place. The single-storyed gray cottage where he lived could be seen from the camp. I pointed it out to Lucie through the wire and explained my plan. She wasn't exactly effusive, and she begged me not to take any risks for her sake. In the end she agreed only because she was no good at resisting.

The appointed day arrived—and brought with it an unexpected incident. Immediately after our return from the pit the boy made us fall in and treated us to one of his frequent addresses. Usually he threatened us with the war which was liable to break out any day and the fate in store for reactionaries—by which he meant first and foremost ourselves. On this occasion he introduced some new ideas. Apparently the class enemy had wormed his way into the Communist Party itself. But let spies and traitors take note that hidden enemies would be dealt with a hundred times more severely than open ones, because the hidden enemy was no better than a rabid dog.

"And we have one of these in our midst," said the boy. Then

he made Alexej take two paces forward. The CO pulled a document from his pocket, and thrust it at him.

"Have you seen this letter before?"

"Yes, sir," said Alexej.

"You're a rabid dog and you're also an informer and a sneak. But a dog's voice can't reach as far as heaven." He tore the letter to shreds. "I have another letter for you," he added, giving Alexej an unsealed envelope. "Read it aloud!"

Alexej drew a paper from the envelope and looked it over. He said nothing.

"Read it!" repeated the CO.

Alexej still said nothing.

"Are you going to read it or not?" asked the captain again, and when Alexej still remained silent, he barked out an order for him to lie flat on the ground. Alexej threw himself flat in the mud. The boy stood over him for a moment, and we all expected a torrent of commands: "Stand up! Lie down! Stand up! Lie down!" Instead the captain turned away from Alexej and began to stroll along the front rank, running a practiced eye over their equipment as he went. When he had reached the end of the rank he strolled back to where Alexej still lay on the ground.

"Right. Read it aloud!" he said, and Alexej lifted his muddy chin off the ground, stretched out his right hand in which he had been clutching the letter all this time, and still lying flat on his belly read:

> *We have to inform you that on September 15, 1951, you were expelled from the Communist Party of Czechoslovakia.*
>
> p.p. Regional Committee

After which the CO ordered Alexej to fall in again and handed us over to the corporal for drill.

After drill there was political instruction, and by the time this ended it was already dark. Lucie was standing by the wire and nodded to show that everything was all right; then she left. After that there was supper, taps, and lights out. I waited for the corporal to go to sleep. Then I pulled on my boots and went out just as I was, in my long white underpants and nightshirt. I walked down the passage and out into the yard, feeling distinctly chilly. My objective was behind the infirmary, which meant that if I met anyone I could say I felt ill and was going to wake the MO. But I reached the infirmary without incident and crouched in the shadow of its wall. The sentry on the watch-tower had evidently stopped taking his job too seriously, and the searchlight was lazily directed on a single spot; now it was just a case of not running into the dog patrol. I waited for about ten minutes until I heard a dog bark, somewhere over on the other side of the camp. Then I dashed across to the wire where, thanks to Honza's management, it stood a little way off the ground. There was no wavering now. I crawled under the wire, covered the few yards to the miner's garden fence, opened the gate, and tapped at a lighted window. Within seconds an enormous man appeared in the doorway and noisily invited me in. I was terrified at the volume of his voice; I couldn't forget that I was a bare five yards from the camp.

The door led straight into a room where there was a table with an open bottle on it and five other men sitting around it drinking. When they saw me they burst out laughing at my outfit. They said I must be cold in my nightshirt, poured me a glass, and told me to drink up. They asked how I had managed the "border crossing," laughed all over again at my ridiculous costume, and called me "the escaping underpants." They were all coal miners in their thirties, and after my initial shock, their friendly, carefree presence set me completely at ease and I let them pour me another glass of their strong, pungent liquor.

Meanwhile the owner of the house had gone into another room and now came back carrying a dark suit. "Will this fit you?" he asked. I could see he was at least five inches taller than me and considerably broader, but I said, "It'll *have* to." I pulled the trousers on over my underpants, but it was no use. I had to hold on to them to keep them from falling. "Has anyone got a belt?" asked my benefactor. No one had. Eventually we found a piece of string, which just about kept the trousers up. When I put the jacket on, the men decided that I looked like Charlie Chaplin, and that all I needed was the bowler and the stick, so to humor them I walked around with my heels together and my toes pointed outward. They poured me a third glass of spirits and saw me out, the owner assuring me I could knock at the window any hour of the night when I wanted to change back again.

I stepped out into a poorly lighted suburban street. To reach the house where Lucie was waiting for me, I had actually to walk the length of the barracks and past the well-lighted gates. But any twinge of alarm I may have felt proved quite unnecessary; my civilian dress constituted a disguise far beyond the sentry's meager powers of penetration. I reached the appointed house safely, opened the door, and faithfully followed the miner's directions: up the stairs on the left to the first floor, first door at the top of the stairs. I knocked. The key turned in the lock, Lucie opened the door, and I took her in my arms.

She asked me if I'd been drinking; I said I had and told her how I'd got there. She said she'd arrived around six, when the owner had left for his night shift, and had been waiting for me ever since, in fear and trembling that anything should happen to me. She was indeed actually shivering. I told her how much I'd been looking forward to seeing her and felt her shudder even more violently.

"What's the matter?" I asked.

"Nothing."

"What are you shaking for then?"

"I was afraid for you," she said and twisted lightly away.

I looked around me. It was a small, austerely appointed room: a table, a chair, a bed made with slightly soiled sheets, a religious picture on the wall above, a cupboard full of preserves

—the only cheerful thing in the room. A naked bulb shone from the ceiling, glaring disagreeably in my eyes and throwing me into a sharp profile whose melancholy clownishness I realized all too painfully at that moment: the enormous jacket, the trousers fastened with a piece of string, and, peeping from under them, the black insteps of my army boots, the entire ensemble crowned by my shaven skull which must have shone like a pallid moon in the glare of the electric light.

"Lucie, please don't take any notice of how I look," I said and explained once again the necessity for my change of clothes. Lucie assured me that it didn't matter, but with alcoholic impetuosity I swore I wasn't going to stand there in front of her like that and threw off the jacket and trousers—forgetting that under the jacket I was wearing my nightshirt and those terrible army-issue long johns, an even more ludicrous costume than the one I'd just shed. I switched out the light, but no concealing darkness came to my rescue, as the streetlight shone right into the room. I was much more ashamed of looking ridiculous than of being seen naked, so I stripped off my shirt and pants and stood naked before Lucie. I took her in my arms and felt her trembling once again. I told her to undress, to remove everything still separating us. I ran my hands all over her, I repeated my pleas again and again, but Lucie only told me to wait a little while, said she couldn't, she couldn't right away, she couldn't so quickly.

I took her by the hand and we sat down on the bed. I put my head in her lap and stayed quietly for a moment. Then I realized the full incongruity of my nakedness—faintly illuminated by the murky glare of the rustic lamp—and the ironic contrast between the dream and the reality. Instead of the naked girl serving drinks to the fully clothed man, a naked man with his head in the lap of a fully clothed woman. Suddenly I had a vision of the naked Christ taken from the cross and lying in the arms of a sorrowing Mary, and the vision horrified me, for I hadn't come for compassion but for something entirely different. And again I began urging Lucie on, kissing her face and clothes, and trying surreptitiously to undo her buttons.

I met with no success. Once more Lucie twisted away from me. I'd lost my original confident impatience, and I remained stretched out on the bed, naked and motionless, while Lucie sat over me and ran her rough fingers over my face. Gradually my accumulated anger and frustration uncoiled inside me; in my thoughts I reminded Lucie of all the risks I'd taken in order to see her today and of all the penalties the excursion might cost me. But these silent reproaches touched only the tip of the iceberg. The real reason for my resentment, the reason I'd have been ashamed to admit, was much deeper. I was thinking of my own misery, the miserable failure of my youth, the endless cheerless weeks, the degrading eternity of unfulfilled desire. I was remembering the fruitless courting of Marketa, the empty encounter with the blonde on the grass-cutter, and again the fruitless attempt on Lucie. And I wanted to cry out: Why must I be an adult in everything, sentenced as an adult, expelled, branded as a Trotskyite, sent down into the mines as an adult? Why is it only in love that I'm not allowed to be an adult, that I have to swallow the full humiliation of my own immaturity? I hated Lucie, and I hated her all the more for the knowledge that she was in love with me, because that made her resistance all the more incomprehensible, unnecessary, and infuriating. And so, after half an hour of sullen silence, I launched a fresh attack.

I rolled over onto her. I used all my strength and managed to pull up her skirt, tear off her bra, and put my hands on her naked breasts, but Lucie resisted all the more furiously, fighting with the same blind strength as I was. Finally she broke free and jumped off the bed.

"Why are you fighting me?" I shouted at her. She told me not to be angry, said she was sorry, but offered no explanation, nothing rational. "Why are you fighting me? Can't you see I love you? You're crazy," I shouted.

"Throw me out then," she said.

"That's exactly what I intend to do. Because you don't love me. Because you're making a fool of me!" And I issued my ultimatum: either she gave herself or I never wanted to see her again.

I went over to her and took her in my arms. This time she didn't resist but stood close up against me as if paralyzed. "What's so special about your virginity? Why are you saving it for?" No answer. "Why don't you answer me?"

"You don't love me," she said.

"*I* don't love you?"

"No, you don't. I thought you did but you don't." And she burst into tears.

I knelt down in front of her, I kissed her feet, I begged and implored her. Still she went on crying and saying I didn't love her.

Suddenly an insane fury gripped me. I felt there was some supernatural force opposing me, tearing from my hands everything I wanted to live for, everything I desired, everything that by rights was mine. It was this force which had stripped away my Party, my Comrades, my studies at the university. Now it was opposing me again in the person of Lucie, and I hated her for having become its instrument. I struck her savagely—for it wasn't she I was fighting, it was that hostile force. I shouted that I hated her, that I never wanted to see her again, never again in my life.

I threw her brown coat at her and ordered her to get out.

She put on her coat and went.

And I lay on the bed and felt an aching void in my soul, and I wanted to call her back because, from the moment I'd driven her out, I knew it was a thousand times better to have a Lucie who was fully dressed and reluctant than not to have any Lucie at all—because to have no Lucie at all meant living in utter desolation.

All this I knew, but I didn't call her back.

I lay for some time on the bed in that borrowed room, because I couldn't at that moment face meeting anyone, turning up at the house outside the camp, joking with the miners and replying to their good-naturedly lewd questions.

Finally, very late at night, I got up and left. I walked the length of the barracks, knocked on the darkened window of the cottage, took off the clothes with the miner yawning away in front of me, made some noncommittal answer to his inquiry about the success of my venture, and back in my nightshirt and underpants, set out for camp. I was in a state of despair and total indifference. I didn't give a thought to the dog patrol or to which way the searchlight was trained. I crawled through the wire and began walking quietly toward my hut. I had just reached the wall of the infirmary when I heard: "Halt! Who's there?" I stopped. A flashlight shone in my eyes, and I heard the snarling of a dog. "What're you doing here?"

"Being sick, Comrade sergeant," I replied, leaning my hand on the wall.

"Get it over with then, man, get it over with!" said the sergeant, and he and the dog continued their patrol.

I got to bed that night without any further complications. The corporal was sound asleep, but my own attempts in that direction were totally unsuccessful, and I was glad when the odious voice of the corporal bawling, "Everybody up! Hop to it!" brought an end to a miserable night. I slipped into my boots and ran to the washroom to splash some cold, refreshing water over myself. When I got back, there was a bunch of half-naked men clustered around Alexej's bed with much muffled laughter. Alexej was sleeping like a log, on his stomach, with his head on the pillow and covered entirely with a blanket. I was reminded at once of Franta Petrasek of C Company who, to spite his company commander, had one morning feigned a sleep so deep that he was shaken by three consecutive superiors without any effect. It was only when he was carried out into the yard and a fire hose was turned on him that he began lazily rubbing his eyes. But with Alexej any sort of insubordination was inconceivable, so his heavy sleeping could only be a consequence of his physical weakness. At this point the corporal came in from the hall, carrying an enormous jug of water in his arms and attended by a few of the men who'd evidently been egging him on to play this stupid prank, so dear to the typical noncom mentality since time immemorial.

I was irritated now by this pathetic reconciliation between the men and the corporal, who at other times was so universally detested—irritated that a common hatred for Alexej had erased all the old scores between them. The CO's little speech yesterday about Alexej's informing had obviously been interpreted to fit their own suspicions, and they'd felt in sudden accord with the CO's brutality. Isn't it, in any case, easier to join the powerful Communist in hating the powerless one than vice versa? I felt a blinding rage at everybody there, at their unthinking tendency to believe every accusation, at their eagerness for the brutality with which they might restore their battered self-esteem—and I went up to the bed and said loudly, "Alexej, you damn fool, get up!"

Someone grabbed my arm, twisted it savagely, and forced me to my knees. It was Pavel Pekny. "Damned Commie, trying to spoil everything!" he hissed at me. I tore myself away and hit him across the face. There would have been a fight then and there if the others hadn't quickly quieted us down in case Alexej should wake up prematurely. Meanwhile the corporal had arrived with his jug. He stepped up to Alexej, bawled, "Out of the sack! Hop to it!" and poured the entire contents of the jug over him—there must have been a good two gallons.

But a strange thing happened: Alexej lay still. For a moment the corporal was at a loss, then he bawled, "On your feet, attention!" But Private Alexej never stirred. The corporal bent down and shook him—the entire bed was soaked through, and pools of water were forming on the floor. He managed to turn Alexej over so that we could see his face. It was sunken, pale, immobile.

The corporal shouted, "Get the MO!" No one moved—
we were all looking at Alexej in his sodden nightshirt—and the
corporal yelled again, "Get the MO!" pointing at one of the
men, who raced out of the room.

Alexej lay there motionless, smaller and frailer than ever before, and much younger, like a child—only his lips were locked
firmly together, as children's never are—and still the water
dripped off him. Someone said, "It's raining."

The Medical Officer arrived and took Alexej's wrist for a
moment. Then he removed the wet blanket and Alexej lay before us in his entire inconsiderable length. We could see his
soaking wet long white underpants with the bare feet sticking
out at the end. The doctor looked around, picked up two cap-
sules from the bedside table, examined them—they were empty
—and said, "There's enough for two men here alone." Then
he pulled a sheet from the nearest bed and covered Alexej with
it.

All this had held things up so we had to eat breakfast on the
double, and in three-quarters of an hour we were already going
underground. Then came the end of the shift, drill time, political instruction and compulsory singing, then cleaning duties,
supper, lights out, and bed. I thought of how Stana had gone,
and my best friend, Honza (I never saw him again and only
heard reports that after completing military service he escaped
across the frontier to Austria), and now Alexej was gone too.
He had assumed his scapegoat role blindly but courageously,
and it wasn't his fault if he'd suddenly been unable to go on
with it, to go on humbly and patiently playing his part as the
laughingstock of them all. It wasn't his fault that he simply
lacked the strength. He was never my friend, he was alien to
me in the toughness of his convictions, but in his life story he
was the closest to me of them all. I felt that even in his death
he had continued to reproach me, as if intending to convince
me that the moment the Party discards a man from its ranks,
that man has no reason to live. I felt suddenly guilty that I

hadn't liked him, because now he was dead and wouldn't come back, and I'd never done anything for him, although I was the only one there who could have helped him at all.

But I hadn't only lost Alexej and the irrecoverable opportunity of offering a man my protection. As I see it today, it was at this point that I lost my sense of companionship and solidarity with my fellow "politicals," and with it any chance of resurrecting and reinvigorating my tenuous faith in men. I began to have doubts about the value of a solidarity which had been forged by mere force of circumstances and the urge for mutual self-protection. And I began to realize that our "black" collective was just as capable of bullying another man, of casting him out and sending him to his death, as was the collective of men who raised unanimous hands in vote, or perhaps as any other collective of men.

During those days I felt utterly empty and desolate and I wanted to call to Lucie. Suddenly I couldn't understand why I'd desired her body so obsessively. Now it seemed to me that she was not a corporeal woman at all, only a transparent pillar of warmth striding through a land of unending chill, a pillar of warmth striding away from me, driven away by me.

One evening, after spending the drill period with my eyes on the wire waiting in vain to see if she would come (the only person to stop by our fence was an old woman who pointed us out to a slovenly-looking child), I wrote a long and sorrowful letter in which I begged Lucie to come back. I said I had to see her, that I didn't want anything from her, only that she should be there, so I could see her and know that she was with me, simply to know she was there at all . . .

As if to mock me, the days grew suddenly warmer, the sky was blue, and we had a glorious October. The leaves on the trees were a blaze of color as nature, that miserable Ostrava nature, celebrated the farewells of autumn with crazy delight. I couldn't consider this as anything but mockery, for no reply came to my despairing letters, and the only people to stop by our wire, under the challenging sun, were utter strangers.

About ten days later one of my letters came back. The address had been crossed out and a message added in ink: GONE AWAY.

I panicked. A thousand times since my last meeting with Lucie I had mentally reviewed everything I'd said to her and she to me, a hundred times I'd cursed myself and a hundred times justified myself, a hundred times I'd assured myself that I'd driven her away forever and a hundred times convinced myself that she'd understand and forgive me. But that message on the envelope had the ring of a final verdict.

I couldn't contain my fears, and the very next day I made another reckless excursion. I say "reckless," but it was no more dangerous than my last escape from the barracks, so the epithet emphasizes in retrospect its lack of success rather than the risks involved. I knew that Honza had done the same thing several times when he'd had a Bulgarian woman in the summer with a husband who spent the mornings at work. I took a leaf from his book. I arrived at the pit early in the morning with the others, collected my number and safety lamp, smudged my face with coal dust—and quietly got lost. I ran to Lucie's hostel and questioned the concierge. He told me Lucie had left two weeks before with her suitcase and all her worldly possessions. No one knew where she'd gone, as she'd said nothing about her plans to anybody. I was beside myself. Had anything happened? The concierge looked at me and said airily with a wave of the hand, "That's what you expect from these drifters. They come and go with never a word to anyone." I went to the place where she worked and made inquiries in the personnel department, but they had nothing to tell me. I wandered all over Ostrava and returned to the mine face at the end of the shift to mingle with the others who'd been underground all morning. But evidently I'd omitted something vital from Honza's escape tactics; they were waiting for me and landed on me like a ton of bricks. In two weeks' time I was hauled before a court-martial and got ten months' jail for desertion.

Yes, it was here, at the moment when I lost Lucie, that the whole long period of hopelessness and barrenness began, that period whose image I'd glimpsed in the dreary provincial scenery of my hometown, to which I'd returned for a particular purpose. Yes, it was from this moment that it all began. During the ten months I was in jail, my mother died and I couldn't even go to her funeral. Then I went back to Ostrava, to the same regiment, and served another full year as a "political." During this period I signed an agreement to work for another three years in the mines after completing my military service, for word was going around that those who didn't would stay on for an extra year or so in the camp. So I spent another three years hewing coal as a civilian.

I take no pleasure in recalling this or talking about it, and I'd go so far as to say that I detest it when I hear men cast out like myself from the movement they believed in boasting of their experiences today. From time to time I've had mercilessly to remind myself that I wasn't assigned to the penal corps for my bravery, for my service in the field or on the battleground of ideological warfare. No heroic drama preceded my fall, I was more the object than the subject of the whole story, and unless one considers trials, heartache, or sheer futility to be virtues I have nothing whatever to boast about.

Lucie? Oh, yes: for those five empty years I never once set eyes on her, and it was a long time before I had any news of her either. After being discharged I heard that she was somewhere in western Bohemia, but by that time I'd ceased asking about her.

IV

Jaroslav

I see a road winding through the field. I see the mud of the track, rutted by the wheels of rustic carts. And I see the verges flanking the road, grassy verges so green that I cannot help caressing their smooth slopes with my hand.

The fields around are small. They are not collective fields. How can this be? Are they not of today, these lands I am passing through? What sort of land is this then?

I walk on and a briar bush appears before me on the grass verge. It is full of small wild roses. I stop beside them and am happy. I sit down on the grass under the bush, and after a while I lie down. I sense my back touching the grassy earth. I feel it with my back. I hold it on my back and beg it not to be afraid of being heavy, of lying on me with its full weight.

Then I hear the clattering of hooves. In the distance a small cloud of dust appears. It comes nearer, becoming progressively more transparent. Horsemen emerge from it. Astride the horses sit young men in white uniforms. But the nearer they come the more evident is the casual disarray of their uniforms. Some coats are buttoned and their gold buttons gleam, some are unbuttoned, and some of the young men are in shirtsleeves only. Some have caps on their heads and some are bareheaded. No, this is no army. These are deserters, turncoats, bandits! They are our cavalry! I raise myself from the ground and watch them ap-

proach. The leading horseman unsheathes his saber and holds it erect. The cavalry come to a halt.

The man with drawn saber leans across the horse's neck and stares fixedly at me.

"Yes, it is I," I say.

"The King!" says the man in wonderment. "Now do I recognize thee."

I incline my head, happy at being recognized. Centuries they have ridden thus and still they know me.

"How farest thou, King?" asks the man.

"I go in fear, my friends," I say.

"Do they hunt for thee?"

"No. Yet it is worse than any hunting. Something is being prepared against me. I do not know those that are around me. I enter my house and within is a different room and a different wife and all things different. I think I have made a mistake, I rush out, but it is truly my house! Without, it is mine; within, it is a stranger's. And so it is where I am going. Something is afoot, my friends, which puts me in great fear."

The man says, "Thou hast not forgotten how to ride?" Only then do I notice that by his steed there stands a saddled and riderless horse. The man indicates it. I put my foot in the stirrups and leap on. The horse starts but I am already firmly in the saddle and gripping his back with my knees in great delight. The man takes a red cape from his saddlebag and gives it to me: "Veil thy face, that they might not know thee!" I veil my face and become at once as blind. "Thy horse will lead thee," I hear the man's voice.

The whole column sets off at a trot, and I feel the riders jogging along on both sides of me. Their calves touch mine and I hear the snorting of their horses. For about an hour we ride thus, body close to body. Then we halt. The same man's voice addresses me again: "We are arrived, O King!"

"Where?" I ask.

"Dost thou not hear the murmuring of the mighty river? We stand on the banks of the Danube. Here thou art safe, King."

"Yes," I say, "I feel that I am safe. But I should like to cast off this cloak."

"Thou must not, King. Thou needest not thine eyes. Thine eyes would but deceive thee."

"But I wish to see the river Danube. It is my river, my mother river. I wish to see it."

"Thou needest not thine eyes, King. Everything there is I shall relate to thee. It is better thus. Around us are plains stretching far out of sight. Pastures. Here and there are bushes, here a wooden stake or well pump juts forth. But we are on the grass by the banks. Not far from us the grass goes into sand, for the river in these parts has a sandy bed. But now do thou dismount, King."

We dismount and sit down upon the ground.

"The men are making fire," I hear the man's voice say. "The sun already merges with the distant horizon and soon it will be cold."

"I should like to see Vlasta," I say suddenly.

"Thou shalt see her."

"Where is she?"

"Not far from here. Thou shalt ride for her. Thy horse shall take thee to her."

I jump up and beg that I may go for her at once. But the man's hand seizes my arm and pulls me to the ground. "Sit, King. Thou must rest and eat thy fill. All the while I shall speak to thee of her."

"Where is she? Tell me that."

"An hour's ride from here there is a wooden cottage with thatched roof. It is encircled by a wooden fence."

"Yes, yes," I affirm and feel a joyous weight upon my heart. "Everything is of wood. Thus it must be. In her cottage there must be not one metal nail."

"Indeed," the voice continues. "The fence is of wooden stakes made ready so hurriedly that one may see the original shape of the branch upon them."

"All things of wood are like to a cat or dog," I say. "They are

beings rather than things. I love the world of wood. Only there am I at home."

"Beyond the fence grow sunflowers, marigolds, and dahlias, and there too grows an old apple tree. While we yet speak Vlasta stands upon the threshold of this house."

"How is she arrayed?"

"She has a skirt of linen, somewhat stained, for she has just returned from the cowshed. In her hand she has a wooden pail. She wears no shoes. But she is beautiful because she is young."

"She is poor," I say. "She is a poor man's daughter."

"Even so, and yet she is a queen. And because she is a queen she must be hidden. Even thou darest not go to her lest she be revealed. Thou canst go to her only under thy veil. Thy horse will lead thee to her."

So fine is the man's narration that I feel myself falling prey to a sweet languor. I lie upon the grass and hear the voice, and then the voice falls silent, and I hear only the murmuring of the water and the crackling of the fire. It is so beautiful that I dare not open my eyes. But there is no help for it. I know it is already time and that they must be opened.

Underneath me there were three cushions on the polished wood. I don't like polished wood—or the curved iron legs on which the sofa stands. A pink glass globe encircled with three white bands hangs above me on the ceiling. I don't like the globe either, or the china closet opposite that displays so much useless bric-a-brac. The only wooden object in the room is the black harmonium in the corner. It's the only thing in the place I like. It was Father's. Father died a year ago.

I got up from the couch, but I didn't feel rested. It was Friday afternoon, two days before Sunday's Ride of the Kings. Everything depended on me. In our district everything connected with folklore depends on me. For a full two weeks I'd been kept awake by all sorts of worries, finding things, debating things, arranging things.

Then Vlasta came into the room. I keep telling myself that she ought to get fatter. Fat wives are usually jolly. Vlasta is skinny and already has a number of fine wrinkles on her face. She asked me if I'd remembered to stop at the laundry for our washing on the way home from school. I had forgotten. "I might have known," she said and asked me if I'd be at home at all to-day. I had to tell her I wouldn't, as I had a meeting in town very soon. A district meeting.

"You promised you'd do Vladimir's homework with him today."

I shrugged my shoulders.

"And who's going to be at this meeting?"

I mentioned those who'd be taking part, and Vlasta interrupted me, "Will Mrs. Hanzlik be there?"

"Yes," I said.

Vlasta assumed her outraged expression, and I knew that I was in trouble. Mrs. Hanzlik had a bad reputation. Everyone knew she slept around. It wasn't that Vlasta suspected me of being involved with her, but she was still irritated at the very mention of her. She scorned any meetings Mrs. Hanzlik attended. There was no use arguing about it—I preferred just to slip out of the house.

At the meeting we discussed the final preparations for the Ride of the Kings. The whole thing was a mess. The local council had begun cutting back on our budget. A few years ago they had supported folk celebrations with large donations. Today we had to support *them*. We'd requested the police to close the road for the duration of the Ride. That very day we'd had a refusal from them. They said it was impossible to disrupt the traffic for the sake of the Ride. But what will it be like with the horses milling among the cars? The whole thing was one big headache.

It was around eight when I left the meeting. I saw Ludvik on the square. I almost stopped dead in my tracks. What was he doing here? Then I caught his glance, which rested on me for a second and quickly shifted away. He pretended not to know me. Two old friends like us. Eight years on the same school bench. And he pretends not to know me!

Ludvik was the first crack to appear in my life. Nowadays I'm used to the idea of my life being none too secure. Not long ago I was in Prague and I went to one of those little theaters that sprang up like mushrooms in the sixties, run mainly by students in a haphazard sort of way. They did a play with very little action in it but with satirical songs and some good jazz. All of a sudden the jazz musicians put on feathered hats like the ones we wear in our folk costume and began doing a takeoff on a cymbalo band. They wailed and squealed, imitated our dance steps and our typical mime gestures. It only lasted a few minutes, but it had the audience rolling in the aisles. I couldn't believe my eyes. Five years ago no one would have dreamed of making clowns of us. And no one would have laughed at the joke. Now we're made to look ridiculous. Why are we suddenly ridiculous?

And Vladimir. I've even had trouble with him the last few weeks. The district council hinted to the Youth League that he should be chosen as this year's King. There is an age-old tradition that the election of the King means honoring the father. This year they were to honor me, to reward me through my son for everything I'd done for folk culture. But Vladimir tried to get out of it, using every conceivable excuse. He said he had to be in Brno on the Sunday of the motorcycle races. He even confessed he was afraid of horses. Finally he said he didn't want to be King if it was going to be a put-up job. He said he didn't want any favors.

I've spent a lot of time worrying about this. It was as if he wanted to erase everything from his life that might remind him of mine. Even as a boy he dragged his feet about joining the children's song and dance group which had been set up at my suggestion in conjunction with our ensemble. He was already making excuses even then. He said he had no musical talent.

Yet he played the guitar quite well and used to go over to his friends' houses to sing American songs.

Of course Vladimir is fifteen now. And he's fond enough of me. He's a sensitive boy. A few days ago we had a little private talk together, and maybe he understood what I was getting at.

I remember it vividly. I was sitting in the rocking chair and Vladimir on the couch. I leaned my elbow on the closed lid of the harmonium, my favorite instrument. Its strains were an intimate part of my childhood. Father played it every day. Mainly folk songs in simple harmonies. To me it sounded like the distant babbling of springs. I only wish Vladimir would think of it like that. I only wish he'd try to understand.

All nations have their popular art. But for the most part it can be distinguished from their culture without much difficulty. Ours cannot. Every western European nation has had an unbroken cultural development, at least since the Middle Ages. Whereas in the seventeenth and eighteenth centuries the Czech nation almost ceased to exist. In the nineteenth century it was virtually re-born. Among the older European nations it was a child. It had its past, and rich culture too, but these were separated from it by an abyss of two hundred years during which neither nobleman nor burgher had spoken Czech. The Czech language retreated from the towns to the countryside and became the exclusive property of the illiterate. Among them, however, it never ceased to continue creating its own culture— a humble culture, completely hidden from the eyes of Europe. A culture of songs, fairy tales, ancient rites and customs, proverbs and sayings. And this was the only narrow bridge which spanned the two-hundred-year gulf. The only bridge, the only crossing point. And so the men who, at the turn of the nineteenth century, began to create a new Czech literature and music grafted it upon this existing culture. That was why the first Czech poets and musicians spent so much time collecting fairy tales and songs. That's why their early poetic and musical efforts were often only a paraphrase of folk poetry and folk melodies.

Vladimir, if only you'd try to understand this. Your father isn't just a crackpot folklore addict. Maybe he is something of an addict but he goes deeper than that. He hears in popular art the sap without which Czech culture would have dried up. He is in love with the sound of its flowing.

This love of mine began during the war. They wanted to show us that we had no right to exist, that we were only Germans who spoke a Slavonic tongue. We had to assure ourselves that we'd existed before and that we still did. We made a pilgrimage to the source. Even the greatest modernists—they all made their humble pilgrimage to popular art.

And my turn came, too. At the time I was playing bass in a small student jazz band. My father was a harsh taskmaster in music, and as a result I could play all the stringed instruments. One day I had a visit from a Dr. Blaha, chairman of a local patriotic organization. He said we should resurrect the cymbalo bands—that it was our patriotic duty. To show that we were Slavs. That we possessed an ancient popular culture. Who at that time could have turned this offer down? I joined them and played the violin.

We awoke folk song from its deep slumbers. Those nineteenth-century patriots had transferred popular art to the songbooks only just in time. Civilization began rapidly to displace the popular traditions. So at the turn of the century we had to take the folk art out of the songbooks and restore it to life again. First in the towns. Then in the country—and especially in our region. Popular feast days were resurrected; the Ride of the Kings and the folk music groups were encouraged. It takes a lot of hard work to preserve a culture. The folklorists couldn't revive traditions as rapidly as civilization had been able to bury them—at least not until the war reinvigorated us.

There are certain merits in having one's back to the wall. A war was on, and the life of a nation was at stake. We heard the folk songs and we suddenly saw that they were the most essential of essentials. I dedicated my life to them. Through them I merge with the stream which flows deep below.

During the war we lived everything more intensely. It was the last year of the occupation, and the Ride of the Kings was staged in our village. There was an army camp in our village, and German officers were jostling the public on the pavements. Our Ride became a demonstration. A host of colorful men on horseback—and carrying sabers. An invincible Czech horde. A deputation from the depths of history. I was fifteen then and I was chosen King. I rode between two pages with my face veiled. And I was proud. And my father was proud, for he knew I'd been chosen King as a mark of respect for him. He was a village schoolmaster and a patriot and liked by everyone.

I believe, Vladimir, that things have their own meaning. I believe that the fates of men are interconnected by the strong strand of wisdom. I see a sign in the fact that it was you they chose to be King this year. I'm as proud as I was twenty years ago. Prouder. Because they want to honor me by choosing you. And I appreciate this honor—why should I deny it? I want to hand over my kingdom to you. I want you to accept it from me.

Perhaps he finally did understand me. He promised to accept his election as King. To take part in the Ride.

At supper tonight I kept seeing Ludvik's eyes shifting away from me, and I felt myself clinging all the more tightly to Vladimir. Suddenly I was afraid that perhaps I'd been neglecting him. Perhaps I'd never tried hard enough to draw him into my world. After supper Vlasta stayed in the kitchen and I went into the sitting room with Vladimir. I tried to tell him something about Moravian folk song. How interesting it all was. And how exciting. But somehow I failed. I felt like a schoolmaster. I was afraid I was boring him. Of course he just sat there saying nothing and looking as if he was listening. He's a good boy. He's always been a good boy to me. But how do I know what goes on inside that head of his?

When I'd tormented him enough with my talk, Vlasta put

her head in the room and said it was time for bed. There was nothing I could do, no resistance I could offer. She is the household's heart and soul, its calendar and its clock. Off you go, Vladimir, good night.

I left him in the room with the harmonium. He sleeps there on the couch with the metal legs. I sleep in the bedroom next door, beside Vlasta on the marriage bed. I won't go to bed yet. I'd be sure to sleep badly. I would twist and turn and wake Vlasta. Instead I'll go and have a look at the garden. It's a warm night and you can see the stars. The garden of the old single-story cottage where we live is full of simple rural smells and quiet night sounds. There is a bench under the pear tree. It was made by my paternal grandfather out of coarse, hardly processed wood. From planks and four logs.

Damn Ludvik. Why did he have to turn up today? I'm afraid it may be a bad omen. My oldest friend! This was the very bench we used to sit on so often when we were boys. I used to like him. Right from our first year in high school when we met. He had more brains in one finger than the rest of us had in the whole of our bodies, but he never made much use of them. He despised the school and the teacher, and he used to love doing anything that was against regulations.

Why did we two become such friends? Destiny must have had something to do with it. We were both half orphans. My mother died when I was born. Ludvik's father was taken away to the concentration camp when he was thirteen and he never saw him again.

Why the Germans locked up old Jahn no one really knows. Some said with a sneer that it was for profiteering and other shady deals. He was employed by a German firm as a bricklayer foreman, and by some irregular means or other he managed to get hold of a mass of groceries. Ludvik said he used to give them to some hungry Jewish family. Maybe he did. The Jews never came back to confirm it.

Ludvik was the eldest son. He was also the only one, because his younger brother died. After his father's arrest he and his mother were left on their own to survive as best they could. It wasn't easy. The high school fees were steep. It looked as if Ludvik would have to leave. Then at the last minute he was saved.

It was a salvation Ludvik hated. His father had a sister who some time before the war had married a rich local builder. After that she'd lost almost all contact with her bricklayer brother. But when he was arrested, her patriotic heart was stirred. She proposed to her sister-in-law that she take on Ludvik as her responsibility. Her only child was a retarded daughter, and the talented Ludvik made her very envious. Not only did she support him financially, but he was invited to their place every day—for lunch and for supper. There he met the cream of local society. Ludvik had to appear grateful to them, for his studies depended on their support.

But at the same time he despised them. They were named Koutecky, and from that time on we regarded the name as synonymous with pompous ass. Builder Koutecky was a great Midas. He bought up masses of paintings by landscape artists in our neighborhood—only the well-known ones, of course. These, God knows, were the worst fakes of all. Mrs. Koutecky would stand in front of a painting and sigh admiringly, "Ah, the perspective!" Her one and only criterion for judging a picture was its perspective.

Mrs. Koutecky's opinion of her sister-in-law was not very high. She'd always claimed loudly that her brother had made a poor marriage. And even after his arrest her attitude remained the same. The heavy guns of her charity were trained on Ludvik. She saw in him a descendant of her own flesh and blood, and she longed to make him her son. The existence of her sister-in-law she regarded as an unfortunate mistake. She never even invited her to the house. Ludvik saw all this and just gritted his teeth. He adored his mother. Often he was driven to the point of defiance. But his mother always begged him tearfully to control himself and to show all possible gratitude to the Kouteckys.

Ludvik much preferred coming over to our place. We were like twins. Father was almost as fond of him as he was of me. When I became active in the student jazz band, Ludvik wanted to join, too. He bought a cheap clarinet at the bazaar and in no time learned to play it competently. We played in the band together, and when Dr. Blaha appealed to our sense of patriotism we joined the cymbalo band together, too.

Toward the end of the war Koutecky's dimwit daughter got married. Mrs. Koutecky decided that the wedding was to be a big one. She wanted to have five pairs of bridesmaids and pages behind the bride and groom. Ludvik was recruited and given the eleven-year-old daughter of the local druggist as partner. He was miserable. He felt ashamed at having to play the fool at a "society" wedding. He wanted to be considered an adult and felt bitterly insulted at having to take the arm of a mere child of eleven. He was furious with the Kouteckys for putting him on display as proof of their charity, and furious at having to kiss the cross during the ceremony after everybody else had slobbered over it. That evening he deserted the festivities and came to see us in the back room of the inn. We played, had a few drinks, and started teasing him. He lost his temper and said he hated the bourgeoisie. Then he cursed the church rites and said he spat on the church and would leave it, too.

We didn't take this too seriously, but a few days after the end of the war Ludvik actually carried out his threat. Of course by doing so he mortally offended the Kouteckys. This didn't bother him. He was delighted to part ways with them. He became avidly pro-Communist. He used to go to their every lecture and buy up their literature. Our area was solidly Catholic and our high school particularly so. This meant we didn't have very much sympathy for Ludvik's Communistic views. But we were all ready to forgive them as an interesting eccentricity. We acknowledged his rights and privileges.

In 1947 we took our finals. The very same day Ludvik, to celebrate his manhood, applied at the local secretariat to join the Party. That autumn we all went our ways out into the world. Ludvik went to study in Prague, I in Brno. We left two poor lonely people at home, Ludvik a mother and I a father. Luckily Brno is only two hours by train. I used to go home every weekend—to see father and to play in the group. I didn't lay eyes on Ludvik for a whole year after our graduation.

It was 1948. Everything was being turned upside down. When Ludvik joined our group during the holidays we were at a loss how to greet him. Not one of us was a Communist. In the February coup we saw the coming of dictatorship. Ludvik brought his clarinet but never needed it. We spent the entire night in debate.

Was it then that the disharmony between us began? I don't think so. That night Ludvik almost entirely won me over. He avoided political arguments as much as possible and spoke about our group. He said we ought to have a more elevated understanding of the meaning of our work than we'd had up till then. What was the sense in merely reviving a lost past? He who looks backward will end up like Lot's wife.

We shouted at him, "So what do you want us to do?"

Of course, he replied, we must cherish our heritage of folk art, but that alone was not enough. We were in a new age now. There were wide horizons opening up for our work. We must take the ordinary everyday musical culture and purge from it the hackneyed hit songs and popular music with which the bourgeois fed the people. Their place must be taken by the real original popular art from which we would create a modern style of art and living.

Strange. What Ludvik was saying was merely the old Utopian dream of the most conservative Moravian patriots. They were always raging against the godless depravity of city culture. In the melodies of the "Charleston" they heard the pipes of the devil. But that's beside the point. It only made Ludvik's words all the more familiar and sympathetic to us.

The rest of his argument sounded more original. He was talking about jazz. How jazz had grown from Negro folk music to conquer the Western world. Forget the fact that jazz had gradually become a commercial commodity. It might serve us as a rousing demonstration of the miraculous power of folk music. The musical style of an entire epoch had stemmed from it.

We listened to Ludvik, and our surprise was mingled with irritation—irritation at his certainty. He was behaving the way all the Communists behaved at that time. As if he'd made a secret pact with the future and had the right to act in its name. Perhaps too he left a bad taste in our mouths because he'd suddenly changed from the Ludvik we'd known. With us he'd always been one of the boys, a joker. Now he was talking in deadly earnest and didn't hesitate to use long and high-sounding words. And of course he also annoyed us by the unhesitating way in which he linked the fate of our band with the fate of the Communist Party, even though not one of us was a Communist.

On the other hand, his words did hold a kind of attraction. His way of thinking corresponded to our most secret dreams. Suddenly they elevated us to a historic greatness. They were too flattering to our love of Moravian song for us to be able to dismiss them. And I personally couldn't on two counts. I liked Ludvik. I liked my father, too, and he had absolutely no use for Communists. Ludvik's talk about music built a bridge across this otherwise impassable ravine.

In my mind I call him the Pied Piper. He blew on his flute and we all flocked after him. He was quite right, we confirmed. There *was* the same strength concealed in the roots of our folk music as there was in the roots of jazz. Only one thing differentiated us from jazz, he contended. Jazz was quick to develop and change. Its entire style was constantly evolving. It was a steep road indeed from the primitive beginnings of New Orleans through hot jazz, swing, to cool jazz, and so on. On the other hand our folk music was a sleeping princess from bygone centuries. We must awaken her. She must merge with the life of today and develop along with it. Folk music must develop as jazz had—only without ceasing to be itself, without losing its unique melody and rhythm. It must create its own new and changing phases of style. It must speak of our twentieth century. It must become its musical mirror. This was an enormous task. And it was a task which could only be carried through under Socialism.

"What's it got to do with Socialism?" we protested.

Patiently, he explained. The old country folk had lived a collective life. Communal rites were observed throughout the rural year. Folk art knew no life outside these rites. The romantics imagined the girl cutting grass as being suddenly inspired and pouring forth song like a stream from the mountainside. In fact the folk song originated in a different way from the artificial poem. The poet created to express himself, his uniqueness and his diversity. In the folk song man did not stand out from the others but joined in with them. Each song had a number of authors, who all disappeared modestly with their creation. No folk song existed just for its own sake. It had its function. There were songs sung at weddings, at harvesttime, songs for Christmas, for haymaking, for dancing, and for funerals. Even love songs did not exist outside certain habitual festivities. The evening rural promenade, the singing under maidens' windows, courtship—everything had its own collective rite and in that rite the songs had their established place.

Capitalism broke up this old collective life. Folk art lost its base, its sense of being, its function. It would be useless to try to resurrect it while there still existed the social conditions in which man lived cut off from man, every one for himself. Socialism, however, liberated man from the yoke of his isolation. People would be living in a new collective system. They would be linked together by a common cause. Their private life would become merged with their public. Again they'd be united by dozens of communal rites and would create their new collective customs. Some they would take from the past—harvesting, haymaking, dancing, work songs. Others they'd create as new— the First of May, meetings, celebrations of the Liberation, rallies. Everywhere folk art would find its place. Here it would develop, change, and be renewed. Did we see what he was driving at?

I remember the day when there were field horses tied to the trees in our streets. A few days earlier the Red Army had broken through to our township. We all put on ceremonial costume, took our instruments, and went out to play in the park. We drank and played nonstop for hours on end. The Russian soldiers responded with their own songs. At the time I had said to myself that a new era was on its way. A Slavonic era. Just like the Roman Empire and the German Empire, we too were the heirs to an antique age. We had slumbered for many centuries. But we had slept well. We were refreshed. We were ready!

And the unbelievable began to come true. No one had ever done a fraction as much for our folk art as the Communist government did. It devoted enormous funds to the setting up of ensembles. Folk music with violin and cymbalo resounded daily from the radio. The universities were inundated with Moravian and Slovak songs. There were the May Day celebrations, young people's festivities, dances. Not only did jazz fall from popularity, but it became the symbol of Western capitalism and its decadence. Young people stopped dancing the jitterbug when they had a party or celebration. Instead they took each other around the shoulders and danced in a circle to Slavonic melodies. The Communist Party was devoting all its efforts to creating a new way of life. Just as it had done in the Soviet Union. It based itself on Stalin's famous definition of the new art: Socialist content in national form. Only our folk art was capable of providing our music, dance, and poetry with this national form.

Our group sailed buoyantly upon the tide of this policy. It soon gained national fame. It added singers and dancers and became a great ensemble which performed on hundreds of platforms and even made an annual tour abroad. We didn't limit ourselves to the traditional songs; we wrote new ones for ourselves, things like, "How good it is there are no masters now," or the "Song of Stalin"—songs about plowed fields and harvests on cooperative farms. No longer were our songs just a memory of the past. They were alive. They belonged to the most contemporary history. They accompanied and celebrated it.

The Communist Party gave us its enthusiastic support, and our political reservations quickly melted away. I joined the Party myself at the beginning of '49. And the others in the ensemble soon followed me.

So we still remained friends. When then did the first shadow fall between us?

I know the answer of course. I know it only too well. It was at my wedding.

I'd been studying the violin at the Academy of Music in Brno and attending lectures on musical theory at the university. When I entered my third year at Brno I was pretty depressed. At home Father was going from bad to worse. He'd suffered a stroke, and though he'd pretty much recovered, he still had to take great care of himself. I kept worrying about his being at home on his own and thinking that if anything were to happen to him he wouldn't even be able to send me a telegram. Every Saturday I'd come home in a state of apprehension, and every Monday morning I'd leave for Brno with new worries. There came a point when I could no longer stand the anxiety. It had been oppressing me on Monday and even more strongly on Tuesday. On Wednesday I threw all my clothes into my bag, paid the landlady, and said I wasn't coming back.

I hurried home from the station, across a field where boys were flying kites. I was happy. I had no regrets about what I was leaving behind. Of course I liked my violin. I even enjoyed musical theory. But I had no career ambitions. Nothing could replace for me the joy of coming home and being surrounded again by the things a man has when he's born: the horizons of his native land, the intimacy of his own few walls, his family. I came home with a profound sense of relief.

When I told Father that I wouldn't be returning to Brno, he

was terribly upset. He didn't want me to ruin my life for his sake. I changed my tactics and managed to persuade him that I'd been thrown out of the college for lack of progress. He finally believed this and was even angrier. Not that that worried me. I hadn't come home to waste my time. I went on playing first fiddle in our band and got a job as violin teacher in the music school. I could devote myself to the things I loved.

One of these was Vlasta. She lived in the next village, which today—like my own village—is a suburb. She danced with our ensemble. I'd met her while studying in Brno, and after my return I was able to see her almost every day. But real love came somewhat later—suddenly, during a rehearsal when she tripped and fell so awkwardly that she broke her leg. I carried her in my arms to the ambulance. I felt her frail, brittle body in my arms. Suddenly I realized with astonishment that I was six feet three and weighed well over two hundred pounds, that I could have been a lumberjack, while she was as light as a broken bird and as pitiful. I cried with sympathy and it made me feel so good that I wished the moment would never end. That it would color everything between us.

It was a moment of revelation. In Vlasta's injured body I suddenly saw another, more familiar figure. How was it that I hadn't seen it before? Vlasta was the "poor man's daughter," the heroine of so many folk songs! The poor girl who has nothing on this earth but her honor, the poor girl who is injured, the poor girl in rags, the poor orphan girl.

Literally, of course, this was hardly the case. She did have parents and they were anything but poor. And precisely because they were a well-to-do farming family the new age began driving them to the wall. Vlasta often came to rehearsals in tears. They'd levied heavy taxes on the family. They'd proclaimed her father a kulak. They'd requisitioned his tractor and implements. They'd threatened him with arrest. I was sorry for Vlasta and comforted myself with the idea that I would protect her—shelter the poor man's daughter.

From the moment I began to regard her in this light I felt as if I were reliving a love I'd experienced a thousand times. As if I were playing it from ancient music. As if it were sung to me from folk songs. Entirely carried away, I dreamed of my wedding and looked eagerly forward to it.

Two days before the ceremony Ludvik appeared out of the blue. I greeted him warmly, told him the great news of my marriage, and asked that, as my best friend, he serve as a witness. He promised to come. And he did.

My friends in the group staged a real Moravian wedding for me. They came for us early in the morning with music and in costume. Fifty-year-old Vondracek, the group's cymbalo player, had the duty of *starosvat,* of giving away. First of all my father regaled everyone with slivovitz, bread, and bacon. The giver then signaled for silence and recited in a loud voice:

> *Well-beloved young men and maidens,*
> *Lords and ladies,*
> *I have summoned you to this abode*
> *Because this young man hath made a request*
> *That we might make the journey with him to the abode*
>   *of the father of one Vlasta Netahal,*
> *Because he has chosen his daughter, a gentle maid, for*
>   *his bride.*

The "giver," *starosvat,* or chief speechmaker is the director, the soul of the entire ceremony. That's the way it's always been. The groom was never the subject of the wedding. He was its object. He was not marrying. He was being married. Someone was using the marriage to possess him and he sailed along on it as though on some great wave. He wasn't the one to act or speak. The giver was his spokesman. But it was not even the giver. It was the age-old tradition, handed down from man to man, that steered him into its honeyed stream—a stream in which everybody became like everybody else, became merged into mankind.

We set off, the giver leading, to the next village. We walked across the fields, and my friends played as we went. In front of

Vlasta's house we were eagerly awaited by a throng of people in folk costume from the bride's side of the family. The giver intoned:

> *We are weary travelers,*
> *And we beseech*
> *That we might gain entrance into this honest abode,*
> *For we are thirsty and hungry.*

An elderly man in costume detached himself from the crowd standing in front of the gate. *"Be ye honest people, then be ye welcome here."* And he invited us in. Silently we crowded into the passageway. We were, as the giver had introduced us, just weary travelers, and so we didn't at first reveal our true intent. The old man in the costume, who was the speaker on the bride's side, challenged us: *"If ye have anything which weighs upon your hearts, speak it now."*

The giver began to speak, at first obliquely and in riddles, and the man in costume answered him in the same manner. Only after considerable circumlocution did the giver reveal why we had come. Now the old man asked him this question:

> *I ask thee, friend,*
> *Why does this honest groom wish to take this honest*
>   *maid as his wife?*
> *Is it for the flower or for the fruit?*

And the giver replied:

> *To each it is well known that the flower advanceth in*
>   *beauty and grace so that it is a pleasure to the heart.*
> *But the flower fadeth*
> *And the fruit ripeneth.*
> *Thus we take not this bride for the flower but for the*
>   *fruit, for from the fruit there cometh goodness.*

The responses continued for a while until the spokesman for the bride concluded: *"Let us call the bride and let her say whether she chooses aye or nay."* He went to the next room and presently returned, leading by the hand a woman in national costume. She was tall, thin, and bony, and her face was veiled with a scarf. *"Here is thy bride."*

But the giver shook his head and with loud murmurs we all echoed his disagreement. The old man spent a little while trying to prevail upon us but finally had to lead the veiled woman away. Only then did he bring in Vlasta. She was wearing black boots, a red pinafore, and a multicolored bodice. She had a garland of flowers on her head. She looked beautiful. I took her hand in mine.

Then the old man turned to the bride's mother and called in a doleful voice: *"Alas, the mother!"*

At these words the bride tore herself from my grasp, knelt on the ground before her mother, and hung her head. The old man went on:

> *Mother, dearest mother, forgive me wherein I have done thee wrong!*
> *Mother, dearest mother, I beg thee before God to be forgiven wherein I have done thee wrong!*
> *Mother, dearest mother, I beg thee by the five wounds of God to forgive me wherein I have done thee wrong!*

We were actors in a play which has been performed for ages past. And the text was beautiful and striking and true in every word. Then our band started to play and we proceeded to the town. The ceremony was held in the guildhall and there was music playing for us there, too. Then came the dinner, and after dinner we all went to the local *buda,* or folk hall. There was music and dancing.

In the evening Vlasta's bridesmaids took her garland of rosemary from her head and ceremonially handed it to me. From her free-hanging hair they made a pigtail, winding it around her head, and they tied her head up in a bonnet. This was the ceremony symbolic of her step from virginity into womanhood.

It had been a long time since Vlasta had been a virgin, so she wasn't strictly entitled to the symbol of the garland. However, I didn't consider this important. At some higher and more binding level she lost her virginity now and only now as the bridesmaids handed me her garland of flowers.

God, why is it that the memory of that garland of rosemary affects me more than our first real love, than Vlasta's real virgin blood? I don't know why but it does. The women used to sing songs in which the garland floated off across the water and the waves weaved it into ribbons of red. I felt like weeping. I was drunk. I saw before my eyes the floating flowers, I saw the brook handing them on to the stream, the stream to the river, the river to the Danube, and the Danube to the sea. It was in this irrevocability that the essence of the whole thing lay. All basic situations in life happen once and are then beyond recall. To be a real man, a man must go through to the end with full knowledge of what he is doing. He must drink to the dregs. He must not cheat. He must not pretend he doesn't see what he is doing. When Vlasta's blood stained the towel I'd placed beneath her, I had no idea that something had been done which was beyond recall. Now there was no escaping it.

Then it was night and the guests accompanied us home. There we stopped, and all Vlasta's friends sang to us about how we should not harm the poor *penniless* girl in her new abode, that as at home she had been loved, even so let us love her here.

I opened the gate. Vlasta stopped on the threshold and then turned again to the cluster of her friends gathered in front of the house. Then one of them intoned the final song:

> *She stood on the threshold,*
> *Lovely she looked then,*
> *Fair as a rose.*
> *She stepped from the threshold,*
> *Lost all her beauty,*
> *My fine young maid.*

They closed the door after us and we were alone. Vlasta was twenty and I was a little older. But I was thinking of how she had crossed the threshold and how from this magic moment onward her beauty would fade from her like the leaves of a tree. I saw that fading in her which lay in the future. That fading which had now begun. For this very reason I loved her now more than anything else in the world. I thought of how she was not just the flower but that in this moment the fruit was already present in her. I felt in the whole thing an unyielding order, an order with which I had merged myself and with which I profoundly agreed. In that moment I was thinking of Vladimir, whom at that moment I could not know, whose existence I could have no idea of. Yet I thought of him and looked through him far into the distance of the generations of his children. I lay down with Vlasta in the high piled bed and it seemed to me to be the wise eternity of human generation which took us into its soft embrace.

What did Ludvik do to me at that wedding? Nothing really. He looked sour and he was in a strange mood. In the afternoon, when the music and dancing began, my friends offered him the clarinet. They wanted him to sit in with them. He refused. Not long afterward he left altogether. Luckily I had plenty to think about and didn't pay any special attention to the incident. The next day, however, I saw that his departure had left a small stain on the day's proceedings. The alcohol circulating in my blood exaggerated this stain out of all proportion. And Vlasta helped in this even more than the alcohol. She had never liked Ludvik. Women instinctively classify their husbands' friends into the harmless and the dangerous. Vlasta had filed Ludvik into the second category and was always glad that he lived in Prague.

When I told her Ludvik would serve as a witness, she hadn't been very pleased. On the day after the wedding she was quick to remind me of his behavior. She said he'd gone around all day, acting as if we were all putting him to considerable inconvenience. He was conceited and difficult and he kept his nose so high in the air it was a wonder he didn't drill a hole in the sky.

However, Ludvik came to see us that very same evening. He brought some presents for Vlasta and made his apologies. Would we please forgive him for acting so strangely the day before? He told us what had happened: he'd been kicked out of the Party and the university. He didn't know what would become of him.

I couldn't believe my ears and hardly knew what to say. Anyway Ludvik didn't want anyone to feel sorry for him and quickly changed the subject. In two weeks our ensemble was due to leave on a big foreign tour, and we were all really looking forward to it. Ludvik began asking me about our trip. I realized at once that he had longed to go abroad ever since he was a child and now the chances of his ever getting out were very slim. At that time, and for a number of years afterward, people with any political blemish were not allowed abroad. I was reluctant to discuss the tour, as that would have illuminated the gulf between our two lives. But I couldn't find a single word which did not do this in some way. Every sentence having anything to do with our lives revealed that we'd taken two completely different roads. Told us that our opportunities and our futures were drastically different. That we were being borne away in opposite directions. I tried to talk about trivial things in hopes of concealing what strangers we'd become. But this was worse still. Our stilted, artificial conversation was in itself unbearably painful.

Ludvik soon left. He volunteered for a labor gang, and I went abroad with the ensemble. From then on, I didn't see him for several years. I sent him a letter or two when he was in the army. After I'd mailed them they always left me with the same sense of dissatisfaction I'd had after our last conversation. I was unable to face up squarely to the fact of Ludvik's failure. The success of my own life embarrassed me. It was unthinkable to be doling out words of encouragement or sympathy to

Ludvik from the heights of my own contentment. Instead I tried to pretend that nothing had changed between us, telling him all the news of the ensemble, the gossip about the new cymbalo player, and so on. I acted as if my world was still one we shared. Yet even at the time, I hated the pretense.

Then one day my father received an obituary announcement. Ludvik's mother had died. None of us had known she was ill. When Ludvik had dropped out of my life, she had vanished with him. I held the obituary in my hand and became aware of my indifference toward people who had, however slightly, withdrawn from my life. My successful life. Even though I'd done nothing wrong, I felt guilty. And then I noticed something that shocked me immeasurably. The obituary notice had been signed on behalf of the next of kin by Mr. and Mrs. Koutecky. There was no mention of Ludvik at all.

The day of the funeral arrived. I felt rather nervous at the prospect of meeting Ludvik again. But he never came. Only a handful of people trudged after the coffin. I asked the Kouteckys where Ludvik was. They shrugged their shoulders and said they didn't know. The pallbearers stopped beside a big marble vault with a white statue of an angel.

This rich builder's family had had everything taken from them and were living on a meager allowance. All they had left was this imposing family vault. I knew all this but had no idea why the coffin was to be placed here. Only later did I learn that Ludvik was at that time in prison. His mother was the only person in town who'd known. She'd kept it hidden from everybody. She lived completely alone with her illness, which had finally brought her to the infirmary and so to the cemetery.

Once she was dead, the flame of family affection was rekindled in Mr. and Mrs. Koutecky. They took charge of the body of a sister-in-law they'd never loved and proclaimed it as their own. At last they were avenged on their ungrateful nephew. They had robbed him of his mother. They covered her with the heavy marble stone guarded by the white angel with his curly hair and his spray of flowers. I have always remembered that angel. A curly-haired angel with his false garland of peace, soaring above the ravaged life of my friend from whom even the bodies of his parents had been stolen. An angel of theft.

Vlasta hates any form of extravagance. For her sitting out in the garden at night just because you feel like it is an extravagance. I heard her banging vigorously on the window. Behind the pane loomed the severe shadow of a woman's figure in a nightdress. I have an obedient nature. I can never say no to those weaker than myself. And because I stand six feet three and can heft a hundred-pound sack with one hand, in all my life I've never yet found anyone I could resist.

So I went in and got into bed beside Vlasta. To break the silence I mentioned that I'd seen Ludvik today. "Oh?" she said, with a display of indifference. There was no denying it: he had got right under her skin. To this day she can't stand the sight of him. I don't see what she has to complain about. Since our wedding she's seen him exactly once. That was in 1956. And that time I was unable to gloss over the gulf that divided us, even to myself.

Ludvik had behind him his military service, the prison, and a few years down in the mines. He'd arranged in Prague to resume his studies and had only come to the town to see about a few legal formalities. Again I was nervous at the prospect of meeting him. However, when I did he was no whimpering wreck. Anything but. Ludvik had changed profoundly. He was tough, touchy, and perhaps a little calmer than I'd remembered him. There was nothing in him that called for sympathy. It seemed we'd quickly vault the gulf I'd feared so much. To make some sort of contact I invited him to a rehearsal of our band. I still thought of it as his band, too. What did it matter that we had different players on cymbalo, bass, and clarinet, and that I was the only one left of the old crowd?

Ludvik sat in a chair next to the cymbalo player and listened to us rehearsing. First we played all his favorite songs, the ones we used to play at school. Then some new ones we'd unearthed

in some remote mountain communities. Finally we reached
the ones that form the mainstay of our repertoire. These are
not real folk songs but ones we composed ourselves in the folk
song spirit. We sang of fields that would be plowed up to make
a single big collective from many small private fields, songs of
the poor who no longer have to be slaves but who've become
masters in their own land, the song of the tractor driver who
does so well at the tractor station. These were all songs whose
music was indistinguishable from that of older folk songs but
whose words were more up to date than any newspaper. Our
favorite was the one about Fucik, the hero tortured by the Nazis
during the occupation. Ludvik just sat there thoughtfully and
never once looked in my direction. After the rehearsal I invited
him over to our place. Vlasta made us some supper and then
went to bed, leaving us alone. Ludvik started to talk about
everything under the sun. But I felt he was intentionally avoiding the very thing I wanted to talk about. How could I be silent
with my best friend on the subject that had been our greatest
shared possession? I interrupted him. What did he think of our
songs? He told me without any hesitation that he liked them.
But I wasn't going to let him get away with easy politeness. I
asked him what he thought of the new songs we'd discovered
in those isolated villages. And what did he think of the ones we'd
composed ourselves?

Ludvik didn't want to enter into a debate. But step by step I
drew him out until finally he started talking. Those few old
folk songs he thought were really beautiful. Otherwise he didn't
care for our repertoire at all. We were accommodating ourselves too much to prevailing tastes. We wanted to be popular,
so we stripped our songs of everything that was unique to them.
We scrapped their inimitable rhythm and adapted it to con-
ventional rhythmic patterns. We chose our songs from the very
recent past, the czardas and that sort of thing, because these
were the easiest to understand and the easiest to like.

I reminded him that we were only at the beginning of our
career. We wanted folk music to spread as widely as possible.

Therefore we must make some concessions to popular taste. The really important thing was that we should create a *modern* folk art form, new folk songs, that would have something important to say about the life we live today.

He disagreed. It was these new songs that grated on his ears. What third-rate imitation! What an out-and-out fake!

To this day it depresses me to remember it. Who was it that warned us that if we went on looking backwards we'd end up like Lot's wife? Who was it who painted such a bright picture of folk music giving rise to the new style of the age? Who challenged us to set folk music in motion and made it stride forward side by side with history?

"It was a Utopia," said Ludvik.

"Utopia? But we have the songs. They exist!"

He laughed in my face. "You sing them in your ensemble. But show me one single person outside the group who does. Show me one collective farmworker who sings your collective farm songs to himself while he plows the fields. They're so unnatural and false, they'd make his voice crack as he sang! The propaganda text sticks out from the pseudo-folk music like a badly sewn-on collar. A pseudo-Moravian song about Fucik! What crap! Fucik was a Prague journalist. What did he have in common with Moravian Slovakia?"

I objected that Fucik belonged to us all and that we had just as much right to sing our own kind of song about him as anyone else.

"Our *own* kind of song? You don't sing them our way—you sing them the way Agitprop directs. Just think of the words. And why a song about Fucik anyway? Was he the only one in the underground? Was he the only one to be tortured?"

"He's the most famous."

"Of course he is. The propaganda machine wants a hierarchy in its dead heroes' gallery. They want a chief hero among heroes so that when the occasion arises they can dredge him up for their own purposes."

"And why not? Every age has its symbols."

"Right, but the really interesting point is—who becomes the symbolic figure? There were hundreds of people just as courageous at the time and now they're forgotten. And some of those who fell were famous men—politicians, writers, scientists, artists. They often have some great work to their credit. Yet none of them became symbols. You don't see their photographs hanging in Party offices and schools. Their very work debars them. What they did is hard to correct or reshape or obliterate. Whatever they did is a hindrance to their getting into the hall of fame."

"None of them wrote *Notes from the Gallows*."

"That's just it! What about the hero who keeps his mouth shut? What about the man who doesn't need to make his last moments an opportunity for theatrical performance? For a public lecture? Fucik, though far from famous, seemed to think that it was of immense importance to inform the world how *he* thought and felt in prison, what *he* was going through and what messages and recommendations *he* had for mankind. He wrote them on little scraps of paper, risking the lives of those who smuggled them out of prison and kept them safe. He had an exaggerated opinion of his own views and impressions—an incredibly exaggerated opinion of himself."

I'd been prepared for Ludvik to be despondent, even bitter. But I hadn't expected this viciousness, this ironic malice. What had Fucik the martyr done to him? I know Ludvik was unjustly punished. But this only made it worse: the motive for his change of views was all too transparent. Is a man to abandon the position he's held all his life just because he was once betrayed?

I said as much to Ludvik's face. And something unexpected happened. He didn't answer. It was as if his feverish anger had left him. He gave me a quizzical glance and then told me very quietly not to be angry, perhaps he was wrong. He said it in such a strange cold voice that I knew very well it wasn't meant sincerely. I didn't want our conversation to end on this false note. Despite my annoyance I still wanted to come to terms with

Ludvik and renew our old friendship. However sharply we'd clashed I still hoped that we might finally find some corner of the common ground we'd once shared where we might be able to coexist again. But my attempts to continue were in vain. Ludvik apologized, saying that he had a tendency to exaggerate and that unfortunately he'd allowed himself to be carried away. He asked me to forget what he'd said.

Forget? Why should we forget a serious discussion? Wouldn't it be better to go on with it? It wasn't until the next day that I worked out the real meaning behind this request. Ludvik slept at our place and had breakfast with us. Afterward we had another half an hour in which to talk. He told me what a job he'd had getting permission to complete his last two years at the university—how his expulsion from the Party had marked him for life. How nobody trusted him. Only with the help of a few of his friends from before the February take-over was he able to gain readmission to the university. Then he talked about a few of his other friends who found themselves in the same spot. He told me how they were followed and how everything they said was carefully noted. How people around them had been interrogated and how some officious or spiteful testimony could easily blight their lives for another decade. Then he abruptly changed the subject, and when we said good-bye he said he was glad he'd seen me, and that I should forget what he'd said the night before.

The connection between his request and the references to the fate of some of his friends was only too clear. I was shocked. Ludvik had stopped talking because he was afraid! He was afraid that our conversation might not remain a secret. He was afraid I might betray him! He was afraid of *me!* This was a terrible and completely unexpected blow. The gulf lying between us was much deeper than I'd thought. It was so deep that it even prevented us from enjoying one of those no-holds-barred theoretical discussions that had been among our chief delights in the old days.

*   *   *

Vlasta's asleep, poor girl, asleep and snoring. They're all asleep. And I'm lying here in my vast bulk and thinking how powerless I am. That last meeting with Ludvik brought it home to me. Until then I'd confidently supposed that the whole thing was well within my grasp. Ludvik and I had never done anything to injure each other. Why shouldn't we be friends again in all good will?

It turned out that this wasn't within my power. Neither our estrangement nor our reconciliation was. I resigned myself to hoping they were in time's hands. Time slipped by. Since our last meeting nine years have passed. Meanwhile Ludvik has graduated and got an excellent job as a scientist in a field that interests him. I follow his progress from across the gulf. I watch it with affection. I can never regard Ludvik either as my enemy or as a stranger. He is my friend, even though he is under a curse. It's almost like the fairy tale of the prince's bride being changed into a snake or a toad. In the fairy tales everything was always saved by the prince's loyalty and patience.

But time hasn't awakened my friend from his spell. Several times during this period I learned that he'd paid a visit to the town. Yet he never came to see me. Today I saw him and he avoided me. Ludvik is one of the damned.

It all began the time we had that conversation. Year after year I've felt the loneliness gathering around me and anxiety growing within. The longer it lasted the more weariness there was and the less joy and success. The ensemble used to go on a foreign tour every year, but then the number of invitations began to dwindle and now we hardly get invited anywhere. We're still working, working harder than ever, but everything around us is silence. I'm standing in a deserted hall. And it seems as if it were Ludvik who gave the order that I should be alone here. For it's not their enemies who condemn men to solitude. It's their friends.

Since that time I've taken refuge more and more in that track across the fields with the lone briar bush growing on the bank. There I meet with the last of my loyal friends. There is the deserter with his men. There is the wandering minstrel. There is the wooden cottage over the horizon and in it Vlasta—the poor man's daughter.

The deserter calls me King and promises me that at any time I may take refuge in his protection. All I need do is go as far as the briar bush, and there we will always meet.

It would be so easy to find peace in the world of fantasy. But I've always tried to live in the two worlds at the same time and not to abandon one for the other. I must not abandon the real world, even if I'm losing everything I have in it. In the long run it will be enough if I manage to do just one thing. One last thing: to present my life as my clear and distinct message to the one person who will understand it and carry it on. Before that I must not join the deserter on his ride to the Danube.

The one person I'm thinking of, my one hope after all my defeats, is only separated from me by a single wall, and he is sleeping. Tomorrow he will mount his brown steed. He will wear ribbons across his face. They will be calling him King. Come, my son. I am slipping away into sleep. They will be calling you by my name. Time to sleep—and to dream of you on your horse.

V
Ludvik

J SLEPT long and fairly well. The bitter memories I'd indulged so freely far into the night before had failed to disrupt the rhythm of my physical life, drilled as it is to the strict routine I imposed on myself when it first occurred to me, on passing thirty, that I wasn't immune to the process of growing old. I woke up some time after eight and couldn't remember having dreamed. I had no headache, but equally I had no desire to get up, and I've never fought this reluctance, which from a certain time onward I've viewed less as a bad habit than as a blessed symptom of indolent youth.

I just lay there. Sleep had erected a sort of windbreak between myself and yesterday's encounter, and behind it I felt—for the moment at least—secure. It wasn't so much, perhaps, that Lucie had dropped out of my consciousness. She'd merely returned to her former state of abstraction.

Abstraction? Yes. When Lucie disappeared from Ostrava so mysteriously and cruelly, I had no practical opportunity to go looking for her. And later, after my release from military service, I discovered that slowly over the years I'd lost the desire for such a search. I told myself that Lucie, however much I'd once been in love with her, and however much she remained the *only* girl, was completely unthinkable outside the context in which we met and fell in love. For what I love in a woman is not what she is in herself and for herself, but the side of her I see turned to me, what she is *for me*. I love her as a character in adventures we've lived through together. What would Hamlet be without the castle at Elsinore, without Ophelia, without all the concrete situations he experiences, what would he be without the *text* of his part? What would remain of the character but an empty, dumb, illusory substance? And so Lucie, stripped of the bleakness of Ostrava, of the roses handed through the barbed wire, of her shabby clothes, stripped of my own endless weeks of despair, would probably cease to be the Lucie I loved.

Yes, this is how I saw it, and as year followed year I was almost afraid of running into her again. For I knew that we'd meet in a place where Lucie would no longer be Lucie, and that I'd lack the imaginative resources to mend the severed thread. Of course I don't mean that I stopped loving her, that I forgot her, or that her image in some way palled. On the contrary, she was always with me. I longed for her nostalgically, as we long for things which are irrevocably lost. And precisely because Lucie had become something belonging definitively to the past, she gradually lost, for me, all corporeal and concrete qualities and became more and more a legend, a myth inscribed on an old parchment and laid in a metal casket at the very foundations of my life.

Perhaps that was why the incredible could happen, why, as I sat in the barber's chair, I could no longer be sure whether it was she or not. Certainly it was the reason why the next morning I was able to feel yesterday's encounter was not even real— that it too was something that took place at the level of legends, oracles, and riddles. If on Friday evening I'd been struck by Lucie's actual presence and abruptly transported to a distant time over which she'd held sway, then this Saturday morning I asked with a calm heart, and after a good sleep: *Why* did I see her? Was the whole Lucie affair to have some continuation? What did this encounter mean and what was it trying to tell me? For I've never been able to rid myself of the need to be continually deciphering my own life, as if there were some sense, meaning, or truth concealed in it. So I lay on the creaky bed, letting thoughts of Lucie pass through my mind, gradually transforming her into a mere idea, a mere question.

The hotel bed was indeed, as I characterized it in the preceding sentence, creaky, and as I became conscious of this property again it evoked with sudden excitement the thought of Helena. As if that creaking bed was a voice summoning me to duty, I heaved a sigh, threw my feet off the bed, sat down on the edge, stretched, scratched my scalp, looked at the sky through the window, and finally stood up. My encounter with Lucie, however insubstantial it seemed in the clear light of morning, had served to muffle my interest in Helena, an interest which a few days before had been so intense. At this moment all that was left of it was the *awareness* that I was interested.

I went over to the washbasin, threw off my pajama top, and turned the tap on full. I splashed handfuls of it on my neck, shoulders, and body; I scrubbed myself down with the towel. I wanted to send the blood coursing through my limbs. Suddenly I realized with a shock that I was completely indifferent to the fact of Helena's coming, and I worried that this momentary indifference might spoil an opportunity that was hardly likely to come again. I told myself I'd have a hearty breakfast and afterward a shot of vodka.

I went downstairs to the coffee shop, but all I found there was a host of chairs lying mournfully, legs in the air, on the unwiped tables, and an old woman in a dirty apron creeping around in their midst.

I went to the reception desk and asked the porter, half asleep in a much-cushioned chair, whether there was any chance of my getting breakfast there. Without moving he said that the coffee shop was closed on Saturdays. I went out into the street. It was a pleasant day, with the clouds scudding across the sky and a gentle wind raising the dust from the pavement. I hurried to the main square. One of the buildings there was a sprawling single-story structure with a self-service cafeteria in front. I went inside. It was a large hall with a tiled floor and tables on long legs, where people were standing eating sandwiches and drinking coffee or beer.

I didn't feel like having breakfast in there. I'd pictured a substantial breakfast with eggs, bacon, and a shot of vodka, to restore my lost vitality. I recalled that a little farther on, in the other square with its garden and the column commemorating the plague, there was another restaurant. It certainly wasn't very prepossessing, but it was enough for me if it had tables and chairs and just one waiter to serve me.

I passed the monument, crossed the garden with its neat lawns and benches (though it was still sufficiently bare not to break the general atmosphere of empty dustiness), and went to the restaurant door. It was closed. I began to realize that my longing for breakfast would remain just that, and this alarmed me, for with childish obstinacy I'd made my mind up that a substantial breakfast was to be the decisive factor for the success of the entire day. I realized that provincial towns take no notice of eccentrics who wish to eat their breakfast sitting down and that they open their restaurants considerably later in the day. I made no attempt to find any other eating place, but turned around and walked back through the park in the opposite direction.

I kept running into people carrying red-crowned ice cream cones, and it struck me that the cones looked like torches and that there might be a symbolic meaning in their shape, because these were not torches but travesties of torches, and the pink token of delight carried triumphantly in the hand was not real pleasure but a travesty of pleasure—which would doubtless accord with the inescapably travestied nature of all torches and pleasures in this dusty little backwater. And then I told myself that since I was walking in the opposite direction from these licking torchbearers they would probably lead me to a candy store where there might be a table and chair and perhaps even black coffee and some kind of snack.

Instead they led me to a milk bar. There was a long line of people waiting for cocoa or milk and rolls with butter, and again there were those high tables where customers stood to eat. In a back room there were tables and chairs—all taken. I joined the line and eventually bought a glass of cocoa and two rolls with butter, took my stand by a table cluttered with used glasses, found a place with nothing spilled on it, and set my glass down.

I ate with uneasy haste and in three minutes or so was back on the street again. It was nine o'clock. Helena had taken the first flight from Prague, and the bus from Brno was due to arrive here around eleven. I could see that these two hours would be utterly empty and wasted.

Of course I could have spent the time taking a look at my childhood haunts, pausing in sentimental meditation by the old family house in which my mother had lived to the end of her days. I often think of her. But in this town, where her remains have been plundered and hidden under alien marble, it's as if all my thoughts were poisoned. If I had indulged them now, they would have been mingled with feelings of my powerlessness at that time and with a terrible bitterness—and this was what I was trying to fight.

So there was nothing to do but sit on a bench in the square. I sat down but almost immediately got up again, went over to the shop windows, read the titles of the books in the bookshop, then finally had the excellent idea of buying a *Rude Pravo* at the newsstand. I ran my eye over the unremarkable headlines, read a couple of interesting reports from the foreign news section, got up from the bench again, folded the *Rude Pravo,* and put it almost untouched into the trash can. I looked at the clock and discovered its hands had barely moved. I tried to focus my thoughts on Helena in order to put the long moments to some use. But the thoughts just wouldn't come, and the most I could do was conjure up a visual image of her. This is in fact a well-known phenomenon: when a man is waiting for a woman, he finds it supremely difficult to think of her and can only walk up and down, calmly or otherwise, with an unmoving picture of her suspended before his eyes.

And so I paced. Opposite the church I was puzzled by the sight of some dozen empty baby carriages standing outside the old guildhall (today the municipal council building). Then a breathless young man pushed another carriage in among the others, the rather nervous woman with him pulled a bundle of white lacy material from the carriage, and they both hurried into the guildhall. Mindful of the hour and a half I still had to kill, I followed them in.

On the broad staircase there was already quite a crowd of idle bystanders, and as I went up the stairs there were more and more of them, especially in the first-floor corridor, while the stairs leading to the second floor were empty. The event all these people were gathered for was apparently to take place here, most probably in a room off the corridor which had its doors wide open and was packed with people. I went in and found myself in a medium-sized hall with some seven rows of chairs, most of them already occupied as if in expectation of some performance. At the front, on a raised rostrum, was a long table covered with a red cloth, and on the table a vase with a big bouquet in it. On the wall behind the rostrum hung the national flag. About three yards from the first row of chairs, in front and rather to one side, were eight other chairs in a semi-circle facing the platform. On the other side of the hall, at the back, stood a small harmonium at which a bald old gentleman sat with bowed head and glasses.

I sat down on an unoccupied chair. For a long time nothing happened, but there was no sign of boredom. The people sat or stood in whispering huddles, evidently full of anticipation. Meanwhile those who'd been standing in groups in the passage had gradually filled the hall, occupying the few remaining chairs and lining the walls.

At last the long-awaited action began. A door near the platform opened, a woman dressed in brown, with steel-rimmed glasses balanced precariously on a long thin nose, appeared in it, glanced around the hall, and raised her right hand. The people around me grew quiet. Then the woman turned back toward the room she'd come from as if making a sign to someone there, but at once she was back, pressing herself against the wall and wearing a fixed and ceremonial smile. Everything appeared to be perfectly synchronized, for at the very instant when the smile appeared, the harmonium started up behind my back.

A few seconds later a flaxen-haired young woman appeared in the door by the platform, very red in the face, with elaborate hairdo and makeup, a terrified expression on her face and a white bundle of infancy in her arms. The bespectacled woman pressed back even farther against the wall so as not to block the way, her smile evidently meant to beckon the young mother forward. She advanced uncertainly, clutching her baby. Another woman with a babe in arms emerged behind her, and after her, in single file, came a whole little troop of them. I kept my eyes on the first one. She was looking somewhere up at the ceiling and failed to wheel in time past the semicircle of chairs, so that the bespectacled woman had quickly and frowningly to detach herself from the wall, go up to her, tap her gently on the shoulder, and remind her which way she should be going. The mother quickly corrected her deviation and walked along in front of the semicircle of chairs, followed by seven other women and their babies. Finally they stood with their backs to the audience, each one in front of a chair. The woman in brown pointed downwards. The women gradually got the message and sat down.

The shadow of dissatisfaction vanished from the face of the bespectacled woman, and she was smiling again as she went back to the half-open door near the platform. For a while she stood there, then again she nodded, backed into the hall and pressed herself up against the wall, while eight men of varying ages but all in dark suits and best shirts filed past her. They too had trouble finding their places, and again the woman, on whose face the now familiar shadow of dissatisfaction immediately appeared, had to shepherd them into position, standing behind their respective wives.

Reassuming her fixed smile, she returned once more to the

door by the platform. This time she didn't need to nod or
make any sign. The new troop was a disciplined and expert
bunch, striding forth without hesitation and with an almost
professional elegance. It comprised eight children of about ten,
boys and girls alternately, each carrying a bouquet of roses and
each dressed in the national colors: dark blue trousers or skirt,
white shirt or blouse, and red kerchiefs folded diagonally,
with one corner hanging down their backs and two others tied
in a knot at their throats. They came forward, as I said, with
confidence, wheeled right in front of the semicircle of chairs
and along the platform, halted, and executed a left turn, so
that they stood in a line before the platform, covering its full
length and facing the semicircle of seated women and the rows
of chairs behind.

Several minutes passed. Then the door by the platform admitted a final figure: a middle-aged man, completely bald, who
headed straight for the platform, mounting the steps and passing behind the long table. He walked erect and with dignity
and wore a black suit; in his hand he held a book bound in
red. Halfway along the length of the table he stopped and
turned to face the audience, bowing to them slightly as he did
so. One could now see the full obesity of his face and a broad
red, white, and blue ribbon around his neck, its two ends
linked by a large gold medallion which hung in the vicinity of
his stomach and bounced gently on the table several times as
he bent forward.

At this point one of the small boys standing below the platform suddenly, and without first requesting permission, started
to speak in a very loud voice. He said that spring had come and
that moms and dads were full of joy, that the whole country
was full of joy. He spoke in this vein for a while and was then interrupted by one of the girls, who made a similar speech, with
no clear meaning but with frequent repetitions of the words
mom, dad, and *spring,* and in addition the word *rose.* Then she
was cut short by another of the boys and he in turn by another of

the girls. One could hardly say that they were in any disagreement, as they were all more or less saying the same thing.
One little boy proclaimed that children were peace. The girl
who followed said that children were flowers; whereupon all
the children were united on this idea, repeating it in unison
and striding forward holding the bouquets in their outstretched
hands, one for each of the women sitting in the semicircle of
chairs. Then they returned to their place below the platform.

Next, the man standing above them on the platform opened
his red book and began to read. He too spoke about the spring
and flowers and moms and dads, about love, and about love
bearing fruit. Then all of a sudden his vocabulary was transformed and in it appeared the words *duty, responsibility, the
State, the citizen.* Also there was no more *mom* and *dad,* but
only *father* and *mother.* He gave the assembled fathers and
mothers a catalog of all the State offered them (as fathers and
mothers), and told them it was their duty to bring up their
children as model citizens of the State. Then he announced that
all parents present should ceremonially confirm this with their
signature, and indicated a large, leather-bound volume lying
on a corner of the table. This was duly done by one couple after another, the woman in brown holding successive babies
while the mothers signed.

Finally the strains of the harmonium sounded again and the
people around me poured forward to the mothers and fathers
and began grasping them by the hand. I too went forward, as
if wanting to shake someone's hand—and suddenly the man
with the ribbon around his neck called me by name and asked
me if I recognized him.

Not wishing to answer his question in the negative, I feigned
surprise and asked how he was. He said things were not too bad,
and then suddenly I knew him: of course, it was Kovalik, one
of my high school classmates, and I recognized all the features
which in his now rather fuller face had become blurred. In
any case Kovalik had been one of the less memorable pupils, be-

ing neither very diligent nor very mischievous, neither very
friendly nor too much the lone wolf. He'd been mediocre at
his studies—in short, a nonentity.

He asked me what I was doing there and whether I had any
relatives among these mothers. I said no, that I'd come simply
out of idle curiosity. He gave me a contented smile and began
to explain that the local council had done a lot to imbue civil
ceremonies with dignity, adding with modest pride that he, as
officer responsible for citizen affairs, took most of the credit
and that he'd been commended for it at district level. I asked
him whether this had been a christening. He told me it
was not a christening, but the *welcoming of new citizens
into life*. He was obviously glad to have a chance of expanding
on the subject. He said that there were two great opposing institutions concerned: the Catholic Church with its ceremonies and thousand-year-old traditions, and the civil institutions
which must displace these ancient traditions with new ones
of their own. He said that people would stop going to church
to have their children christened or to be married only when
our civil ceremonies had as much dignity and beauty as did
those of the church.

I said that this was evidently not entirely easy. He agreed
and said he was glad that the officers for citizen affairs, of whom
he was one, were at last finding a measure of support among
our artists, who had perhaps realized that it was their honorable
task to give our people really Socialist funerals, weddings, and
christenings—here he corrected himself and said "welcomings
of new citizens to life." He added that the verses the young
pioneers had recited today were truly beautiful. I acknowledged
this and asked if it might not be a more effective way of educating people away from the religious ceremonies if we gave them
a chance to avoid *any* sort of ceremony whatsoever. Didn't he
think that the distinguishing feature of the modern man is a
dislike for ritual occasions, and that if there was one thing
which should be supported it was this general dislike?

He told me that people would never let their weddings and

LUDVIK   **⊷§ 165**

I asked my old classmate what he did with people who didn't want to take part in this sort of ceremony, and whether there were any who refused. He said that of course there were, since not everybody had yet begun to think in the new way, and that if they didn't turn up they kept receiving more and more invitations, so that most of them came sooner or later. I asked him whether attendance at the ceremony was compulsory. He replied with a smile that it wasn't, but that the national committee adjudged people's sense of citizenship and attitude toward the State according to their attendance and that in the end every citizen would realize this and come.

I said this meant that the national committee was just as strict with their believers as the church with theirs. Kovalik laughed and said this couldn't be helped. Then he invited me to come and sit in his office. I said that unfortunately I was a little pressed for time, as I had to meet someone off a bus. He asked me if I'd seen any of the "boys," meaning our friends from school. I said that unfortunately I hadn't but I was glad I'd seen him at least, and that whenever I had a child to christen I'd come straight to him. He laughed and clapped me on the shoulder. We shook hands and I emerged into the square again in the knowledge that there was another quarter of an hour before the bus arrived.

A quarter of an hour is not a long time. I crossed the square, went past the barber's shop, peered through the window (although I knew that Lucie would not be there until the afternoon), and strolled over in the direction of the bus station. I imagined Helena to myself: her face hidden under a layer of dark powder, her reddish, obviously dyed hair, her figure far from slim, though retaining the modicum of proportion necessary for our acceptance of a woman as a woman. And I re-

hearsed to myself all the features that placed her on the provocative borderline between the repellent and the attractive: her
voice, louder than necessary, her exaggerated gestures that in-
voluntarily betrayed a pathetic desire to continue being attractive to men.

I'd only seen Helena three times in my life, and whenever I'd
wanted to recall her my memory had emphasized one of her
points so much that for me she'd gone through a gradual trans-
formation into a caricature of herself. But however inaccurate
my impressions might be, they had undoubtedly managed to
catch some essential feature, something hidden beneath the
outward form.

This time in particular I couldn't rid my imagination of an
image of Helena's bodily blurriness, which I felt to be a characteristic not just of her age, her motherhood, but in particular
of some psychological and erotic defenselessness—almost help-
lessness—which was unsuccessfully concealed beneath a confident manner. Was this in fact an essential part of Helena, or
was it a symptom of my own attitude toward her? Who knows?
The bus was nearly due, and I longed to see Helena just as my
imagination had interpreted her to me. I hid in the doorway
of one of the houses on the square which enclosed the bus station. I wanted to stand there for a few minutes and watch her
looking *defenselessly* around and suddenly thinking she'd
wasted her time coming, since I wasn't there.

A large long-distance coach pulled into the square. Helena
was one of the first off. She was dressed in a blue Italian trenchcoat of the type currently popular in the foreign-currency stores.
They gave their wearers a youthful, sexy look. Even Helena,
with her collar turned up and belt drawn in tightly, looked excellent in it. She surveyed the square, she even took a few steps
forward to see the areas obscured by the bus, but instead of
standing there helplessly, she turned on her heel without hesitation and headed for the hotel where I was staying, where she
had a room booked for the night.

I was convinced once again that my imagination had offered

me Helena only in a distorted form. Luckily she was always more attractive in the flesh than in my imagination, as I realized once again when I saw her from behind, striding toward the hotel on her high heels. I started off in pursuit.

She was already in the lobby, leaning her elbow on the reception desk while a listless clerk signed her in. She was spelling out her name to him: Helena Zemanek, ZE-MAN-EK. I stood behind her and listened as she gave her particulars. Then she asked, "Is there a Comrade Jahn staying here?" The receptionist mumbled that there wasn't. I went up to Helena and put my hand on her shoulder.

Everything that occurred between myself and Helena was part of a precise and deliberate plan. Helena, of course, had not entered into the relationship without designs of her own, but these barely went beyond a vague female desire to hold onto her youthfulness, her sentimentality, and stopped short at any attempt to stage-manage events. I, on the other hand, had from the moment we met acted as meticulous stage manager of the course on which I was embarked, and had left to chance neither my choice of words and proposals nor of the room in which I intended to be alone with Helena. Nonetheless I was afraid of letting the opportunity slip, an opportunity which meant so much to me, not because Helena was especially young or especially attractive, but for one reason and one reason only: that she had the surname she had, that her husband was a man I hated.

The day at the institute when I was informed that a Comrade Zemanek from the broadcasting company was coming to see me, and that I was to give her some information on our research, I thought of my former student friend for a moment but quickly dismissed this coincidence of names as a mere trick of chance. And if I disliked her being sent to me, it was for other reasons entirely.

It had become an invariable custom in our institute that all journalists were routed to me and I was the one who was always sent to lecture on behalf of the institute when we were requested to do so by various educational bodies. This apparent honor was a matter of some sadness for me. I'd begun my own research almost ten years later than my colleagues—I had been only an undergraduate in my thirties. For a few years I'd tried desperately to bridge the gap but had then realized the futility of devoting the second half of my life to a pathetic pursuit of lost years, and so I resigned myself to it. Luckily this had its compensations: the less I chased after success in my own narrow field, the more I could allow myself the luxury of looking out onto other areas of research, onto man's being and the existence of the world, and could experience the joys—among the sweetest there are—of speculation and reflection. My colleagues, however, knew well that if such contemplation gives a man personal pleasure, it's of little use for a modern scientific career, which demands that the scientist burrow zealously in his own field or subfield like a blind mole and never lose a minute lamenting lost horizons. For this reason my colleagues half envied me my resignation and half despised me for it, they let me know with gentle irony, calling me the institute's "philosopher" and sending me journalists and news editors from the broadcasting companies.

Perhaps for this reason, and certainly because they're for the most part shallow, loudmouthed, and insolent, I don't like journalists. The fact that Helena was a features editor for the radio and not for a newspaper only heightened my aversion. In my eyes newspapers have one extenuating feature: they make no noise. When they're tedious, they're at least quiet about it. They never intrude; they can be put aside or thrown in the wastebasket. On the other hand, the radio persecutes us in coffee shops, restaurants, trains, even when we visit friends. For there are many people unable to live without this continual aural massage.

I was equally irritated by Helena's manner of speaking. All too obviously, she'd had her feature fully thought out even before she came to the institute, and now was only looking for some concrete data and examples to go with all the usual, tired phrases. I tried to complicate her job for her as much as possible. I deliberately spoke in an involved and unintelligible way and tried to upset all her preconceived views. Whenever there was any danger of her actually understanding anything, I tried to sidestep it by becoming familiar. I told her how much red hair suited her (though I thought the exact opposite); I asked her how she liked her work in radio and what sort of books she preferred. And in the quiet calculation of probabilities I was making, far below the surface of our conversation, I came to the conclusion that her surname could not be mere coincidence. This pretentious, loudmouthed, prosperous woman journalist seemed to me decidedly akin to the man I'd also known as pretentious, loudmouthed, and prosperous. In the light, almost flirtatious tone the conversation had assumed, I asked her about her husband. The clues all fitted neatly into position, and a few further questions identified Pavel Zemanek with absolute certainty.

Of course I can't say that it occurred to me at that moment to become as intimate with her as I later did. On the contrary, the revulsion I'd felt for her the moment she walked in only deepened with this discovery. At first I began to look for a pretext to break the interview off and hand her over to some other member of the staff. I even thought what a pleasure it would be to take her with her flirtatious smiles and her know-it-all air and throw her out of my office, and I regretted that this was impossible.

However, at the very moment when I was most filled with dislike, Helena, stirred by my sudden familiarity and innocent of its intent, surprised me with a few completely natural feminine gestures, and my hatred suddenly assumed a new cast; behind the veil of this comic-strip journalist I saw in Helena the *woman*, the flesh-and-blood woman, capable of functioning as a woman. Sneering to myself, I had thought this was exactly the woman Zemanek deserved, and she was no doubt an adequate punishment for him. Now suddenly I had to amend my first

contemptuous impression as too subjective. Clearly this woman
had once been very pretty, and there was no reason to suppose
that Pavel Zemanek shouldn't be enjoying her as a wife to this
very day. I sustained the lighter tone of the conversation without giving any indication of what I was thinking. Something was
forcing me to learn more about the woman sitting opposite me,
especially about her femininity.

Meditation on the feminine can cause hatred to be tempered
with certain qualities more symptomatic of affection: curiosity, understanding, the urge to cross the threshold of intimacy.
I was in raptures; I imagined Zemanek, Helena, their whole
alien world. With intense delight I indulged in my hatred—
my attentive, almost tender hatred of Helena's appearance, hatred of her red hair, hatred of her blue eyes, hatred of her short
bristling lashes, hatred of her round face, hatred of her up-
turned sensuous nostrils, hatred of the gap between her two
front teeth, hatred of the ripe fleshiness of her body. I was
watching her as if watching a woman I loved, as if I wanted
everything about her to be etched indelibly on my memory. And
to disguise the spiteful nature of my interest I chose my words
in an ever more familiar, teasing vein, so that Helena became
increasingly feminine. Her mouth, breasts, eyes, and hair belonged to Zemanek. In my mind's eye I took them all in my
hands, weighed them up and balanced them, testing them to
see whether they would be better crushed in my fist or shattered against the wall, and then I carefully reexamined them,
trying to see them first with Zemanek's eyes and then again
with my own.

Perhaps I did have the fleeting, utterly impractical idea that
it might be possible to move this woman from the plane of our
flirtation straight toward the target area of bed. But that was
only one thought, one of many that flash through the mind
like a spark and are quickly extinguished. Helena announced
that she thanked me for the information I'd put at her disposal
and that she wouldn't take up any more of my time. We said
good-bye and I was glad to see her go. My strange elation had

passed, leaving utter distaste. And I felt uncomfortable for having acted toward her with such confidential interest and simulated friendliness.

This meeting of ours would certainly have remained without a sequel had Helena not telephoned a few days later and asked whether she might see me. Perhaps she really did want me to check the text of her feature, but at the time it seemed to me more like a pretext, and the tone she used harmonized more with the intimate part of our last conversation than with the technical and serious part. I had adopted this tone quickly and without thinking, nor did I now abandon it. We met in a coffeehouse. With deliberate provocation I ignored everything concerning Helena's feature and made fun of her interests as a journalist. I could see that these tactics were throwing her off balance, and that I was beginning to gain control. I invited her to come out to the country with me. She protested, reminding me she was a married woman. No words could have given me greater pleasure. I lingered on this delightful objection, playing with it, returning repeatedly to it, joking about it. Finally she was glad of the opportunity to change the subject and quickly acceded to my proposal. After that everything went precisely according to plan. I had worked it out with the force of fifteen years of hatred, and I felt unaccountably confident of its success.

And certainly things were moving now. I took Helena's small overnight case from her at the reception desk and accompanied her upstairs to her room, which was just as hideous as my own. Even Helena, who had a rare capacity for romanticizing, had to admit it. I told her that nothing could be done about it, that we would work things out between us. She gave me a glance full of meaning. Then she said she wanted to wash up, and I said I'd wait for her in the lobby.

She came downstairs, wearing a black skirt and pink sweater under her unbuttoned coat, and I was able to assure myself again of how elegant she was. I said we'd have lunch at the People's House—an indifferent restaurant but the best there was in town. She said since I came from these parts she put herself entirely in my hands, and that she'd offer no resistance to anything I proposed. It looked as if she was trying to choose her words for the sake of double entendre—a ridiculous but gratifying attempt on her part. We followed the route I'd taken that morning in my vain quest for a decent breakfast, and Helena kept reiterating how delighted she was to be seeing my hometown for the first time. She did not, however, bother to look around her or to ask about the various buildings or in any way to behave like a visitor seeing an unfamiliar town for the first time. I wondered whether her lack of interest stemmed from that form of spiritual decay that causes normal curiosity toward the outside world to atrophy, or whether it meant that Helena had all her attention on me and none left for anything else. I favored the second possibility.

Again we walked past the memorial to the plague: a saint supporting a cloud, the cloud supporting an angel, the angel another cloud, and the other cloud another angel. Helena took off her coat, threw it over her arm, and said how warm it was. The warmth merely increased the pervasive sense of dusty emptiness. The sculpture group jutted up in the middle of the square like a piece broken off the sky which couldn't be put back. I told myself that the two of us had been cast irrevocably into this strangely deserted square with its park and restaurant —that we, too, had been broken off something, that man was wasting his time imitating the heavens, that no one was fooled by it, when our deeds were as low as the earth itself.

Yes, it was an awareness of my own *lowness* that had taken me by surprise. But what surprised me even more was that I wasn't shocked by it but accepted it with a certain pleasure, if not with joy or relief, and that this pleasure was increased by the certainty that the woman walking by my side was driven to the dubious hours of this afternoon by motives not much higher than my own.

The People's House was already open. The tables were laid.

Opposite every chair was a soup bowl covered by a paper nap-kin on which lay knife, fork, and spoon. The place was de-serted. We sat down, picked up our napkins and implements, put them by our plates, and waited. A few minutes later a waiter appeared in the kitchen doorway, surveyed the dining hall wearily, and was about to go back into the kitchen.

"Waiter!" I called.

He turned back into the room and took a few steps in the direction of our table. "Did you want anything?" he asked when he was still about fifteen feet away.

"We'd like to have lunch," I said.

"Twelve o'clock for lunch," he replied and turned to go back to the kitchen.

"Waiter!" I called him again. He turned. "Have you got any vodka?" I had to shout, as he was some distance away.

"No, no vodka."

"What have you got?"

"We have," he replied from the distance, "rye or rum."

"I don't think much of that," I shouted, "but give us two ryes anyway."

"I didn't even ask you if you drank rye," I said to Helena.

Helena laughed. "Only infrequently."

"Never mind," I said. "You'll get used to it. You're in Mora-via now, and rye whiskey is the Moravian's favorite spirit."

"Excellent," said Helena delightedly. "That's what I like best of all, just an ordinary sort of bar where truck drivers and mechanics go and where there's just ordinary things to eat and drink."

"Have you ever put rum in your beer?"

"Never," said Helena.

"But you said you liked these proletarian sort of places."

"I do," she replied. "I can't stand those chic places with a dozen waiters circling around you and serving you from a dozen dishes . . ."

"Of course, there's nothing like those old taverns where the waiter doesn't even see you for the smoke. And there's nothing better than rye. That's what I drank when I was a student. I didn't have the money for anything else."

"And I like simple food too, like potato pancakes or liver sausage and onions. I can't think of anything better . . ."

I've become so suspicious that when anyone, especially a woman, starts telling me what he or she likes or dislikes I'm unable to take it seriously, or to put it more precisely, I accept it only as indicating what might be called their self-image. I didn't believe for a minute that Helena breathed more freely in dirty ill-ventilated dives (of which this country has no shortage) than in clean, well-aired restaurants, or that she liked raw alcohol and cheap food better than haute cuisine. However, she'd revealed her predilection for a certain pose, a pose long outdated and going back to the years when revolutionary snobbery delighted in anything that was "common," "proletarian," or "raw," just as it loved to despise everything that was "refined" or "pampered" or suspiciously associated with the idea of the dinner jacket and exaggerated good manners. In Helena's pose I recognized the period of my own youth, and in Helena I recognized more than anything else—Zemanek's wife. My preoccupations of the morning vanished and I began to concentrate.

The waiter brought us two glasses of rye on a tray and then handed us a sheet of paper on which was typed, evidently through several carbons, an illegible copy of the day's menu.

I raised my glass and said, "Let's drink to rye, the common man's rye!"

She laughed and we touched glasses, and then she said, "I've always longed for a man who was simple and direct. Unaffected. Straightforward."

We took a swig of the stuff and I said, "There aren't many like that."

"They do exist," said Helena. "And you're one of them."

"I wouldn't have thought so," I said.

"You are."

Again I was filled with horror at the endless human capacity for self-delusion, for transforming reality into a likeness of our own desires, but I accepted unfalteringly Helena's characterization of myself.

"Who knows—maybe I am plain and straightforward," I said. "But what is plain and straightforward? It's all a question of a man being what he is, not being ashamed to want what he wants or to have the aspirations he has. People are often the slaves of convention. Someone tells them what they ought to be like and they try to be like it, and to the day they die they don't even find out who they were and who they are. They're nobody and nothing; they live a double, confused life. First and foremost a man must have the courage to be himself. I want to tell you, Helena, right away, that I like you and that I desire you, even though you're a married woman. I can't put it any other way, and I can't let it remain unsaid."

It was a fairly ticklish sort of thing to say—although Helena, who'd lowered her head as I spoke, failed to notice my embarrassment—but it had to be done. The conquest of a woman's mind has its own inflexible rules. Anyone who decides to seduce her with rational argument is unlikely to get anywhere. It's much wiser to determine a woman's self-image—her basic principles, ideals, and convictions—and then to try, with the aid of sophistry, illogical rhetoric, et cetera, to steer her into a harmonic relationship with this image. Helena, for instance, had raved about "simplicity," "unaffectedness," "straightforwardness." Her ideals undoubtedly had their roots in the revolutionary puritanism of the early days and were associated with the idea of the "pure," "unsullied," high-principled, and strictly moral man. But since Helena's principles, like most people's, were based not on rational thought but on irrational suggestion, nothing was simpler than to enlist the aid of crude rhetoric in undermining them—in combining the idea of the "straightforward man" with behavior that was altogether unpuritanical, immoral, and adulterous, and to prevent Helena's desired, *i.e.,* adulterous, behavior from subsequently finding itself in neurotic conflict with her inward ideals. A man can ask anything of a woman, but unless he wants to act like a brute, he must make it possible for her to act according to her own most profound self-deceptions.

Meanwhile people had been trickling into the restaurant, and by now most of the tables were occupied. The waiter came out of the kitchen again and began taking orders. I handed Helena the menu. She said I knew more about Moravian cuisine than she did and handed it back.

You didn't, of course, need to be an expert on Moravian cuisine, since the menu was exactly the same in all eating houses of this type and comprised a narrow selection of stereotyped dishes, all equally unalluring. I gazed glumly at the smudgy sheet of paper. The waiter was already standing over me, waiting impatiently.

"Just a moment," I said.

"You wanted your lunch a quarter of an hour ago and you haven't even decided what you want yet," he reminded me and left.

To my relief he came back fairly soon, and we ventured to choose the Spanish fowl and two more ryes with soda. The liquor had already affected Helena, and she announced that life was good in spite of all the inequalities that were still with us. In any case it was up to individuals what sort of life they made for themselves. I chewed at the stringy Spanish fowl and proclaimed, with my mouth full, that the place became really beautiful when I was sitting there with her.

Helena's cheeks were flushed (clearly a result of the liquor), which emphasized their roundness and detracted from her elegance. But I magnanimously ignored this (clearly a result of the liquor), telling myself with malicious glee that it was a mercy of the fates that Helena was at least as presentable as she was, since even if she'd been hideous, hunchbacked, or crippled I'd still have made an attempt on her and tried to get her into my power.

Helena remarked, chewing energetically, how splendid (a favorite word) it was that we were here, sitting in a strange

place of which she'd dreamed so often when she'd been in the
ensemble and sung our regional songs. Then she said that it
was probably wrong of her but that she felt happy with me and
that she couldn't help it—it was against her will, but it was
stronger than her will and that was that. I told her she ought
never to be ashamed of her honest feelings. Then I called the
waiter and asked for the bill.

As we left the restaurant there was the memorial to the
plague confronting us again. It looked so ridiculous that I
pointed it out. "Look, Helena, look at those saints clambering
up there. Look at them fighting their way up! How they'd love
to get to heaven! And heaven couldn't care less about them.
Heaven knows nothing about them, those winged yokels!"

"True," said Helena, in whom the fresh air was reinforcing
the good work wrought by the alcohol. "Why are these statues
of saints here at all? Why don't they put something here to celebrate life instead of this mysticism?" She was not quite sure of
herself and added, "Or am I talking nonsense?"

"No, Helena, you're quite right. Life is a beautiful thing and
we can never celebrate it enough."

"Yes," said Helena. "Let them say what they like, life is a
splendid thing. I hate pessimists. Even if I have plenty to complain about, still I don't complain. Why should I complain,
tell me, why should I complain, when life can bring a day like
this? It's so splendid—a strange town, and me here with
you . . ."

I let Helena ramble on, and whenever a pause occurred in
her romantic monologue, I said something to start her up again.
Soon we were standing in front of the new block of apartments
where Kostka lived.

"Where are we?" asked Helena.

"Those public bars are completely useless," I said. "I know a
small private bar in this apartment building. Let's go up and
have a drink."

"Where are you taking me?" Helena protested, following
me.

"A genuine Moravian wine bar. Haven't you ever been in one?"

"Never," said Helena.

On the third floor I unlocked the door and we went inside.

"This isn't a bar—it's an ordinary apartment," said Helena, when she'd gone in and looked down the hallway into Kostka's room.

"It's not an ordinary apartment. It would be if you or I lived in it. The special thing about this place is that it's neither mine nor yours—there's none of my washing lying around here, or yours, or my memories or your memories, it doesn't have the air of my home or of your home. It's a stranger's apartment, and because of that it's *pure* as far as both of us are concerned and so we can both feel free in it."

I'd managed to extemporize a rather remarkable defense of the very principle of the borrowed apartment. But my eloquence was quite superfluous. Helena had no objection to my leading her into a strange apartment and needed no apologia. On the contrary, it appeared that from the minute she'd crossed the threshold she was determined to proceed from flirtation, which speaks in double entendre and pretends to be a game, to that act that has only one meaning and significance and that creates the illusion that it is not a game but life itself. She stopped in the middle of Kostka's room to look back at me, and I could read in her eyes that she was already waiting for me to take her in my arms. In that moment she was precisely the Helena I'd imagined to myself: a Helena utterly defenseless.

I went up to her; she lifted her face. But instead of kissing her as she expected I smiled and took the sleeves of her blue trenchcoat in my fingers. She understood and unbuttoned it. I carried it to the closet in the hall. At this stage, when everything was ready—my desire and her willingness—I didn't want to proceed too fast and risk missing in my haste a single nuance of my desire. I started a meaningless conversation. I told her to sit down and drew her attention to all the details of Kostka's

apartment. I opened the cupboard with the bottle of vodka inside, the one Kostka had pointed out the day before, and pretended to be surprised. I uncorked the bottle, put two small
glasses on the table, and poured some out.

"I shall be drunk," she said.

"We'll both be drunk," I said, though I knew that *I* wouldn't
be drunk, that I had no intention of being drunk, because I
wanted my memory of this encounter to be preserved intact.

Helena didn't smile. She took a drink and said seriously,
"Ludvik, you know I'd be terribly unhappy if you thought I
was just one of those bored married women who long for
any adventure. I'm not so naïve as not to realize that you've
known a good number of women and that women themselves
have taught you to take them in your stride. But I'd be so unhappy . . ."

"I'd be unhappy too," I said, "if you were one of those
married women looking for just another romantic adventure
to divert them from their marriage. If you were, then our meeting would have had no meaning for me at all."

"Do you really mean that?"

"Yes, Helena, I do. You're right when you say that I've
known a lot of women and that they've taught me not to be
afraid to keep moving from one to another, but my meeting
you is something different."

"You're not just saying that?"

"No. When I first met you I realized that I'd been longing
for years—many years—just for you."

"You wouldn't say that if you didn't feel it?"

"No. I can never conceal my real feelings from women—
that's the one thing they've never taught me. So I'm not lying
to you, Helena, even if it doesn't sound very convincing. When
I first met you I knew I'd been waiting for you for years, waiting
for you without knowing you. And I knew that now you had
to be mine. That it was as inevitable as fate."

"God," said Helena and closed her eyes. Her face was flecked
with red, perhaps from the alcohol, perhaps from excitement.

"If only you knew, Ludvik, I felt just like that, too. From the first moment I knew that meeting you like this was no mere flirtation. And that was what I was afraid of, because I'm a married woman and I knew that this with you was true, that you are my truth and there's nothing I can do about it."

"Yes, Helena, and you are my truth too," I said.

She was sitting on the couch, with her big eyes looking at me unseeingly, and I was sitting in the chair opposite her and watching her greedily. I put my hands on her knees and slowly turned up her skirt until her stocking tops and garters appeared, and her sadly wasted thighs. Helena sat there, not reacting to my touch with either word or movement.

"If only you knew . . ."

"Knew what?"

"About me. The way I live. The way I've been living."

"How have you been living?"

She smiled bitterly.

Suddenly I was afraid Helena was going to trot out that banal rationalization of all unfaithful wives and begin to make light of her marriage—robbing me of its value at the very moment when it had become my prey. "For God's sake don't tell me you have an unhappy marriage, that your husband doesn't understand you."

"I didn't want to say it," said Helena, confused by this sudden attack, "even though—"

"Even though at this moment that's what you're thinking. Every woman starts to think that way when she's alone with another man, but that's where all the lies begin, and you want to stay truthful, Helena, don't you? You certainly must have loved your husband, you're not a woman to give yourself without love."

"No," said Helena quietly.

"Who is your husband?" I asked.

She shrugged her shoulders and smiled. "Just a husband."

"How long have you known each other?"

"We've been married for thirteen years and we knew each other before that."

"You must have been a student then."

"Yes. I was in the first year."

She wanted to pull her skirt down, but I caught her hand, preventing her. I asked again, "Tell me about him. Where did you meet him?"

"In the ensemble."

"The ensemble? Did your husband sing then?"

"Yes. Like all of us."

"So you met in a musical ensemble. What an appropriate setting for falling in love."

"Yes."

"That was a good time."

"Do you have nice memories of it, too?"

"It was the best time of my life. Was your husband your first love?"

"I don't want to think of my husband right now," she said.

"I want to get to know you, Helena. I want to know everything about you. The more I know you the more you'll be mine. Did you have anyone before him?"

Helena nodded. "Yes."

I felt almost disappointed that Helena had known some other man, diminishing the significance of her attachment to Pavel Zemanek. "Was it serious?"

She shook her head. "Just idle curiosity."

"So your first real love was your husband."

She nodded. "But that was a long time ago."

"What did he look like then?" I asked quietly.

"Why do you want to know?"

"I want you to be mine with everything in you, every thought, every memory." I stroked her hair.

If there's anything that prevents a woman from telling her lover about her husband, it's rarely refinement or tact or genuine bashfulness; it's simply the fear that it might somehow wound the lover. Once the lover has dispelled this fear, the woman is deeply grateful to him and feels freer; she has something to talk about. Topics of conversation are not unlimited, and for a woman her husband is the safest of topics, because it's the only one on which she feels secure, on which she feels an *expert*. So as soon as I had assured Helena that it didn't disturb me, she started speaking with complete freedom about Pavel Zemanek, letting herself be so carried away by her memories that she didn't add a single false shadow to the portrait, telling me in an earnest and matter-of-fact way how she'd fallen in love with him—that straight-backed fair-haired youth—how she'd looked at him with respect when he became political head of their ensemble (not one of those dry-as-dust officials but a thousand times livelier, in fact, than any of these young people today!), how she and all her girlfriends looked up to him (he had the most charming way of talking), and how their affair was in complete harmony with the whole epoch, in whose praise she also had a few things to say (how were *we* to know that Stalin was having loyal Communists shot?)—not, perhaps, because she wanted to divert the conversation into political channels, but because she considered herself personally concerned in this matter. Her emphatic defense of the period of her youth and the way she identified herself with it, as if it had been her home, a home she'd since lost, was almost a sort of challenge: Take me as I am and with no conditions save this one—you must let me be the way I am, you must take my opinions with me. This fierce avowal of the value of opinions in a situation in which opinions don't matter—when only the body matters—had an element of the abnormal in it, suggesting that it's opinions that make women neurotic. Either she was afraid I might suspect her of having no opinions at all and so was hastily inventing some or, more likely in Helena's case, she had gnawing doubts about her views and wanted to regain her certainty at all costs, even if she had to gamble for it with what was for her an indisputable value, the act of love itself—perhaps with the cowardly subconscious certainty that her lover

would set more store by her lovemaking than her political
theories. This demonstration of Helena's delighted me, since
it brought me nearer to the core of my passion.

"The young people of today are different from us," she said.
"They've had everything free, everything handed out to them,
and they can't understand why even to this day I'm moved
when I hear a Russian chastushka."

"But you had everything handed out to you, too. You were
only fourteen at the end of the war and seventeen in February
of forty-eight."

"I know, but even so all that is a part of my life. Do you see
this?" She pointed to a small silver disc she kept attached to
her wristwatch by a short chain. I leaned over it, and Helena
explained to me that the design carved on it represented the
Kremlin. "Pavel gave that to me," she said, and she told me the
whole story of the ornament. Apparently a lovesick Russian
girl had given it years and years ago to a Russian boy named
Sasha who had gone off to fight in the war, at the end of which
he found himself in Prague, which he protected against destruction but which destroyed him. In the villa where Pavel Zemanek lived with his parents, on the floor above, the Red Army
had set up a small hospital, and here a badly wounded Russian lieutenant named Sasha had spent the last days of his life.
Pavel became friendly with him and spent whole days by his
bedside. When he was dying, Sasha gave Pavel the ornament
with the Kremlin engraved on it that he'd carried right through
the war on a piece of string around his neck. Pavel kept this gift
as a treasured memento. Once—when they were still only engaged—Helena and Pavel had quarreled and thought they
were going to split up. But then Pavel had come over and given
her this cheap ornament and treasured keepsake as a peace offering, and from that time on, Helena had never taken it off
because the tiny object seemed like a mission (I asked her what
sort of a mission and she said "a mission of joy") or like a baton
which she must bear to the goal post.

She sat facing me, with her skirt turned up, revealing garters attached to fashionable black panties, and her face slightly flushed with the alcohol, and perhaps with the excitement of the moment. But for me the moment had caused her image to disappear behind that of another person. Helena's story about the locket and how it changed hands three times had suddenly, even violently, evoked the entire existence of Pavel Zemanek.

I had no faith at all in the existence of any Red Army soldier named Sasha. Anyway, even if he *had* existed his real existence would have completely vanished behind the grand gesture Pavel Zemanek had used to transform him into a character in his own legend, a sacred figure, a sentimental instrument to touch the heartstrings, and an article of religion which his wife, evidently more constant than he, would worship, devoutly and defiantly, until the day of her death. It was as if Pavel Zemanek's vilely exhibitionistic heart was with us in the room. At once I was in the midst of that scene fifteen years ago: the great lecture hall of the natural sciences department; on the rostrum Zemanek sitting behind a long table; beside him a fat girl with a round face, pigtail, and shapeless sweater; on his other side a youth representing the district committee. Behind the platform was a large blackboard and a framed portrait of Julius Fucik. Opposite the table were the benches of the lecture hall rising in tiers, myself sitting among them. And now, fifteen years later, I clearly saw Zemanek in front of me announcing that "the case of Comrade Jahn is open for discussion . . . I shall read you letters written by two Communists." After these words he paused theatrically, picked up a slim volume, ran his fingers through his long, wavy hair, and began reading in an ingratiating, almost tender voice.

"Death, you have been a long time coming. Yet it had been my hope that I would meet you many years from now, that I would continue living as a free man, would continue to work and to love, to sing and to travel the world. . . ." I recognized Fucik's *Notes from the Gallows*. "I have loved life and for the sake of its beauty I went to war. People, I have loved you and was happy when this love was returned, and I suffered when you did not understand me. . . ." This text, written secretly in prison and illuminated by the glow of the man's heroism, was at that time perhaps the most widely read book in the country. Zemanek had just read us the most famous passages, the ones everyone knew by heart. "Let sadness never be linked with my name. That is my last will and testament to you, father, mother, and sisters, to you, my Gustina, to you, Comrades, to everyone I have loved. . . ." Fucik's handsome face hung on the wall just as it hung in a thousand other public places in our country, and it was so handsome that when I looked at it I felt inferior, not just because of my guilt but because of my appearance as well. Zemanek read on: "They can take our lives, Gustina, as you see, but our honor and love, those they cannot take away from us. Oh, people, can you imagine the way we would live if we met again after all this suffering, met again in a free life, a life made beautiful by liberty and creation? The life that will come into being when all that we have yearned for, fought for, and that I now die for, takes place?" Zemanek read these last sentences with feeling, and stopped.

Then he said, "That was a letter written by a Communist in the shadow of the gallows. Now I shall read you another letter." And he read out the three brief, stupid, ghastly lines from my postcard. Then he fell silent, there was a general hush, and I knew I was lost. Zemanek, that inspired showman, deliberately allowed the silence to last some time before calling on me to speak. I knew I had no defense; what chance did I have when Zemanek had put my postcard in the scales against the absolute weight of Fucik's agony? Of course I had no other option but to stand up and say my piece. Once again I said that the message was meant as a joke. I condemned the unsuitability and crudity of the joke, spoke of my individualism, intellectualism, isolation from the people, even uncovered in myself complacency, skepticism, and cynicism, but vowed that in spite of it all I was still a devoted Party man and not its enemy.

Next came the discussion, in which the Comrades convicted me of inconsistency. How could a man be devoted to the Party when he himself admitted he was a cynic? One woman member reminded me of my frivolous pronouncements about women and asked me whether that was the way a Communist should talk. Others made general remarks about the petty bourgeois, which they illustrated by insinuating me into their number. There was general agreement that my self-criticism had been superficial and insincere. Then the girl with the pigtail sitting next to Zemanek asked, "What do you think would be the reaction to your words on the part of those Comrades who were tortured by the Gestapo and who did not survive?" I realized they were all pretending not to know how my father died. I said nothing. She repeated her question and urged me to answer.

I said, "I don't know."

"Think," she insisted. "Perhaps you may think of something." She wanted me to pass severe sentence on myself from the imaginary lips of dead Comrades.

But I suddenly felt a wave of anger wash over me, completely unforeseen and unexpected anger, and reversing my self-critical statements of many weeks I said, "They stood between life and death. There could be no question of their being so small-minded. If they had read my postcard, it might even have made them laugh."

A moment previously the pigtail had given me a last chance to salvage at least something from the wreck, to understand the criticism of my Comrades, to identify myself with it, to accept it, and on the basis of this identification to gain in turn a measure of understanding. But my unexpected reply had suddenly excluded me from the sphere of their thinking. I had refused to play the part which was generally played at many hundreds of meetings, hundreds of disciplinary proceedings—and not long after at hundreds of trials in a court of law—the part of the accused who is also the accuser and by the very ardor of his self-accusation, his absolute identification with the accusers, asks that mercy be granted him.

There was another moment of silence. Then Zemanek spoke

again. He said he was unable to imagine what could possibly be funny about my anti-Party pronouncements. He referred again to Fucik's words and said that in critical situations, wavering and skepticism were quickly transformed into treachery and the Party was a stronghold in which no traitor was permitted. Then he said that my answer clearly proved that I had failed to learn anything, that not only was I unfit to be in the Party but also I did not deserve that the working class should continue to devote their funds to my studies. He proposed a motion that I be excluded from the Party and expelled from the university. The people in the room all raised their hands, and Zemanek told me I was to surrender my Party card and leave.

I stood up and placed my Party card in front of Zemanek. Zemanek didn't even look at me. He no longer saw me. But I can see his wife now. She is sitting right in front of me, drunk, with her face red and her skirt wound up around her waist. Her heavy legs are topped by the black of her lace-trimmed underpants—those legs whose opening and closing marked the rhythm that pulsated through a decade of Zemanek's life. On these legs I now put the palms of my hands, and it was as if I had Zemanek's very life in my grasp. I looked at Helena's face, into her eyes, which reacted to my touch by closing ever so slightly.

"Get undressed, Helena," I said quietly.

She got up off the couch, and the hem of her skirt slipped back down to her knees. She gazed fixedly into my eyes, and then without a word, and without taking her eyes off me, began to unbutton her skirt down the side. When it slid down her legs onto the floor, she stepped out of it with her left foot and with her right passed it up to her hand and laid it on the chair. She was now standing in her sweater and slip. Then she pulled the sweater over her head and threw it over to join the skirt.

"Don't watch," she said.

"I want to see you," I said.

"I don't want you to see me undressing."

I went over to her. I took her from both sides under the armpits and as I let my hands move down to her hips I felt her soft strong body under the silk of the slip, now somewhat damp with sweat. She bent her head down and her lips opened slightly in the habit (a bad one) of many years, ready for a kiss. But I didn't want to kiss her; I wanted to go on looking at her for as long as I could.

"Get undressed, Helena," I said again and I stepped back and took off my own jacket.

"Too much light here," she said.

"That's all right," I said and hung my jacket over the back of the chair.

She pulled the slip over her head and threw it across to the sweater and skirt. She unfastened her stockings and slid them off her legs one after the other, but instead of throwing the stockings she took two steps toward the chair and placed them carefully on it. Next she strained her chest forward and put her hands behind her back; it took a few seconds and then her arms, which had been stretched behind her back as if to launch herself forward, came free and fell forward and with them fell her bra, sliding off her breasts, which were pressed into one another, big, full, pale, and naturally somewhat heavy and fallen.

"Get undressed, Helena," I repeated for the last time. Helena looked me in the eyes and then pulled off the black underpants, throwing them on top of the pile on the chair. She was naked.

I am not dragging out the individual details of the scene out of any special predilection for the process of female undressing, but because I took careful note of each one of these details. This wasn't a case of achieving quick pleasure with a woman (*any* woman) but of mastering a very particular alien intimate world in the space of a single afternoon, in the course of a single act of love in which I was to be not just a man carried away by the process of lovemaking, but a man who is ravaging and

guarding a fleeting prey and for this reason must be absolutely
on the alert.

So far I'd gained mastery of Helena just by looking at her.
Now again I remained a step or two away from her, while she
longed for the speedy application of warm caresses which would
conceal her body from the frank coldness of my stare. I felt
from my distance the moisture of her mouth and the sensual
impatience of her tongue. Another second, two, and I went up
to her. We held each other close, standing in the middle of the
room between the two chairs covered by our clothes.

"Ludvik, Ludvik, Ludvik," she whispered. I took her to the
daybed. I laid her on it. "Come," she said, "come, come to me,
come to me."

There is nothing uncommon about the union of two strange
bodies. Occasionally, perhaps, we may also find the union of
souls. What is a thousand times more rare is for the body to
unite with its own soul and be at one with it in a shared passion.
But sometimes it does happen, when a man is really in love.
Perhaps. I believe it does. I want to go on believing it.

But what was my soul doing during the moments my body
spent in physical lovemaking with Helena?

My soul had seen a female body. It was indifferent to this
one. It knew this body had meaning for it only as one that had
been seen and loved in just the same way by a third party who
was not present. And therefore the soul strained to look at this
body with the eyes of this third, absent person. The naked
body, the bend of the legs, the curve of the belly and breasts:
all gained significance only in the moments when my eyes were
transformed into the eyes of the third absent person. In these
moments my soul suddenly entered into, and became, this
alien; it not only mastered the bend of the legs, the curve of
the belly and breasts but it mastered them in the way that they
were seen by the third party.

Not only did my soul become the medium for this third absent person but it urged my body to become the medium for

his body. Then it stood back and watched the squirming struggle of the two bodies, the two conjugal bodies. Then it suddenly commanded my body to be itself again, to enter into this
conjugal coitus and brutally disturb it.

A vein showed blue on Helena's neck and a convulsion ran
through her body; she turned her head to one side and her
teeth bit into the pillow.

Then she whispered my name and her eyes begged a few moments' respite.

But my soul commanded me not to stop; to drive her from
pleasure to pleasure; to hunt her down; to change the position
of her body so that not a single look given her by that third absent party should remain veiled or hidden. No, grant her no
respite, repeat that convulsion over and over again, that moment in which she was real and exact, authentic, in which she
feigned nothing, in which she was engraved in the memory of
this third person, this third man who was not there, like a stamp,
a seal, a cipher, a badge. Steal this secret cipher, this royal seal!
Ransack Pavel Zemanek's marriage bed! Rummage through everything! Leave everything in a shambles!

I looked at Helena's face, flushed and disfigured by a gri-
mace. I put the palm of my hand on this face, as one puts one's
hand on an object that can be turned over or upside down,
smashed or crushed, and I felt that her face accepted my hand
in the same way: as something that wants to be turned over
and smashed. I turned her head first to one side, then to the
other. And then the turning motion was transformed into a first
hard slap, then a second and a third. Helena began to sob and
scream, not with pain but with excitement. Her chin came up
to me, and I hit her and hit her and hit her; then I saw not only
her chin but her breasts coming up to me, and hoisting myself
slightly over her, I beat her on her arms and flanks and
breasts . . .

Everything comes to an end; even this delectable devastation
was over at last. She lay crosswise over the daybed on her stom-

ach, exhausted. I could see the brown round birthmark on her back, and below, on her buttocks, the red blotches from my beating.

I got up and lurched across the room; I opened the door and went into the bathroom; I turned on the tap and washed my face, hands, and body in the cold water. I raised my head and saw myself in the mirror: my face was smiling. I thought how funny it looked and burst out laughing. Then I dried myself with a towel and sat on the edge of the bath. I wanted to be alone just for a few seconds, to savor the rare delight of sudden solitude.

Yes, I was satisfied. I was even perhaps completely happy. I felt myself the victor. As for the ensuing minutes and hours, they were superfluous and held no interest for me.

Then I went back into the room.

Helena was now lying not on her belly but on her side, looking at me. "Come here, darling," she said.

Many people believe, without giving it much thought, that when they are united physically they are united spiritually, too. And so they automatically feel justified in using a more intimate form of speech. For my part, never having shared this erroneous belief, I viewed Helena's words with embarrassment and distaste. Instead of accepting her invitation I went over to the chair where I'd thrown my clothes, and picked up my shirt.

"Don't get dressed," begged Helena. She stretched her arm out toward me and repeated, "Come here."

I didn't want to touch her body again. I was horrified at the thought of any show of affection—at the same time I was equally horrified at the thought of any tension or dramatics. So I unwillingly renounced my shirt and sat down with Helena on the daybed. It was terrible. She pushed up against me and put her head on my leg. Then she began kissing me, and soon my whole leg was wet—but not from her kisses. Helena raised her head and I saw that her face was wet with tears. She wiped them away and said, "Don't be angry, darling, I can't help crying, I can't," and she pushed closer again, put her arms around me, and burst into sobs.

"What's the matter?" I said.

She shook her head, said, "Nothing, stupid, nothing," and began ardently kissing me all over my face and body. "I'm in love," she said, and when I was silent, she went on, "You'll laugh at me but I don't care. I'm in love, I'm in love." When I still said nothing, she said, "I'm so happy." Then she got up and pointed at the table with the unfinished bottle of vodka on it. "Pour me out a drop of that."

I didn't feel like pouring any, either for myself or for Helena. I was afraid that any further alcohol might bring a dangerous sequel to the afternoon's work—whose excellence was conditional on its being already over and done with.

"Please, love." She was still pointing at the table, and added apologetically, "Don't be angry. I'm just happy. I want to be happy."

"You don't need vodka for that," I said.

"Don't be cross. I just feel like it."

There was no remedy; I poured her a glass of vodka. "Don't you want any more?" she asked. I shook my head. She gulped the glass down and said, "Put it down for me over there." I put the bottle and glass down on the floor by the daybed.

She was very quick to recover from her momentary exhaustion. Suddenly she'd become a little girl; she wanted to enjoy herself and to make it obvious that she was doing so. She evidently felt completely free and natural in her nakedness—all she was wearing was her wristwatch with the picture of the Kremlin jingling and swinging from it—and she was trying out different positions for comfort. She crossed her legs under her and sat there like a Turk; then she drew them out again and leaned on her elbow; then she lay on her belly and pressed her face into my lap. With the most diverse variations she told me how happy she was and, in between, she kept wanting to kiss me. I endured her with considerable self-restraint, for her mouth was too wet and she was not content with my shoulders and cheeks but tried to touch my lips as well—and I loathe wet kisses, except when I'm blinded by physical desire.

Then she told me that she'd never known anything like this before, and I told her, for the sake of saying something, that she was exaggerating. She began to swear that in matters of love she never lied and that I had no reason to doubt her. She insisted that the body has its own foolproof instinct; that I had, of course, impressed her with my intelligence and zest (yes, zest—I can't think how she discovered *that* in me), but that between our bodies had immediately arisen that secret pact which the human body signs perhaps only once in a lifetime. "And that's why I'm happy, you see," and she hung her legs over the edge of the bed, squatted down for the bottle, and poured herself another glass. She drank it and said, laughing, "What am I to do if you don't want any more? I'll have to drink it all by myself!"

Even if I'd considered the incident closed I won't deny that I was glad to hear Helena talking like this; it confirmed the success of my project and my satisfaction with it. And because I didn't know what to say and didn't want to seem too morose, I suggested she was exaggerating when she talked about an experience which occurs only once in a lifetime. Hadn't she, as she herself had confided, lived through a great love with her husband?

Helena thought seriously about this—she was sitting on the daybed with her legs slightly apart and resting on the ground, her elbows on her knees and an empty glass in her hand—and said quietly, "Yes."

Perhaps she thought that the intensity of the experience she'd enjoyed a moment before bound her to an equally intense sincerity. She repeated, "Yes," and then said that perhaps it would be unfair and wrong to disparage something that once had been, in the name of the miracle that had happened to-day. (This was her way of referring to our lovemaking.) She took another swig and went on about how the most powerful experiences were the hardest to compare—and that for a woman there was a great difference between love at twenty and at thirty, physically as well as mentally. And then, illogically and without any connection, she announced that in any case there was a resemblance between myself and her husband! She said she wasn't quite sure where it lay; admittedly we looked completely different, but she had a foolproof instinct which enabled her to look more deeply into men, behind their outward appearance.

"I'd love to know what it is about me that makes me resemble your husband," I said.

She told me there was no need for me to be angry; I'd been the one who wanted to hear about him, and that was the only reason she'd brought him up at all. But if I wanted to hear the real truth then she must tell me: only twice in her life had she been attracted to anyone so strongly and unconditionally—to her husband and to me. What we had in common, she said, was some secret zest for life—the joy that emanated from us—eternal youth, strength.

Helena's attempts to explain my resemblance to Pavel Zemanek may have been incoherent, but there was no denying that she saw and felt, and even *lived,* this resemblance and clung tenaciously to it. Apparently we were so similar that perhaps she hadn't really been unfaithful in making love with me. I won't say that this hurt or offended me, but I was shocked at her clumsiness and boundless stupidity. I went over to the chair with my clothes on it and started slowly to dress.

"Did I say something wrong, darling?" Helena had sensed my displeasure. She got off the couch and came over to me. She began stroking my face, begging me not to be angry with her. She tried to stop me from dressing; for some mysterious reason she regarded my pants and shirt as her enemies. She began telling me that she really loved me, that she wasn't just using empty words, that perhaps she might have an opportunity to prove it, that when I asked her about her husband she'd known right away there was no sense in talking about him, that she didn't want any man, any stranger, to come between us—yes, stranger, for her husband had been a stranger to her for a long time. "But I haven't lived with him for three years, silly. The only reason we don't divorce is because of the children. He has his life and I have mine. Today we're just two strangers. He's simply my past, something that happened a long time ago."

"Is that true?" I asked.

"Of course it is."

"You're lying."

"I'm not. We live in the same apartment but not as man and wife. It's been years since we really lived together."

She was looking at me with the imploring face of a woman miserably in love. Again and again she kept assuring me that what she said was true, she wasn't trying to deceive me, I needn't be jealous of her husband . . . her husband was merely the past . . . today she hadn't even been unfaithful, because she had no one to be unfaithful *to* . . . I needn't be afraid . . . our lovemaking was *pure* as well as good.

Suddenly I realized with terrifying clarity that I had no reason to doubt her. When she saw this she became more at ease and begged me several times to say in so many words that I believed her. Then she poured herself another glass of vodka and wanted us to drink a toast. I refused. She kissed me. I was appalled, but I couldn't turn away. I was fascinated by her idiotic blue eyes and her still-twitching body.

But this time I saw her naked body in a completely different light. I saw it as a body which had been *stripped,* stripped of the sensual allurement which until then had blurred over all the faults of age—corpulence, sagging, overripeness. Now that Helena stood before me bare, without a husband or any links binding her to a husband, without marriage vows, just *in herself,* her bodily unloveliness lost all its ability to excite and became merely ugly.

Helena was unaware of the change and became more and more drunk and contented. She was happy that I believed her assurances of love and hardly knew how to give vent to her happiness. For no apparent reason she decided to turn on the radio, squatting in front of it with her back to me as she moved the dial. There was jazz on one station. Helena stood up and her eyes gleamed. She made a clumsy imitation of the undulating movements of the twist. I stared at her breasts as they flew from side to side. "Is that right?" she laughed. "You know, I've never tried these dances." She laughed again, very loudly, and came for me with her arms outstretched. She asked me to dance with her and was angry when I refused. She told me that she didn't know the new dances but she wanted to learn and I must teach her. She expected me to teach her a lot of things— she wanted to be young again when she was with me. She begged me to assure her that she was still young (which I did). She realized that I was dressed while she was naked and started to laugh again at that. It seemed to her inconceivably odd. She asked if there was a mirror so that she could see what we looked like. There was no mirror, only a glass-fronted bookcase. She tried to see us in the glass but the image was too shadowy. Then she went to the bookcase and laughed over the titles of the books: the Bible, Calvin's *Institutes, Epistles Against the Jesuits,* Jan Hus. She took out the Bible, struck a theatrical pose, opened it at random, and began reading in an exaggerated clerical voice. She asked me if she made a good priest. Yes, admirable, I told her, but now she must get dressed because Mr. Kostka would be arriving at any moment. "What's the time?" she asked. "Half past six," I said. She seized my left wrist, looked at my watch, and cried, "Liar! It's only a quarter to six! You want to get rid of me!"

I did indeed wish she was gone, that her wretchedly material body might dematerialize, melt, turn into a river, and flow away, into steam and fly out of the window—but her body was *here,* a body I'd stolen from no one, in which I'd vanquished no one, destroyed no one, a body abandoned, deserted by her husband, a body I'd intended to use but which had used me and was consequently now in transports of insolent delight.

There was no way of cutting short my bizarre torment. It

was almost half past six before she started to dress. As she did so she noticed a red mark on her arm where I'd hit her, stroked it, and said she'd wear it as a memento until she saw me again. Then she quickly corrected herself: she'd certainly see me long before the memento had disappeared. She stood facing me, with one stocking on and the other in her hand, and wanted me to promise we'd see each other before then. I nodded. That wasn't enough for her; she wanted me to promise we'd see each other *lots of times* before then.

She took a long time getting dressed. She left a few minutes before seven.

I opened the window, because I longed for a wind to waft away all memories of that wasted afternoon, every trace of odor and emotion. Then I put the bottle back in the cupboard, smoothed the cushions on the daybed, and when I thought all traces had been removed, I slumped in the armchair by the window and waited, almost imploringly, for Kostka. I looked forward to the sound of his masculine voice, his long skinny frame with its flat chest, his quiet way of talking, eccentric and wise—looked forward to his telling me something about Lucie, who, by contrast to Helena, was so sweetly bodiless, so abstract, so far removed from all conflicts, tensions, and dramas, and yet not without influence on the course of my life. As I sat sunk in the armchair, under the open window through which I'd banished all scent of Helena, it occurred to me that I knew why Lucie had flashed across the stage during the last few days: it was just so that she could take my revenge and annihilate it, transform into smoke all I'd come here to do. For Lucie, whom I'd loved so much and who at the last moment had run away from me so incomprehensibly, was the goddess of escape, the goddess of the race run in vain, the goddess of smoke—and she still held my head in her hands.

VI
Kostka

*I*T'S a good many years now since we last saw each other, and in fact we've only actually met a few times in our lives. This is rather strange, because in my thoughts I meet Ludvik Jahn very frequently indeed, and I turn to him in my soliloquies as to my chief adversary. I've grown so accustomed to his imagined presence that I found myself in some confusion yesterday on suddenly meeting him again after all these years as a real man of flesh and blood. I call Ludvik Jahn my adversary. Have I the right to do so? By coincidence I've run into him every time I've found myself in real need of assistance, and he was the one who always came through for me. But beneath this outward alliance there was always a depth of inward disagreement. I don't know whether Ludvik was as intensely aware of it as I was. He definitely attached a greater significance to our superficial rapport than to our deeper differences. He was merciless toward outward adversaries and tolerant toward inward disharmonies. I wasn't. I am the complete opposite. I don't mean by this that I dislike Ludvik. I love him, as one loves one's adversaries.

I first met him in 1947, at one of those stormy meetings the institutes of higher education seethed with in those days. The future of a nation was being decided. Everyone realized it, myself included, and in all the discussions, arguments, and balloting I was on the side of the Communist minority against the majority, which in the universities at that time was made up of adherents of the People's and Socialist parties.

Many Christians, both Catholics and Evangelists, bore me a grudge for this. They considered it a betrayal for me to have allied myself with a movement that bore atheism inscribed upon its shield. When I see these people today they imagine that after fifteen years I must at last have seen the error of my ways. But I have to disappoint them. To this day I haven't altered my position one iota.

Of course the Communist movement is atheistic. But only those Christians who refuse to acknowledge the beam in their own eye can blame Communism for this. I say "Christians." But who are they? All around me I see only the most superficial Christians living in exactly the same way as the unbelievers. But being a Christian means living differently. It means taking the path Christ took, *imitating* Christ. It means giving up our private interests, our comfort and power, and turning our face toward the poor, the downtrodden, and the suffering. But do the churches do this? My father was a working man, continually unemployed and with a humble faith in God. He turned his pious face toward Him, but the church never met his eyes. He remained forsaken among those near him, forsaken within the church, alone with his God, until at last he fell ill and died.

The established churches failed to realize that the working-class movement was the movement of the downtrodden and those that groan for justice. Utterly contrary to the spirit of Jesus, the churches turned their backs. They weren't interested in striving with them and for them, for a kingdom of God here on earth. They allied themselves with the oppressors and deprived the working-class movement of God. And now they want to reproach it for being godless. The hypocrites! Yes, the working-class movement is atheistic, but in this I see God's reproach to us, the Christians! A reproach for our hardheartedness toward the poor and the suffering.

And what am I to do in this situation? Am I to feel shocked

at the dwindling support for the churches? Am I to feel shocked that the schools bring up our children in an irreligious frame of mind? How silly! True religion doesn't require the sanction of secular power. Secular disfavor only strengthens the faith.

And am I perhaps to fight against Socialism because it is, thanks to us, atheistic? Sillier still! I can only lament the tragic error that led Socialism away from God. All I can do is explain this error and work for its correction.

And anyway, why this disquiet, brother Christians? Everything is done according to God's will, and I often wonder whether it's God's design not to let mankind know that man cannot with impunity take his seat on His throne and that even the most just disposition of secular conditions will without His participation fail and become corrupt.

I remember those years when people here felt themselves to be but a few steps from paradise. And they were proud because it was *their* paradise for which they needed no one in heaven above. And then suddenly it slipped from their grasp.

In any case, until the February coup my being a Christian suited the Communists quite well. They loved to hear me explaining the social content of the Gospel, inveighing against the rottenness of the old world of property and wars, and demonstrating the affinity between Christianity and Communism. It was, after all, their concern to win over the broadest possible section of the population, and this of course included the believers. Soon after that February, however, things began to change. As a lecturer at the university I took the side of some of my pupils who were to be expelled because of the political convictions of their parents. I protested this and came into direct conflict with the university. Suddenly it began to be said that a man with such a distinct Christian orientation was not properly capable of educating Socialist youth. It appeared that I'd have to fight for my very livelihood. Then I heard that a student by the name of Ludvik Jahn had stood up for me at a plenary meeting of the Party. He said, apparently, that it would be base ingratitude to forget what I'd meant to the Party before February. And when they referred to my Christian beliefs he said that they must surely be a passing phase in my life, one that, thanks to my youth, I would undoubtedly outgrow.

I went to see him and thanked him for his support. I told him, however, that I didn't want to disappoint him, warning him that I was older than he and that there was no hope at all of my "outgrowing" my faith. We then began to debate the existence of God, the finite and the infinite, Descartes' views on religion, whether Spinoza was a materialist, and so on, long into the night. We came to no agreement. Finally I asked Ludvik whether he regretted standing up for me now that he saw how incorrigible I was. He told me my Christian faith was my own private affair and that all in all it was no business of anyone else's.

From that time on I didn't see him at the university again. And yet the pattern of our lives became more and more similar. About three months after our conversation Jahn was expelled from the Party and university, and another six months later I too had to leave the faculty. Was I thrown out? Driven out? Impossible for me to say. All I can say for certain is that there were more and more voices raised against me and against my convictions. It's true that some of my colleagues suggested that I ought to make some public statement along atheistic lines. It's also true that I had some unpleasant scenes at lectures with aggressive Communistic students who wanted to insult my faith. My status at the college was decidedly precarious. Yet it's also true that I still had plenty of friends among the Communists on the faculty and that they respected me for my attitude before the February coup. Perhaps it would have taken very little; I'd only have had to start defending myself and they would certainly have all backed me up. But this I didn't do.

"Follow me," said Jesus to His disciples, and without demur they left their nets, their boats, their homes, and their families and followed Him. "No man having put his hand to the plow and looking back is fit for the kingdom of God."

If we hear Christ's challenge we must follow it unconditionally. This is clear from the Gospel, and yet in modern times the whole thing sounds like something from a fairy tale. Where is the challenge in these prosaic lives of ours, who is there to follow? With whom are we to leave our nets and whither shall we go?

And yet the voice can reach us even here if our hearing is keen. The challenge doesn't come to us through the mail like a registered letter. It comes disguised. Rarely does it come in alluring guise. "Not the deed that thou choosest, but that which befalls thee against thy will, thy thinking, and thy desire, this is the path thou must enter upon, this is whither I call, there be thou the disciple, that is thy time, this is the way the Master trod."

I had a number of reasons for clinging to my lectureship. It was reasonably comfortable, it gave me plenty of free time for my own research, and it held the promise of a career as a university teacher. Yet I was alarmed when I saw a number of valuable people, both teachers and pupils, being forced in those days to leave the universities. I was alarmed at my attachment to my comfortable life, distancing me as it did with its calm security from the anything but calm fate that befell those near me. I recognized in the proposals that I should leave the faculty a *challenge*. I heard someone calling to me. Someone warning me against the comfortable career that would restrict my mind, my faith, and my conscience.

Naturally my wife, by whom I already had a five-year-old child, insisted repeatedly that I should defend myself and do everything possible to remain at the university. She was thinking of our son and the future of our family. For her nothing else existed. When I looked into her already aging face I was alarmed at that eternal anxiety, anxiety about tomorrow, about next year, that pervasive anxiety about all tomorrows and all years stretching out beyond count. I was alarmed, and in my mind I heard Jesus' words: "Take therefore no thought for the morrow; for the morrow shall take thought for the things of itself. Sufficient unto the day is the evil thereof."

My enemies were expecting me to be bowed down with worry, while I actually experienced an unexpected absence of care. They thought I'd feel limited in my freedom, while on the contrary I'd just discovered for myself the real meaning of freedom. I saw that man has nothing to lose and that his place is everywhere, everywhere that Jesus went, which means: everywhere among men.

After my initial surprise and regret I went forward to meet the malice of my enemies. I accepted their injustices as a challenge written in code.

Communists hold the entirely religious belief that a man who's committed some wrong against his Party may find absolution if he leaves for a period to work among agricultural or industrial laborers. During the years after February a number of intellectuals went off in this way for short or longer periods to the mines, factories, building sites, and state farms, so that after mysterious purification through work they might be allowed to return to their offices, their educational or political posts.

When I announced to the university senate that I'd be leaving the university and wouldn't be applying for another scientific post, as I wanted to "go to the people," preferably as technical adviser to some state farm, the Communists in my institute—friends and enemies alike—regarded this not in light of my own faith but theirs: as the expression of an unprecedented example of self-criticism. They applauded my decision and helped me find a very good post on a state farm in western Bohemia, under a competent manager and in a beautiful part of the country. They sent me on my way with the gift of an uncommonly favorable testimonial.

I was actually happy in my new position. I felt myself reborn. The state farm had been set up in a derelict and underpopulated border village from which the Germans had been expelled after the war. There were hills all around, most of them bare pastureland. In the valleys the cottages of a number of small, straggly villages were dotted at widespread intervals. Frequent mists swirling across the countryside drifted between me and populated land, so that the world was as it was on the fifth day of creation, when God was perhaps still undecided whether He should hand it over to man.

And people here were much more like original man. They confronted nature face to face, endless pastures, herds of cows and flocks of sheep. I felt at home among them. I soon had a number of ideas about how the vegetation in this hilly country might be put to better use, ideas about manuring, storing the hay, experimental fields of medicinal herbs, a greenhouse. The manager was grateful for my ideas and I was grateful to him for making it possible for me to earn my bread by useful work.

It was in 1951. September was cool, but halfway through October it suddenly warmed up and there was a superb autumn lasting well into November. The stacks of hay dried on the hilly meadows and their perfume spread far over the land. Delicate little clusters of meadow saffron appeared in the grass. It was then that in the surrounding villages word began to spread about the lost girl.

Some youngsters from a neighboring village went out into the flat mown fields. They were talking noisily, shouting at each other, and then apparently they saw a girl crawl out of a stack, tousled and with straw in her hair, a young girl none of them had ever seen before. She looked around in alarm and started running toward the woods. Before they could decide whether to pursue her or not they'd lost her.

A farmer's wife from the same village said that one afternoon when she was busy with something in the yard, suddenly a girl, about twenty and dressed in a threadbare coat, appeared from nowhere and asked with bowed head for a crust of bread. "Where are you going, girl?" asked the woman.

The girl replied that she had a long way to go.

"And are you going on foot?"

"I've lost all my money," she replied.

The woman asked no more questions and gave her bread and milk.

A shepherd from our estate reported that one day when he was in the hills he'd put a piece of bread and butter and a jug of milk in a tree stump for safekeeping. He left for a minute to follow his flock, and when he returned, the bread and the jug had mysteriously vanished.

The children immediately seized on these episodes and multiplied them with their eager fantasy. They saw the girl in the evenings bathing in the fishing lake beyond the village, although it was the beginning of November and the water was already very chilly. When anyone lost anything the children immediately took it as proof of her existence. At other times, in the evenings, a song, sung in a clear female voice, would echo from somewhere in the distance. The adults said that some cottage on the hill had had the radio turned up full, but the children knew it was she, the wild girl, treading the ridge along the hills, her hair hanging free, singing her song.

One evening a fire was made outside the village, and potato stalks and leaves were placed on top of it and potatoes thrown into the glowing ash. Then they looked toward the woods, and one little girl began to shout that she could see the wild girl looking at them from the shadows. A small boy picked up a clod of earth and threw it in the direction the girl was pointing. Strangely enough, there was no answering shriek, but something else happened. All the children shouted at the boy and almost beat him up.

Yes, indeed, the customary cruelty of children had never reared its head in the story of the lost girl, even though there were a number of small thefts associated with her growing legend. From the beginning she'd had their secret sympathies. Perhaps it was the innocent insignificance of the thefts that had won people's hearts. Or was it her tender years? Or was she protected by an angel's hand?

Whichever way it was, the throwing of that lump of earth kindled in those children a feeling of love for the lost girl. The same day they left a heap of baked potatoes around the embers of the fire, covered them with ashes to keep them warm, and thrust a broken fir branch into the pile. They even found a name for the girl. On a piece of paper torn from an exercise book they wrote in big penciled letters: LITTLE WAIF, THIS IS FOR YOU. They put it up against the mound and weighed it down with earth. Then they left and hid in the surrounding bushes, watching for the timid girl to appear. Evening became night, and still no one came. Finally the children had to desert their hiding place and go home. At crack of dawn they were back at their posts. It had happened. The pile of potatoes had disappeared and so had the paper and the fir branch.

The girl became the children's own pampered fairy. They left her jugs of milk, bread, potatoes, and messages. And they never repeated the same place twice for their gifts. They avoided leaving her provisions in a definite spot as though it were put out for the beggars. They were playing a game with her. A game of hidden treasure. They moved from the place they'd originally left the pile of potatoes and went farther away from the village into the country. They left their treasures by the tree stumps, by the big rock, by the wayside cross, by the briar bush. To nobody did they ever betray the spot where they'd hidden their gifts. Never did they violate the spider's-web delicacy of the game; never did they lie in wait for the girl or jump out at her. They allowed her to keep her invisibility.

The whole story was short-lived. One day the manager of our estate went on a trip far into the country with the chairman of the local council. They were to look over some still-uninhabited cottages left behind after the German evacuation, with the thought of setting them up as overnight hostels for farm laborers working on a job a long way from the village. On the way they were overtaken by rain which soon became torrential. Nearby there was a low-lying clump of firs with a grayish barn at the edge—a hayloft. They ran over to it, opened the door that was secured only by a wooden stake, and crawled inside. The light filtered through the open door and the holes in the roof. In the straw they saw a smoothed-over area. They stretched out on it, listened to the raindrops falling on the roof, breathed the intoxicating scent, and started to gossip. Suddenly the chairman felt something hard under the dry straw. It was a suitcase. An old, ugly, cheap suitcase made of cardboard. How long they brooded over the mystery I don't know. One thing is certain. They opened the case and found in it four outfits, all of them new and pretty. The fineness of the clothes was apparently in strange contrast with the drabness of the case, and their suspicions of a theft were aroused. Under the clothes were a few more articles of girl's underwear, and hidden among them a bundle of letters tied with a blue ribbon. That was all. To this day I know nothing of the letters and don't even know whether the manager and the chairman read them. I only know that the letters helped them to discover the name of their recipient: Lucie Sebetka.

While they were contemplating their unexpected find the chairman discovered something else in the straw. It was a cracked milk container. The same blue enamel jug whose mysterious loss the shepherd had been retelling in the tavern every evening for the past two weeks.

After this the whole thing ran along predictable lines. The chairman hid in the fir trees to wait, and the manager went down to the village and sent the village constable up after the chairman. Toward dusk the girl returned to her perfumed bower. They let her go in, allowed her to close the door, waited half a minute, and went in after her.

Both the men who trapped Lucie in the barn were good men. The chairman, a village official under the old regime, honest, father of six, reminded one somehow of the old-time village chroniclers. The policeman was a naïve, coarse, good-natured fellow with an immense mustache. Neither of them would have hurt a fly.

And yet it tore strangely at my heartstrings when I heard how Lucie was trapped. To this day I feel a twinge in my heart to think of the manager and the chairman rummaging in her suitcase, taking all her most intimate objects into their hands, the delicate mysteries of her dirty linen, looking into forbidden things. And it hurts to this day when I imagine the little lair made in the straw, from which there was no escape, whose only doors were blocked by two large men.

When, later, I learned more about Lucie, I realized with astonishment that in both aspects of this agonizing situation the very essence of her fate had been made clear to me. Both were illustrations of her *defilement*.

That night Lucie slept not in the hut of straw but on an iron bed in the shop the police had set up as their daytime office. The next day her case was heard before the council. They learned that until then she'd worked and lived in Ostrava. She'd run away because she couldn't stand it there any longer. When they tried to find out something more specific, they were met with stubborn silence.

Why run this way, to the west of Bohemia? She said that her parents lived in Cheb. Why didn't she join them? She'd got off the train a short distance before her home station because on the way she'd begun to feel afraid. All her life her father had done nothing but beat her.

The chairman of the council informed Lucie that they'd be sending her back to Ostrava, since she'd come from there without a proper discharge. Lucie insisted she'd run away from the train at the first stop. For a while they tried to shout her down but soon saw that this would solve nothing. They asked her if they should send her home, to Cheb. She shook her head furiously. For a while they were severe with her again, and then the chairman succumbed to his own softheartedness. "What do you want then?" She asked whether she mightn't be allowed to work here. They shrugged their shoulders and said they'd ask at the state farm.

The manager was fighting a constant battle against an acute labor shortage. He accepted the council's proposal with alacrity. Then he told me I'd finally be getting the greenhouse assistant I'd long been looking for. The same day the council chairman came to present me with Lucie.

I remember that day well. It was the second half of November, and an autumn which had so far been sunny was for the first time showing its windy and misty aspect. It was drizzling. She stood there in a brown coat with her little case, her head bowed and an absent look in her eyes, the tall council chairman by her side. The chairman, holding the blue jug in his hands, announced ceremoniously, "If you've done anything wrong we have forgiven you and we trust you. We could have sent you back to Ostrava, but we've left you here. The working class requires honest people everywhere. Do not let it down."

He then went into the office to hand over the shepherd's jug, and I took Lucie into the greenhouse, introduced her to the two girls she'd be working with, and explained to her what she would be doing.

In my recollection of those days Lucie overshadows everything else. Despite this, the figure of the council chairman stands fairly clearly outlined in her shadow. When you were actually sitting opposite me in the armchair, Ludvik, I didn't want to offend you. Now that you are opposite me again in the form in which I know you best, as a figment and a shadow, I shall tell you: this former local official, who'd wanted to create a paradise for those near him who were suffering, this honest man, with his enthusiasm and naïvely high-sounding words about forgiveness, trust, and the working class, was a lot nearer my heart and my way of thinking than you were, even though he never once showed me any personal favor.

You once stated that Socialism grew from the stem of European rationalism and skepticism, a stem which was nonreligious and antireligious, and that it is otherwise unthinkable. But do you seriously maintain that it is impossible to build a Socialist society without faith in the supremacy of matter? Do you really think that men who believe in God are incapable of nationalizing factories?

I am altogether certain that that line of European thought stemming from the teaching of Jesus leads far more naturally to social equality and Socialism. And as I recall the most ardent Communists from the earlier period of Socialism in this country of mine, the chairman for instance, who delivered Lucie into my care, they seem to me to be much more like religious zealots than Voltairean skeptics. The revolutionary era from 1948 to 1956 had little in common with skepticism and rationalism. This was the time of the great collective faith. The man who strode forward in unison with the age had feelings very much like religious ones; he renounced himself, his person, his privacy, for the benefit of something higher, something more than personal. Marxist teachings were in origin entirely secular, but the significance assigned them was similar to the significance of the Gospel and the Biblical commandments. We saw the evolution of a body of thought that was inviolate or, in our terminology, sacred.

This was a cruel religion. It didn't elevate you or me among its high priests; perhaps it injured both of us. Yet despite this, the age that has just passed was a hundred times nearer my heart than the age that seems to be approaching today: an age of ridicule, skepticism, and corrosion, a petty age with the ironic intellectual in the limelight, and behind him the mob of youth —coarse, cynical, and bitter, without enthusiasm or ideas, ready to mate or to kill on sight.

The age which is passing, or which has already passed, had something of the spirit of the great religious movements. It's a pity that it wasn't able to follow its religious self-revelations to their conclusion. It had religious ritual and emotion, but it remained empty and godless within. Yet I still believed that God would have mercy, that at last He would sanctify this great world faith. For this I waited in vain.

This age finally betrayed its religious nature and paid its

debt to the rationalistic heritage to which it swore allegiance
—and only because it didn't understand its own true nature.
This rationalistic skepticism has been corroding Christianity
for two millennia. Still, it hasn't eaten it away completely.
But the Communist theory—its own creature—it will destroy
in a few decades. In you, Ludvik, it has already done so. As you
well know.

When people are able to transport themselves in fantasy to a
fairy-tale land, they are full of nobility, sympathy, and poetry.
Unfortunately, in the realm of everyday life they are more
prone to caution, mistrust, and suspicion. This was revealed in
their behavior toward Lucie. As soon as she'd left the children's
fairy tales and become a real girl, one who worked and lived
with people, she immediately became the object of a curiosity
which was not without its touch of malice, just as people behave
toward angels flung down from paradise and fairies driven from
fairyland.

Lucie's being so tight-lipped didn't help her much either. A
month or so later, the estate had her file from Ostrava. We
learned she'd started work in Cheb as an apprentice barber.
After an immorality charge she'd spent a year in a reformatory
and then gone to Ostrava. In Ostrava she'd proved a good
worker. Her behavior in the hostel was exemplary. Before her
flight there'd been only one completely unexpected conviction against her: she'd been caught stealing flowers in a cemetery.

The reports were fairly bald, and far from unraveling the
mystery surrounding Lucie, they only deepened it.

I promised the manager I'd take Lucie into my care. I rather
liked her. She worked quietly and with concentration. She was
calm in her shyness. I found in her none of the strangeness you'd
expect in a girl who had lived for several weeks alone in the
woods. She declared several times that she was happy on the
farm and didn't want to leave us. She was placid and ready to
give way in any argument, and because of this she gradually

won over the girls who worked with her. However, there remained something in her quietness that betrayed a life of suffering and a wounded soul. I would have liked nothing better than for her to have confided in me, but I knew that she'd had enough questioning and quizzing in her life and that she probably associated them with police interrogation. So instead of questioning her I began to tell my own story. Every day I used to talk with her. I told her of my plans to start the planting of medicinal herbs on the estate. I told her how in the old days country people used to cure themselves with decoctions and solutions of various herbs. I told her about burnet, with which people used to cure cholera and the plague, and about breakstone, which breaks up stones in the bladder and bile. Lucie would listen. She liked herbs. But what innocence. She knew nothing about them and could hardly name one.

Winter was already coming on, and Lucie had only her pretty summer things. I helped her to budget. I prevailed upon her to buy a trenchcoat and a sweater and other things later: boots, pajamas, stockings, and overcoat.

One day I asked her whether she believed in God. She answered in a way I thought peculiar. She said neither yes nor no. She shrugged her shoulders and said, "I don't know." I asked her whether she knew who Jesus Christ was. She said she did. But she knew nothing about Him. In her His name was vaguely associated with the idea of Christmas, which she had somehow muddled up with the crucifixion in a haze of two or three impressions that came together and made no sense. Until then Lucie had known neither belief nor unbelief. At that moment I felt a slight dizziness—perhaps something akin to that experienced by the lover when he finds that no male body has preceded him in his beloved. "Do you want me to tell you about him?" I asked, and she nodded. By then the pastures and hills were covered in snow. I began the story. Lucie listened . . .

She had had too much to bear on her slender shoulders. She needed somebody to help her, but there'd been nobody capable of doing so. Lucie, the help offered by religion is simple: Yield thyself up. Yield thyself up together with the burden under which thou stumblest. This is the greatest relief, to live, giving yourself to others. I know that you never had anyone to give yourself to, because you were afraid of people. But God is here. Give yourself to Him. Then you will feel lighter.

To yield oneself up means to lay aside one's past life. To pluck it out of one's soul. To confess. Tell me, Lucie, why did you run away from Ostrava? Was it because of those flowers on the grave?

That was part of it.

And why did you take the flowers?

She had felt depressed, so she put them in a vase in her room in the hostel. She picked flowers in the open field, but Ostrava is a black place with hardly any open fields around it, just dumps and fences and here and there a few bushes covered with coal dust. Beautiful flowers were found only in the cemetery. Elegant flowers, flowers for an occasion. Gladioli, roses, and lilies. Chrysanthemums too, with their immense blooms and brittle leaves . . .

And how did they catch you?

She often went to the cemetery and liked it there. Not only because of the flowers she took but because it was nice and quiet, and the quiet was comforting to her. Every tomb was like a private garden, and she liked to stand by the individual gravestones and read their sad inscriptions. So as not to be disturbed, she imitated some of the visitors to the cemetery, especially the older ones, by kneeling before particular stones. Once she took a fancy to a grave that was almost fresh. The coffin had been buried there only a few days before. The earth on the grave was loose and there were wreaths lying on it, and in front of them in a vase stood a magnificent spray of roses. Lucie knelt, and a weeping willow inclined over her like an intimate, whispering heaven. Lucie dissolved away in unspeakable rapture. It was at this point that an elderly gentleman arrived at the tomb with his wife. Perhaps it was the grave of their son or brother, who knows. They saw an unfamiliar girl kneeling by the tomb and stopped in horror. Who was this girl? To them there must have been something ominous in her appearance. Who was she—an unknown relative or an abandoned lover of the deceased? They stopped short, afraid to disturb her, and watched her from a distance. Then they saw her stand up, take the fine spray of roses from the vase—the one they had placed there themselves a few days before—turn, and leave. At that they ran after her. "Who are you?" they asked. She became confused and didn't know what to say. When they realized that the unknown girl hadn't known the deceased at all, they called the cemetery attendant to their aid. They demanded identification. They shouted at her and said there was nothing worse than robbing the dead. The attendant confirmed that this wasn't the first flower theft in her cemetery. Then they called a policeman and Lucie confessed everything.

"Let the dead bury their dead," said Jesus. Flowers on graves are the property of the living. Lucie, you didn't know God, but you yearned for Him. It was the unearthly revealing itself to you in the beauty of earthly flowers. You didn't need those flowers for anyone. Only for yourself. To fill the emptiness in your soul. And they caught you and humiliated you. And was that the only reason for your running away from that black town?

She was silent. Then she shook her head.

Someone hurt you?

She nodded.

Tell me, Lucie!

It was a very small room. There was a light bulb in the ceiling, it had no shade, and in its lewd nakedness hung crookedly from the fixture. A bed by the wall, a picture hanging over it, and in the picture a handsome man in a blue robe, kneeling. It was the Garden of Gethsemane, but Lucie wasn't to know that.

THE JOKE

This is where he brought her, and she fought and screamed. He wanted to rape her, he ripped off her clothes, but she tore away from him and ran.

Who was he, Lucie?

A soldier.

Did you love him?

No, she didn't love him.

Then why did you go with him into that room with nothing but the bare bed?

It was just the emptiness in her soul that drew her to him. All she could find in her misery was an adolescent, a national serviceman.

But there's one thing I still don't understand, Lucie. Since you went with him into the room with just its bare bed, why did you run away from him afterward?

Because he was nasty and fierce like all of them.

Of whom, Lucie? All of whom?

Silence.

Who did you know before the soldier? Speak, Lucie! Tell me the truth!

There were six of them and just one of her. Six of them between sixteen and twenty. She was sixteen. They were all in the same gang at work and they spoke of their gang with awe, as if it were some pagan sect. On that day they were talking about initiation. They brought along a few bottles of cheap wine. She took part in the drinking with a blind obedience in which she had placed all the unrequited love of a daughter for her father and mother. She drank when they drank and laughed when they laughed. Then they ordered her to strip. She'd never done that in front of them before. But when, as she hesitated, the gang's chief took the initiative and undressed first, she saw that the order was not directed at her alone and complied obediently. She trusted them, she trusted their roughness, they were her shield and protection, and she couldn't imagine what there would be if she lost them. They were her father and her mother.

They drank and laughed and gave her more instructions. She opened her legs. She was afraid, she knew what it meant, but she obeyed. Then she was screaming and there was blood coming from her. The lads roared and raised their glasses and poured the coarse sparkling wine down the back of the chief, over her body and between their legs; they were shouting some words about christening and initiation, and then the chief got up and the next member of the gang went over to her and then they all came in order of seniority with the youngest last, and he was sixteen like her, and Lucie couldn't stand any more, couldn't stand any more pain, wanted to rest, wanted to be by herself, and because he was the youngest she dared to thrust him off. But just because he was the youngest he didn't want to be humiliated. He was a member of their gang, a fully fledged member! He wanted to prove it, and so he hit Lucie across the face, and none of the gang stood up for her because they all knew that the youngest man was in the right and was claiming what was rightly his. Lucie wept but lacked the courage to resist further, and so she opened her legs for the sixth time . . .

Where was this, Lucie?

One of the laborers' apartments, his parents were both on night shift, there was a kitchen and one room, in the room a table, a couch, and a bed, over the door a framed motto saying GOD GRANT HAPPINESS and over the bed in a frame a beautiful lady in a blue robe holding a child to her breast.

The Virgin Mary?

She didn't know.

And then, Lucie, what happened then?

Afterward it happened again, many times in the apartment and in other apartments and out in the fields. It became a custom with the gang.

And did you like it, Lucie?

She didn't. From that time on they had treated her arrogantly and coarsely, but there was no way out, forward, backward, anywhere.

And how did it end, Lucie?

One evening in one of those empty apartments. The police came and took everyone away. The gang had a few thefts to answer for. Lucie wasn't aware of it, but it was known that she went around with the gang and gave them everything that as a young girl she was capable of giving. She was the shame of Cheb, and at home she was beaten black and blue. The boys got varying sentences and she was sent to a reformatory. She stayed there for a year—until she was seventeen. She didn't want to go home again for anything in the world. So she went to the Black City.

I was surprised and startled when Ludvik revealed to me on the telephone day before yesterday that he knew Lucie. Luckily he had only a fleeting knowledge of her. Apparently he'd had some superficial relationship in Ostrava with a girl who lived in the hostel with her. When he asked me about her again yesterday I told him the whole story. I had long needed to throw off that burden, but until now I'd never found a man I could trust with the confidence. Ludvik is well disposed toward me and at the same time is sufficiently distant from my life and even more removed from Lucie's. I had no need to fear that I'd be putting her secret in jeopardy.

Of course everybody on the farm knew from her file about her having been in a reformatory and stolen flowers from a cemetery. They were friendly enough, but they constantly reminded her of her past. The manager talked of her as "the little grave robber"! He meant it in fun, but this sort of talk kept Lucie's past sins constantly alive. She felt continuously and endlessly guilty. And at the same time she needed nothing other than complete forgiveness. Yes, Ludvik, she needed forgiveness, she needed to go through that mysterious purgatory which to you is unfamiliar and incomprehensible.

For people themselves are not capable of forgiveness. It's not in their power to annihilate the sin that has been. Not within the power of man alone. To deprive a sin of its validity, to undo it, to rub it out of time, to make something into nothing, is a mysterious and supernatural feat. Only God, because He is beyond earthly laws, because He is free, because He can work miracles, may wipe out a sin, dispel it, forgive it. Man can forgive man only insofar as he founds himself on God's forgiveness.

Nor can you, Ludvik, forgive, because you don't believe in God. You still remember the plenary meeting when everyone raised his hand against you and resolved that your life should be destroyed. You've never forgiven them that. And not only as individuals. There were about a hundred of them there, and that is a quantity which can become a sort of microcosm. You've never forgiven mankind. From that time on, you've ceased trusting men, and you still feel bitterness toward them. I can understand you in this, but it doesn't alter the fact that such general bitterness toward people is evil and sinful. It has become your curse. *Because to live in a world in which no one is forgiven, where all are irredeemable, is the same as living in hell.* You are living in hell, Ludvik, and I pity you.

Everything that on this earth belongs to God may also belong to the devil. Even the movements of lovers as they make love. For Lucie they had become a thing of disgust. For her they were associated with the faces of the savage adolescents from the work gang and later with the face of the soldier as he forced himself on her. I can see him before me quite clearly, as if I knew him. He mingles his banal love words with the rough violence of the male caged without women behind the barracks wire. Lucie sees that the tender words are only the mask on a vulgar wolfish face. And for her the whole world tumbles downward into a pit of loathing.

Here was the source of the disease. Here was where I had to begin. The man walking along the seashore and madly waving a lantern in his outstretched hand may be a lunatic. But on a night in which a boat has gone astray he is a protector. The land we live in is the borderland between heaven and hell. No act of itself is either good or bad. Even physical love, Lucie, is not of itself good or bad. If it is in accordance with the system created by God, if you love with an eternal love, the loving too will be good and you'll be happy. Because God so decreed it that "a man shall leave his father and his mother and shall cleave unto his wife; and the two shall be one flesh."

I spoke to Lucie every single day. Every single day I reassured her that she was forgiven, that she wasn't to writhe inwardly, that she must unloose the straitjacket of her soul, that she must humbly yield herself to God's order, in which even the love of the body will find its place.

And so the weeks went by.

Then came the first days of spring. Apple trees bloomed on the hilly slopes, and in the gentle wind their crowns looked like swinging bells. I closed my eyes to hear their velvet tones. Then I opened them and saw Lucie in her blue overalls, with a hoe in her hand. She was looking down the valley and she was smiling.

I saw that smile and drank it in eagerly. For before then Lucie's soul had been in eternal flight, a flight from both past and future. She was afraid of everything. The past and the future for her were watery depths. She clung desperately to the present as to a precarious haven.

And now today she was smiling. For no apparent reason. Just like that. And that smile told me she was looking into the future with confidence. And in that instant I felt like a mariner who's spent many months sailing to a longed-for land. I was happy. I leaned on the crooked stem of the apple tree and again for a moment I closed my eyes. I heard the breeze in the white tree-tops, I heard the trilling of the birds, and behind my closed eyes their song was transformed into thousands of lanterns and candles carried by invisible hands toward a great ceremony. I didn't see those hands but I heard the high-pitched tones of the voices and I saw them as children, a happy procession of chil-dren. . . . Then I suddenly felt a hand on my cheek. A voice: "Mr. Kostka, you are so good to me . . ." I didn't open my eyes. I didn't move my hand. I still saw the birds' voices as a host of lights. I still heard the ringing of the apple trees. And the voice added more faintly, "I love you."

Perhaps I should have waited only for that moment and then quickly left; for now my job was done. But before I could reflect I was seized by a delirium of weakness. We were completely alone in the wide open country between the piteous little apple trees, and I took Lucie in my arms and sank with her into the bower of nature.

What shouldn't have happened had happened. When I saw in Lucie's smile the reconciliation of her soul, I had reached my goal and should then have departed. But I didn't depart. And what happened was wrong. We went on living together on the same farm. Lucie was happy, she was aglow, she was like the spring that was gradually changing into summer all around us. But instead of being happy myself I was horrified at this exuberant female spring beside me, that I myself had awakened and that turned to me with all its blooms opening out, while I knew that they were not and must not be mine. In Prague I had a son and a wife who waited patiently for my infrequent visits home.

I was afraid to break off the intimacies I'd entered into with Lucie for fear of hurting her, but neither did I dare continue with them, because I knew I had no right to them. I desired Lucie, yet at the same time I was afraid of her love, because I didn't know where to direct it. It was only with the greatest effort that I maintained our previous naturalness. My doubts came between us. It seemed to me that my spiritual assistance to Lucie was a mask now removed. That I'd desired her physically from the first moment I saw her. That I'd acted like a seducer disguised as comforter and preacher. That all that talk about Jesus and God has been only a veil for the most earthly bodily desire. It seemed to me that in the moment I yielded to my sexuality I'd violated the purity of my original intentions and been stripped of my merit before God.

Yet no sooner had I arrived at this conclusion than my train of thought made an about-turn. What vanity, I accused myself, what selfish desire, to want to be worthy, to be pleasing to God! What are the merits of man before Him? Nothing! Lucie loves me and her health depends on my love! What if I were to hurl her back into despair just so that I should be pure? Wouldn't God despise me for it? And if my love is a sin, which means more, Lucie's life or my own spotlessness? It will be *my* sin, only *I* shall bear it, only *I* shall condemn my own sin!

Suddenly these thoughts and considerations were disturbed by outside intervention. The people at the center had trumped up some charge against the manager. He was defending himself tooth and nail, and to strengthen the case against him his enemies accused him of being surrounded by suspicious elements. One of these was myself, a man said to have been expelled from the university for anti-State thinking, a cleric. The manager unsuccessfully argued that I wasn't in fact a cleric, that I hadn't been expelled from the university. The more he stood up for me the more he demonstrated his close ties with me and the more he harmed himself. My situation was almost hopeless.

Injustice, Ludvik? This is the word you use most often when you hear about this or similar incidents. But I don't know what injustice is. If there were nothing else above human affairs and if actions had only the significance ascribed to them by those who performed them, then the concept of injustice would be warranted, and I could speak of injustice when I was more or less thrown out of the state farm where I'd been working with such devotion. Perhaps it would have been logical too if I'd defended myself against this injustice and fought furiously for my puny human rights.

Yet events for the most part have a meaning different from the one their agents ascribe to them; they're often disguised instructions from above, and those men who've allowed them to occur are only the unwitting agents of a higher will of which they have no conception.

I was certain that this was how it was in this case too. So I accepted the events on the estate with relief. In them I saw a

clear order: Leave Lucie before it's too late. You have completed the task set you. The fruits of the task are not thine.
Thy path leads elsewhere.

And I did the same thing I'd done two years before in the
natural history department. I said good-bye to a weeping and
desperate Lucie and went to confront apparent disaster. I volunteered to leave the farm. The manager did try to stop me,
but I knew that he was only doing so out of decency and that in
the depths of his soul he was pleased at my departure.

Only this time my voluntary resignation impressed no one.
My Communist friends of the pre-February period who'd
strewn the path of my retirement with good advice were absent.
I left the farm as a man who admits he's unfit to carry out any
work of significance in this State. And so I became a bricklayer.

It was an autumn day in 1956. I'd met Ludvik for the first
time in five years, in the restaurant car of the Prague-Bratislava
express. I was traveling to work on the construction of some
factory in eastern Moravia. Ludvik had just completed his work
quota in the Ostrava mines and had applied to Prague for
permission to resume his studies. He was now traveling home
to eastern Moravia. We hardly knew each other. And when
we did recognize each other we were astonished at the way
each other's lives had turned out.

I well remember the concern with which you listened, Ludvik, when I told you how I left the university and of the intrigues on the state farm that had led to my becoming a bricklayer. Thank you for that concern. You were enraged, you
spoke of injustice, wrong, lack of respect for intellectuals,
and the absurd policy of personnel vetting. You were angry with
me too; you reproached me for not defending myself, for
giving up. You said we should never walk out of anywhere
voluntarily. Let our opponents be driven to do their very worst!
Why make their consciences any easier?

You down in the mines, myself on the building sites. Our
stories have been fairly similar, and yet we are so utterly dif-

ferent. I the forgiving, you the implacable; I the humble, you the proud. How outwardly similar we are and how inwardly remote!

You were far less aware of this internal distance than I was. When you gave me the full details of why you'd been excluded from the Party in 1950, you took it for granted that I'd be on your side and just as indignant as you at the bigotry of the Comrades who punished you just for making fun of something they held sacred. Referring to the postcard, you asked in open surprise: "What of it?"

I'll tell you something. In Geneva, in the days of Calvin's rule there, there was a young man, in a sense similar to yourself, an intelligent boy immensely fond of jokes, on whom was found a notebook full of satire and attacks on Jesus Christ and the Gospel. What of it? was most probably his thought, too. He'd done nothing wrong—it was all in fun. He knew little of hatred. He apparently knew only disrespect and indifference. He was executed.

Please don't think I support such cruelties. I only mean that no great movement designed to change the world can bear to be laughed at or belittled, because laughter is a rust corroding everything.

Keep on thinking as you do, Ludvik. They excluded you from the Party, expelled you from the university, in military service they assigned you to the black brigade, and then they sent you for another two or three years down into the mines. And you? You became bitter to the depths of your soul, convinced of being immensely wronged. This sense of wrong determines your every attitude to life to this very day. I cannot understand you! Why do you speak of wrong? They posted you among the black brigades, among the enemies of Communism. Granted. And was that wrong? Wasn't it more like a great opportunity for you? You could have worked among those enemies. Wasn't that a greater mission? Didn't Jesus send His disciples as "sheep in the midst of wolves"? "They that be whole need not a physician, but they that are sick," Jesus said. "For I am not come to call the righteous, but sinners to repentance." But you didn't want to go out among the sinful and infirm!

You'll argue that my comparison is inept. That Jesus sent His disciples "in the midst of wolves" with His blessing, whereas you were ostracized and cursed and then sent among the enemies as an enemy yourself, as a wolf among the wolves, as a sinner among the sinning.

But why deny that you were a sinner? Were you utterly blameless before your committee? Where do you get your arrogance? The man devoted to his faith is humble and must in humility bear even an unjust punishment. The humiliated will be raised up. The repentant will be purified. Those that are wronged have the opportunity to prove their loyalty. If you became bitter at your group only because too great a burden was placed on your shoulders, then your faith was weak and you failed in the test set you.

I'm not on your side in your quarrel with the Party, Ludvik, because I know that great things can be done in this world only by a band of men of infinite devotion who humbly lay down their lives for the greater cause. Your devotion, Ludvik, is finite. Your faith is feeble. How could it be otherwise when you were eternally appealing only to yourself and your own wretched reason?

I am not ungrateful, Ludvik. I know what you've done for me and for many others who've been injured in some way by today's regime. You make use of your present position and your acquaintance with high-ranking Communists you knew before the revolution in order to intercede, intervene, and assist. I like you for this. But I tell you again for the last time: Look into the depths of your soul! Deep down behind your good work, the motive is not love but hatred. Hatred of those who once did you wrong, who raised their hands against you in that hall! Your soul knows not God and therefore knows not forgiveness. You yearn for retribution. You identify those who wronged you with those who wronged others, and you revenge yourself on them. Yes, revenge! You're full of hatred even when you help people! I feel it radiating from you. I feel it in your every word. But what are the fruits of hatred other than hatred returned and a chain of further hatreds? You live in hell, Ludvik, I repeat this again, you are living in Hell and I pity you.

Had Ludvik heard my monologue, he might have said that I was ungrateful. I know that he's rendered me great assistance. At that time in 1956 when we met on the train, he was distressed at the life I was leading, showed concern for my capabilities, and immediately began to think how he might find employment for me in which I'd find greater fulfillment. He surprised me then by the speed and drive with which he acted. In his hometown he had a few words with a friend of his. He wanted me to teach natural history in the high school. This was an act of courage. Antireligious propaganda was at its height, and to accept a Christian teacher in a high school was almost impossible. In any case Ludvik's friend considered the matter and came up with another solution. This was how I obtained my post in the virological department of the local hospital, where I've been breeding viruses and bacteria on mice and rabbits for the last eight years.

That's the way it is. If it weren't for Ludvik I wouldn't be here, and Lucie wouldn't be living here either.

A few years after my leaving the farm she married. She couldn't stay on the estate, for her husband was looking for a job in town. After some uncertainty about where they'd settle, she prevailed on her husband to move here, to the town where I was living.

I've never received a greater gift, a greater reward, in all my life. My little lamb, my dove, the child I'd healed and nurtured with my soul, was returning to me. She wants nothing of me. She has her own husband. But she wants to be near me. She needs me. She needs to hear my voice sometimes. To see me at the service on Sundays. To meet me in the street. I was happy, and in that instant I felt I was no longer young, I was older than I thought, and Lucie was perhaps the only achievement of my life.

Is that too little, Ludvik? Not at all. It is sufficient and I am happy. I am happy, happy, happy . . .

Oh, how I deceive myself! How stubbornly I attempt to re-affirm to myself the wisdom of my life's path! How I boast of my faith before the unbeliever!

Yes, I did manage to bring Lucie to a faith in God. I was successful in calming and healing her. I rid her of her disgust for physical love. In the end I stepped out of her path. But what good did I bring her by this step?

Her marriage hasn't turned out well. Her husband is a brute, he's publicly unfaithful to her, and there are rumors that he ill-treats her. Lucie has never complained. She knows it would distress me. She presents her life to me as a model of happiness. But we live in a small town where nothing remains secret.

How I manage to deceive myself! I interpreted the political intrigues against the manager of the state farm as a sign from God that I should leave. But how can God's voice be distinguished from so many others? What if the voice I heard was only the voice of my own cowardice?

I had a wife and child in Prague. I wasn't particularly devoted to them, but I was unable to part from them either. I was afraid of an impossible situation. I was afraid of Lucie's love and didn't know what I should do with it. I was scared of possible complications.

I set myself up as the angel bringing her salvation, when in fact I was merely another of those who corrupted her. I loved her once and then I turned from her. I acted as if I were bringing her forgiveness, while in reality she had the cause to forgive me. She was desperate, she wept when I left, and yet after a few years she came after me again and settled down here. She'd forgiven me. That much is clear. It hasn't happened to me often in my life, but this girl was in love with me. I held her life in my hands, her happiness in my power. And I ran away. No one ever wronged her as I did.

And now I find myself using supposed challenges from God as mere pretexts to extract myself from my human obligations. I'm afraid of women. I'm afraid of their warmth. I'm afraid of their constant presence. I was terrified of a life with Lucie just as I'm terrified at the thought of moving permanently into the teacher's two-room apartment in the next town.

Why did I volunteer to resign from the university fifteen years ago? I wasn't in love with my wife, who was six years older. I couldn't bear either the sound of her voice or the sight of her face. I couldn't stand the monotonous tick-tock of the clock at home. I couldn't live with her, but neither could I inflict on her the injury of a divorce, because she was a good girl and had never done me any wrong. And so I suddenly heard the saving voice of a challenge from above. I heard Jesus calling to me to forsake my nets.

God, is this really so? Am I really so miserably absurd? Deny it! Reassure me! Speak, God, speak louder! I cannot hear Thy voice among the babel of tongues!

VII

LUDVIK

WHEN, late that evening, I got back from Kostka's place to my hotel I was determined to leave for Prague first thing in the morning, since I had nothing left to hope for here. My ill-conceived mission in my hometown had come to an end. Unfortunately my thoughts were in such a whirl that I spent half the night tossing and turning on my creaky bed, unable to sleep. When I finally did drop off it was a disturbed sleep, and it wasn't until the early hours that I achieved anything deeper. I woke up late, almost nine o'clock, when the morning buses and trains had already left and there was no means of starting for Prague until around two in the afternoon. I was almost beside myself, like a man who's been shipwrecked; and suddenly I felt a great hunger for Prague, for my work, for the desk in my apartment, for my books. There was nothing to do about it; I had to grit my teeth and go down to the restaurant for my breakfast.

I entered with some caution, as I was afraid of bumping into Helena. She wasn't there, however. Evidently she was already romping around the next village with her tape recorder over her shoulder, annoying all the passersby with her microphone and her stupid questions. On the other hand the dining room was packed with people sitting noisily and smokily by their beers, black coffees, ryes, and cognacs. I could see that on this occasion, too, my hometown begrudged me a decent breakfast.

I went out into the street. The blue sky, the ragged clouds, the incipient closeness, the dust rising slightly, the wide, level square with its soaring tower—all this washed over me with the gloom of desolation. From the distance echoed a drunken chorus of some drawn-out Moravian chant; then Lucie emerged in my mind, and that incident of long ago spoke to my heart, through which so many women had passed without leaving a trace.

I strode across the dusty cobbles of the square and felt the oppressive weightlessness of the vacuum that lay over my life: Lucie, goddess of smoke, had yesterday turned to ashes a carefully calculated vengeance and in no time had turned even my own memories of myself into something pitiful and ridiculous, into a grotesque delusion, because what Kostka had told me testified that in all those years I'd never really known who Lucie was.

I'd always told myself with satisfaction that for me Lucie was something abstract, a legend and a myth, but now I knew that these would-be poetic terms hid an entirely unpoetic truth: I'd never known Lucie the way she really was, the way she was in and for herself. In my blind egoism I'd been aware only of those aspects of her being that were turned toward myself— my loneliness, my captivity, my yearning for tenderness and affection. She'd never been anything for me but a function of my own situation. So it was entirely logical that the instant the situation changed, *my* Lucie should vanish with it, that after fifteen years I shouldn't even have recognized her. She had long been for me—and I'd never thought of her except as a "being for me"—a different person, a stranger.

The message of my defeat had been trailing me for fifteen years, and now it had caught up with me. Kostka the eccentric, whom I'd never taken more than half seriously, had meant more to her, had done more for her, knew more about her, and loved her better than I'd ever done. To him she had revealed everything—to me nothing. He'd made her happy—I'd made her miserable. He'd known her physically—I'd never done so. And yet all I'd needed in order to possess the body I so desperately desired was one simple thing: to understand her, to learn how to treat her, to love her not only for what she was to me but for everything in her that didn't directly concern me, everything in which she existed as and for herself. I'd been unable to do this and had hurt both of us. A wave of self-reproach washed over me.

I remembered the bleak room with its single bed and the streetlamp shining into it through the grimy glass. I remembered Lucie's ferocious resistance. It was all like a bad joke. I'd taken her for a virgin, and she'd fought me because she wasn't and feared the moment when I'd discover the truth. Or her resistance had another explanation, one that corresponds to Kostka's view of Lucie. Her initial drastic sexual experiences had sickened her of the love act and had deprived it of all the significance most people ascribe to it, had emptied it entirely of affection and love. For this half woman, half child, the body was something ugly and love was something incorporeal; the soul engaged the body in a silent and dogged combat.

From the distance the drunken roar of the Moravian lament droned on, mingling with the dusty emptiness of the square and with my low spirits, reinforced by the hunger clamoring rudely from my insides. I tried the door of a milk bar but found it shut. A passerby told me, "The whole milk bar's at the festival today."

"At the Ride of the Kings?"

"Yes. They've set up a stall there."

I cursed and set off in the direction of the dirge. My rumbling stomach was leading me toward the folk festival—the festival I'd so studiously tried to avoid.

*   *   *

JAROSLAV

Tired. Tired ever since morning. As if I'd been carousing
all night. Yet I'd slept all night. Except that the way I slept
was like the skimmed milk of real sleep. Over breakfast I had
to struggle with my yawns. Then people began slowly drifting our way. There were Vladimir's companions and various
spectators. A young boy from the farm cooperative brought the
horse for Vladimir over to our backyard. Then in the midst of
it all Kalasek suddenly appeared, the cultural adviser to the
district council. I'd been at loggerheads with him for two years.
He was dressed in black and wore a ceremonial air. With him
was an elegant-looking woman, a features editor for Prague
radio. Apparently I was to go with them. The lady wanted to
tape some interviews for a program about the Ride of the
Kings.

Leave me out of it! I'm not going to play the fool. The radio
woman was all enthusiasm at meeting me personally, and of
course Kalasek joined in. He said it was my political obligation
to go. Silly fool. I began by resisting. I told them my son was to
be King today and that I wanted to be there while he was being dressed. Then Vlasta stabbed me in the back. She said it
was her job to get Vladimir ready. I was to go and do the tap-
ing.

In the end I went with them obediently. The radio woman
was staying in a room belonging to the rural council. There
she had her tape recorder and a young man to run errands for
her. She talked obsessively and kept laughing all the time.
Then she lifted the microphone to her mouth and asked
Kalasek the first question.

Kalesek coughed and began. The cultivation of folk art
was an inseparable constituent of Communist education. The
rural national committee understood this perfectly. For this
reason it lent its full support. It wished them every success and
had every sympathy with them. It thanked all those who took

part. The enthusiastic organizers and the enthusiastic school-children, whom we fully . . .

Boring. Boring. Always the same. For fifteen years I'd heard the same old crap. And now to hear it from Kalasek, who had absolutely no concern for folk art. For him it was simply a means to an end. A new charity to boast about. A directive to fulfill. A gimmick for boosting his own prestige. He hadn't lifted a finger for the Ride of the Kings and had honed our budget down by every penny he could. Yet the Ride of the Kings would be a feather in his cap. He was the lord and master of local culture. A former shop assistant who didn't know a violin from a guitar.

The interviewer stuck the microphone to her mouth. How well satisfied was I with this year's Ride of the Kings? I felt like laughing at her. The Ride hadn't even started yet! But it was her turn to laugh at me. I was such an experienced folk expert that I was certain to know how it would turn out.

I had an impulse to tell her exactly what I felt. That the Ride wouldn't be as good as in previous years. That every year folk art loses more supporters. That it was nearly moribund. The fact that some form of folk music was continually being played over the air shouldn't delude us. All those folk instrument bands and folk song and dance ensembles were more like opera or operetta or musical comedy—certainly not folk music. Imagine a folk instrument orchestra with a conductor, a score, and music stands. An almost symphonic instrumentation. What desecration! Real folk art is dead—yes, madame, dead.

I wanted to spill it all out into the mike, but in the end I said something completely different. The Ride of the Kings was splendid. The strength of folk art. The blaze of color. Congratulations and thanks to all those who took part. The enthusiastic organizers and schoolchildren, whom we fully . . .

I felt ashamed for talking the way they wanted me to. Am I such a coward? Or so well trained? Or so tired?

I was glad to get to the end of my piece, and made a hasty exit. I was looking forward to getting home again. There were quite a few idle spectators standing in the yard and all sorts of assistants decorating the horse with bows and ribbons. I wanted to see Vladimir getting ready. I went into the house, but the door to the living room, where he was being robed, was locked. I knocked and called out. Vlasta answered from inside, "You shouldn't be here. The King is being robed!" Why shouldn't I be there, damn it! "It's against the tradition," Vlasta answered. I don't know why it should be against the tradition for a father to be present while the King is being robed, but I didn't say so. I heard the concern in her voice and I was pleased that they were concerned with my world. My miserably lonely world!

So I went back into the yard and chatted with the people who were decorating the horse. It was a hefty cart horse from the farm. Patient and placid.

Then I heard crowd noises drifting from the street over the closed gates. There was shouting and banging. My moment had come. I was excited. I opened the gates and went out. The Ride of the Kings was marshaled in front of our house. Horses adorned with ribbons and streamers. Young riders in colorful costumes. It was just like twenty years ago, when they came for me. When they asked my father to give them his son to be King.

Right in front, up against the gates, were two pages on horseback, in women's costumes and with sabers in their hands. They were waiting for Vladimir, to accompany and guard him all day. Now a young man rode out of the band of riders, halted his horse just before me, and began with these verses:

> *Hear, everyone, hear!*
> *Gentle father, we have come hither to ask*
> *Whether you will give us your son to be King!*

Then he promised that the King would be well guarded. He would be conducted safely among the armies of his enemies. He would not be delivered up into their hands. They were armed for the fray. *Hear, oh, hear!*

I looked back. In the dark driveway of our house sat a figure on a beribboned horse. He was in woman's costume, with puckered sleeves and colored bands across the face. The King. Vladimir. Suddenly I forgot my weariness and dejection and felt at ease. The old King was sending the young one out into the world. I turned and went over to him. I was standing right by the horse and stood on tiptoe so that my mouth was as near as possible to the hidden face. "Good luck, Vladimir," I whispered to him. He didn't reply. He didn't move. Vlasta told me with a smile, "He's not supposed to answer you. He mustn't say a word until evening."

LUDVIK

It took me barely a quarter of an hour before I found myself in the village. In my youth it had been separated from the town by a belt of fields, but now the two had merged. The singing I'd heard from the town, tipsy and melancholy, now resounded in full force and proved to be a recorded voice issuing from loudspeakers fastened to houses or telegraph poles. Just outside the village they'd erected a triumphal arch with an immense paper banner bearing, in red ornamental letters, the inscription: WELCOME.

The people were crowded more thickly here, dressed for the most part in everyday clothes but with here and there a few old men in folk costume: high boots, white linen trousers, and embroidered shirts. Here the street widened into the village green. Between the road and a terrace of cottages there was now a wide swath of grass with trees dotted around, between which a few stalls had been set up, selling beer, lemonade, peanuts, chocolate, gingerbread, and frankfurters with mustard. In one the town's milk bar had its stand. The only alcohol being sold was beer, but most of the people looked drunk to me. They were jostling around the stands, getting in one another's way, gaping vacantly. Now and then someone would break into loud song, but this was always a senseless straining of the voice

(accompanied by a drunken raising of the hand), two or three
bars of song immediately drowned by the uproar in the marketplace and the invincible blast of the folk song from the loudspeakers. Although it was early and the Ride hadn't begun yet,
the marketplace was littered with waxed paper beer mugs and
paper plates covered with mustard.

The stand with milk and yogurt had a temperance aura
about it that discouraged business, so I was easily able to get
a mug of milk and a buttered roll before moving to a less
crowded spot. As I was drinking my milk, there was a com-
motion from the other end of the green. The Ride of the Kings
had entered the village.

Black hats with cockerel feathers, wide frilled sleeves on
white shirts, blue waistcoats with red tufts of wool, colored
paper ribbons fluttering from the horses—all these filled the
arena of the green. And now the buzz of voices and the song
from the loudspeakers were joined by new sounds: the whinny-
ing of horses and the calling of the horsemen.

> Hear, everyone, hear,
> Ye from up village, down village, here and across the fields,
> Ye that are gathered together this saint's-day Sunday,
> We have a pauper king, but greatly righteous,
> A thousand oxen he's had stolen
> From an empty farmyard . . .

Ear and eye alike were assaulted by confusion, in which everything competed for attention with everything else: the
folklore from the loudspeakers with the folklore on horseback;
the vivid colors of the costumes and horses with the ugly browns
and grays of the badly cut clothes worn by the spectators; the
artificial spontaneity of the fancifully attired men on the horses
with the artificial officiousness of the organizers as they ran
around in their red armbands among the horses and people,
trying to keep the chaos within bounds—by no means a simple
task, not just because of the unruliness of the spectators but
especially because the road hadn't been closed to traffic. The

organizers were merely standing at either end of the troop of riders and signaling the cars to slow down, so that cars and trucks and roaring motorcycles squeezed their way between the procession, spooking horses and riders alike.

Quite frankly, in trying so stubbornly to avoid taking part in this (or any other) folk event I'd been afraid of something quite different from what I now saw. I'd been prepared for tastelessness, for an unholy alliance of real folk art with fake, for inaugural addresses by stultifying orators, for all kinds of absurd modernizations—I wouldn't have been surprised to find the Ride of the Kings turned into something like the Ride of the Partisans. I'd been prepared for the worst kind of bombast and hypocrisy, but I hadn't expected this mournful, almost moving, *pathos*. It was in everything: in the handful of stalls, in the small but unruly and inattentive crowd, in the battle between the everyday traffic and the anachronistic ritual, in the frightened horses, in the loudspeakers bellowing their two unchanging folk songs and mingling with the racket of the motorcycles, completely drowning the young horsemen as they shouted their lines, the veins standing out on their necks.

I threw away my paper cup, and the Ride of the Kings, having displayed itself to the spectators on the village green, set off on a lengthy tour of the village. I knew it all well, because once, the last year of the war, I myself rode as a page, dressed in ceremonial woman's garb and with sword in hand, at the side of Jaroslav, who was then the King. I had no desire to indulge in sentimental memories, but somehow disarmed by the pathos of the Ride, I slowly made my way in the wake of the riders, who now spread out. In the center of the road was a cluster of three riders; in the middle the King and on either side a page, wearing a sword and dressed in women's clothes. Beside them trotted a few other riders from the King's company—the so-called ministers. The rest of the throng split into two independent wings, riding on either side of the street, and within each wing the duties of the riders were precisely defined. There were the standard-bearers, with their red flags stuck

into their thigh boots and fluttering along the horses' flanks;
the callers, crying out before every house their rhymed message about the *righteous yet pauper King* who'd had *three
thousand* stolen from an empty *coffer,* and three hundred *oxen*
stolen from an empty *farmyard;* and finally the collectors, who
called for gifts (*"For the King, old lady, for the King!"*) and
held out their cane baskets for contributions.

HELENA

Thank you, Ludvik. I've known you for just eight days and
I love you as I've never loved anyone else. I can think of nothing else, and I trust you, because if my mind deceived me, if
my emotions deceived me, if my soul deceived me, the body at
least is without deceit. The body is more honest than the soul,
and my body knows that it has never experienced anything
like yesterday—sensuality, affection, cruelty, pleasure, pain—
my body never dreamed of anything like it. Our bodies made
their vows, and now let our heads follow their dictates obediently. I've known you just eight days and I thank you, Ludvik.

I thank you too for coming at the most opportune moment,
for protecting me. Today the weather has been fine since early
morning, the sky is blue, everything went well in the morning,
and we walked over to the parents' house to record the Ride,
the calling upon the King, and on the way he came up to me
suddenly, and I was afraid. I didn't know he was here already,
that he'd come up from Bratislava so quickly, and I didn't expect he'd be so cruel. Imagine, Ludvik, he was mean enough to
bring her with him.

And like a fool, I'd believed to the last that my marriage was
not yet completely lost, that it could still be saved. Like a fool,
I'd almost have sacrificed even you for that ruined marriage
and would have refused to see you here. Like a fool, I almost
let myself be taken in by that sugary voice of his telling me he'd
stop off here for me on the way from Bratislava and that he
had a lot to say to me, that he wanted a candid talk. And then

he brought her with him, that child, that slut, a girl of twenty-two, thirteen years younger than me. It's so degrading to lose simply because I was born earlier. I felt so helpless I could have screamed. But I mustn't. I had to smile and shake hands with her politely. Thank you, Ludvik, for giving me that strength.

When we were alone for a moment, he told me that now we had a chance to talk it all over frankly among the three of us and that this would be the most honorable way. Honorable, honorable, I know all about his kind of honor. For two years now he's been angling for a divorce and he knows that with just the two of us he'll achieve nothing. He's relying on my embarrassment at confronting his girlfriend. He thinks I won't have the nerve to play the degrading role of the obstinate wife, that I'll break down and given in. I hate him. He calmly slips the knife between my ribs when I'm on an assignment, when I need to be calm and collected. He ought at least to have some respect for my work, to give it some consideration, yet this is the way it's been for years and years, I've always been bullied by him, I always lose, I'm always humiliated. But now I've learned to show a little spirit, now I've felt you and your love behind me, I felt you still in me and on me, and those fine colorful horsemen were all around me shouting lustily as if crying out that you are here, that life is here, that there *is* a future. I felt pride within me, the pride I'd nearly lost, pride that flooded over me, and I managed to smile sweetly and tell him, "I don't think there's any need for me to go to Prague with you. I wouldn't want to put you out and anyway I have the company car here. As for the agreement you wanted to discuss, that can be settled very quickly. I can introduce you to the man I want to live with and I'm sure that we can all come to an amicable arrangement."

Perhaps it was a crazy thing to do, but if it was, then let it stand. It was worth it for that moment of sweet pride, it was worth it. He immediately became far more amiable, was obviously relieved but was afraid I might not really mean it. He

asked me to repeat it and I told him your full name: Ludvik
Jahn, Ludvik Jahn, and finally I told him explicitly, "Don't
worry, honestly, I'm not going to stand in the way of our divorce. Don't worry, I wouldn't want you, even if you wanted
me." He replied that he was sure we'd remain good friends. I
smiled and said I didn't doubt it.

LUDVIK

Years ago when I played the clarinet in the band we used to
wonder just what the Ride of the Kings meant. Apparently
when the defeated Hungarian King Matyas was fleeing from
Bohemia to Hungary, his cavalry had to hide here, in rural
Moravia, from their Czech pursuers, and to maintain him and
themselves by begging. The Ride of the Kings is said to be a
reminder of this historic event, but you need only do a bit of
delving into old documents to realize that it's much older than
this. Where then did it come from and what does it mean?
Does it perhaps date from pagan times and is it a survival of the
rites of initiation at which boys were accepted as men? And
why are the King and his pages in women's attire? Is it a por-
trayal of how some army (either Matyas' or a much more ancient one) once led its leader through enemy country in disguise, or is it a survival of some old pagan superstition according to which transvestism protects one from evil spirits? Why
must the King not speak a word throughout? And why is the
event called the Ride of the Kings when there is only one king
involved? What does it all mean? There are a number of hy-
potheses—none of them proved. The Ride of the Kings is a
mysterious rite. No one entirely comprehends it, but just as
Egyptian hieroglyphs are the more beautiful for those who cannot read them and accept them as mere fanciful sketchings,
the Ride of the Kings is a beautiful thing perhaps for the same
reason—that its precise meaning has long since been lost.

And so, to my astonishment, the initial mistrust with which
I watched the Ride as they raggedly set out vanished, and all

at once I was completely enthralled by the colorful cavalcade
as it slowly moved from house to house. Also the loudspeakers
had finally grown silent and I could hear (if I ignored the occasional clatter of vehicles, which I've long since learned to do)
only the strange, polyphonic music of the verse invocations.

The Ride of the Kings straggled down the main street, being continually startled by the traffic, and then at a corner it
split up, one wing continuing straight ahead while the other
turned off into a little street, at whose end was a small yellow
cottage with a fence and a small front garden ablaze with flowers. After a certain amount of byplay a plump middle-aged
woman standing in front of the cottage went in and quickly returned with a bottle and a glass, into which she poured some
slivovitz and handed it to the horseman.

While the King's army was drinking and joking, the King
himself stood motionless and grave a short distance away with
his two pages, as if it was part of a king's lot to be swathed in
gravity and to stand alone and aloof in the midst of his clamorous troops. All three speechless horsemen were, as I said, in
women's clothes. They wore wide skirts and puckered
starched sleeves. On their heads the pages had richly orna-
mented bonnets, while the King wore a brilliant silver tiara,
hung with three long wide ribbons, blue on the edges and red
in the middle, which completely covered his face and gave him
a solemn and mysterious appearance.

I stood enchanted by this solemn trio; twenty years ago I
myself had sat on a garlanded horse just like them, but because on that occasion I'd experienced the Ride from the inside,
it was only now that I was really seeing it, and I couldn't tear
my eyes away. The King was only a few yards from me, looking like a statue under guard. Suddenly it occurred to me that
perhaps this was not a king at all, perhaps it was a queen; perhaps it was Queen Lucie who'd come to reveal herself to me in
her real form, because her real form was her hidden form.

And at the same moment it occurred to me that Kostka was
a crank, and that although everything he'd told me might con-

ceivably be true, it was quite uncertain. He knew Lucie, of course, he might even have known a lot about her, but he didn't know the vital fact: Lucie had really loved that soldier who'd attacked her in that borrowed apartment. I could scarcely take seriously Lucie's picking flowers out of some vague religious longing, when I remember that she picked them for me. And if she'd kept this hidden from Kostka as an inviolable secret, and also the whole sweet six months of our love together, then even he didn't know her. Moreover, it was quite uncertain whether she'd really moved to this town because of him; it could have been a mere coincidence. But it was also quite possible that she came here because of me, since she did after all know that this was my hometown! I felt that the report of her original raping was substantially true, but I now doubted its precision of detail. In Kostka's narrative truth and fairy tale mingled to produce a new legend—perhaps closer to the truth, perhaps more beautiful, perhaps more profound—which superimposed itself on the old.

I looked at the veiled King and I saw Lucie, unrecognized and unrecognizable, riding ceremoniously and mockingly through my life. Then something caught my attention, and my gaze fell directly on that of a man who'd evidently been watching me for some time and smiling. He said hello and walked up to me. He offered his hand and I pressed it. Then he turned and called to a girl whom I hadn't noticed. "What are you standing there for? Come on, I want to introduce you." The girl, lanky but good-looking with dark hair and dark eyes, came up to me and said, "Miss Broz." She gave me her hand and I said, "Jahn. Pleased to meet you."

"God, man, it's been years," said the man genially. It was Zemanek.

JAROSLAV

Tired. Tired. I couldn't stop feeling tired. The troupe had set out with the King for the village green, and I strolled slowly after them. I took deep breaths to overcome my fatigue.

I stopped with the neighbors who'd come out of their cottages to watch. Suddenly I felt I was just another staid, complacent old neighbor. That I'd never think of traveling again or any form of adventure. That I was hopelessly bound to the two or three streets where I lived.

I reached the green when the troupe had already started down the long main street. I wanted to wander along after them, but then I saw Ludvik. He was standing by himself on the grass verge, looking thoughtfully at the young fellow on the horse. Damn Ludvik! Why can't he go to hell! So far he's been avoiding me. Today it's my turn to avoid him. I turned my back on him and went over to a bench on the green under an apple tree.

I sat, listening to the invocations and watching. The Ride of the Kings gradually drifted away. It clung pathetically to both sides of the highway along which the cars and motorcycles were continually passing. A bunch of people were trailing after it. A miserably small crowd. From year to year fewer people came to the Ride. Though this year Ludvik is here. What *is* he doing here? Damn you, Ludvik! It's too late now. It's too late for everything. You've come like a bad omen. A dark foreboding. Seven crosses. Now of all times, when my Vladimir is King.

I averted my eyes. There was only a handful of people standing on the green by the stalls and around the tavern door. Most of them were drunk. Drunkards are the most loyal supporters of revivalist folk ventures. The last supporters. After all, they provide a noble pretext for getting drunk.

Then old man Pechacku came and sat beside me on the bench. He said it wasn't like old times. I had to agree. It wasn't. Gingerbread hearts on the horses' breasts! Tons of paper ribbon bought in the department store! Yes, old fellow, it was better centuries ago. No one then had to search for young men who might deign to take part in the Ride. No one then had to spend days beforehand holding meetings and arguing who should organize the Ride and who should receive the proceeds.

The Ride of the Kings used to gush forth over the life of the village like a spring. And after the war we wanted to help. We eagerly organized popular festivals. But a spring can't be organized. Either it gushes or it doesn't. You see, old fellow, now we're just squeezing it out, these songs of ours and the Rides and all that. These are just the final drops.

Ah, well. The Ride was no longer in sight. It had probably turned into some side street. But we could still hear the shouting. The invocations were magnificent. I closed my eyes and imagined myself for a moment living in another time. Another century. A long time ago. Then I opened them and told myself it was good after all that Vladimir was King. He is King of an almost extinct kingdom, but a most magnificent one. A kingdom to which I shall remain loyal to the end.

I got up from the bench. Someone called out a greeting. It was old Koutecky, Ludvik's adoptive father. I hadn't seen him for a long time. He was walking with difficulty, leaning on a stick. I'd never liked him but I suddenly felt sorry for his old age. "Where are you off to?" I asked. He said he took a constitutional every Sunday. "How did you like the Ride?" I asked him.

He shrugged elaborately. "Didn't even watch it."

"Why not?" I asked.

Again he shrugged in annoyance and it dawned on me then why he didn't watch it. Ludvik was among the spectators. Koutecky didn't want to meet him any more than I did.

"I'm not surprised," I said. "My son's in the Ride of the Kings, but even so I don't feel like trailing after it."

"Your son? What, your Vladimir?"

"Yes," I said, "he's riding as the King."

Koutecky said, "That's interesting."

"Why's that?" I asked.

"Very interesting," said Koutecky, and there was a twinkle in his eye.

"Why?" I asked again.

"Vladimir's with our Milos," said Koutecky. I had no idea

which Milos this might be. He explained that it was his grandson, his daughter's son.

"It's impossible," I said. "I saw him—I saw him a moment ago riding off on his horse!"

"I saw him too. Milos brought him over from your place on the back of his motorcycle," said Koutecky.

"Nonsense," I said, but then I asked, "Where did they go?"

"Well, since you don't know anything about it, I'm not going to be the one to tell you," said Koutecky, and he hobbled away.

LUDVIK

I'd never expected to meet Zemanek—Helena had told me he would be here, but not until the afternoon—and of course it was extremely unpleasant running into him. But there was no avoiding it. There he was standing in front of me, just as he used to be. His blond hair was as blond as ever, even though he no longer combed it back in long curls but had it cut short and brushed fashionably forward. He stood as erect as ever and he still arched his neck back in the same convulsive fashion, always with his head slightly inclined. He was just as jovial and complacent, invulnerable, endowed with the good favor of angels and with a young girl whose beauty immediately trained my recollections on the painful imperfection of the body with which I'd spent yesterday afternoon.

Hoping our encounter would be as brief as possible, I tried to answer all the trite conversational banalities he heaped on me with equally trite responses. He proclaimed again the fact that we hadn't seen each other for years and his surprise that after such a long interval we should meet "in such a godforsaken dump." I told him I was born here. He asked me to forgive him and said that in that case it was certainly not so forsaken as all that. Miss Broz laughed. I said I wasn't surprised to see him here because, if I remembered rightly, he'd always been a folklore enthusiast. Miss Broz laughed again and said

they hadn't come for the Ride of the Kings. Didn't she like
the ceremony? I asked. She said it didn't interest her. I asked
her why not. She shrugged her shoulders, and Zemanek said,
"Ludvik, old friend, times have changed."

Meanwhile the Ride had progressed, and two of the horsemen were struggling with their mounts, which had begun to
get nervy. One rider was shouting at the other, scolding him for
poor control of his mount, and the cries of "idiot" and "damn
fool" mingled drolly with the ritual of the festival. Miss Broz
said, "Funny if they were to bolt!" Zemanek laughed gaily at
this, but by this time the horsemen had managed to calm their
horses down, and again *"Hear, oh, hear,"* resounded calmly
and majestically through the village.

As we slowly followed the clamorous troupe through a side
street lined with gardens full of flowers I started hunting for
some natural and spontaneous pretext for saying good-bye to
Zemanek. Meanwhile I had to walk dutifully alongside his
pretty companion and continue the meaningless conversation.
I learned that in Bratislava the weather had been just as fine
early that morning as it was here. I learned that they'd come
in Zemanek's car and that just outside Bratislava they'd had to
change spark plugs. Then I learned that Miss Broz was one of
Zemanek's pupils. I knew from Helena that he lectured in
Marxism-Leninism at the university, but this didn't stop me
from asking him what he taught there. He told me he was
teaching philosophy, and his use of this word struck me as
symptomatic; a few years ago he would have said "Marxism,"
but in recent years this subject had declined so much in popularity, especially among the young, that Zemanek, for whom
popularity had always been of paramount importance, chastely
concealed Marxism behind the more general term. I expressed
surprise and said that I thought his field was biology.

Miss Broz now entered the conversation, announcing that
most teachers of Marxism had political pamphlets in their
heads instead of brains but that Pavel was entirely different.
Her words delighted Zemanek. He protested mildly, demon-

strating his modesty and at the same time inciting the young lady to further praise. In this way I learned that Zemanek was one of the most popular teachers in the university and that his pupils worshiped him for not being popular with university authorities, for always saying what he thought, for being courageous and sticking up for the young. Zemanek continued protesting mildly, and so I learned further details of the various battles Zemanek had fought in recent years—how the authorities had even wanted to throw him out for not sticking to the rigid, outdated curriculum and for wanting to acquaint the young people with everything taking place in modern philosophy (apparently this had led to a charge of wanting to smuggle "hostile ideology" into the country); how he'd defended a pupil from expulsion for some boyish prank (a fight with a policeman) which the chancellor, Zemanek's enemy, had characterized as a *political* misdemeanor; how afterward the girl students had held a secret poll to choose their favorite teacher, and how he'd won it. Zemanek was by now not even attempting to protest against this flood of praise, and I said, with an irony too subtle (alas) to be perceptible, that I could see what Miss Broz meant, as I remembered that Zemanek was immensely popular back in my own student days. Miss Broz agreed enthusiastically; she wasn't in the least surprised, as Pavel was a fabulous speaker and could cut any opponent to ribbons in debate. "What of it?" laughed Zemanek. "Even if I destroy them in debate they can cut *me* to ribbons in different and much more effective ways than any debate."

In the cocksure complacency of this last remark I saw the Zemanek I knew. But the *content* of it staggered me. It was evident that he'd completely abandoned his former views, and that if today I had anything to do with him I would in any conflict, like it or not, find myself on his side. This was horrible and completely unexpected, even though such an about-face was nothing miraculous. On the contrary, it was very common and had been performed by many others, while the whole society was doing the same thing more gradually. It was only in Zemanek that I hadn't expected such a change. He'd become petrified in my memory in the form in which I'd last seen him, and I now furiously denied him the right to be any different.

There are people who claim to love humanity, while others hint that you can love only in the singular, only individuals. I agree with this latter view, and would add that what goes for love goes for hate, too. Man, pining for equilibrium, balances the weight of the evil which has been piled on his back with the weight of his hatred. But just try directing hatred at mere abstract principles—at injustice, fanaticism, cruelty—or, if you've managed to find the human principle itself hateful, then try to hate mankind! Such hatreds are beyond human capacity. And so man, conscious of his limited power, in the end always seeks to relieve his anger by concentrating it upon a single individual.

This was why Zemanek's reversal had given me such a shock. It suddenly occurred to me that he was capable any minute now of admitting the profound change in himself and of asking me for forgiveness in its name. This was terrible. What was I to say to him? What answer should I give? How was I to explain to him that I couldn't make my peace with him? That in doing so I'd immediately lose my inner balance? That one of the arms of my internal scales would suddenly have shot upward? That by hating him I was balancing the weight of evil that had smothered my youth, my life? That in him I saw personified all evil? How was I to explain to him that I *needed* to hate him?

JAROSLAV

The narrow street was full of horses. I saw the King from a few yards away. He was sitting on his horse some distance from the others. Two other boys on horseback, his pages, were at his side. I was confused. True, he had Vladimir's slightly bent back. He was sitting calmly as if without interest. Is it he? Perhaps. But it might just as easily be someone else.

I worked my way closer to him. I had to recognize him. Didn't I have the way he held himself, his every gesture, inscribed in my memory? Besides, I love him, and love has its own instinct.

I was standing right beside him. I could have spoken to him. It was so simple. But it would have been no use. The King is not supposed to speak.

Then the Ride of the Kings swept on to the next house. Now I'd know him! The horse's sudden movement forward was bound to make him move in some way that would betray him. As the horse stepped forward the King did in fact straighten up slightly, but the movement gave me no indication of who was behind the veil. The garish ribbons across his face were frustratingly opaque.

LUDVIK

The Ride of the Kings had advanced past a few more houses and we continued to follow it, while our conversation leaped to other topics. Miss Broz had shifted from Zemanek to herself and was holding forth about how much she loved hitchhiking. She spoke about it with such enthusiasm (somewhat affected) that I could see at once that she was making a case for her generation. Every generation has its own particular passions, loves, and interests, which it clings to tenaciously, to differentiate it from older generations and to confirm itself in its uniqueness. I've always disliked kowtowing to the mentality of a whole generation, and as Miss Broz developed her argument, which I've now heard at least ten times from people her age, about how mankind is divided into those who give lifts (freethinking, adventurous, humanists) and those who don't (inhumane, monstrous, Socialist bourgeois), I jokingly named her the "hitchhiking dogmatist." She answered sharply that she was no dogmatist, or revisionist or sectarian, or deviationist, that she was neither class-conscious nor otherwise, that these were all terms invented by us, which belonged to us, and which to *them* were alien.

"Yes," said Zemanek, "they are different. I'm *glad* to say they are different. Even their vocabulary is different. Neither our successes nor our failures interest them. You wouldn't believe this, but in the entrance exams for the university the young people don't even know what the Trials were. Stalin is just a name to them, and Bukharin, Kamenev, Rajk, are not even names. Just imagine, most of them do not even know who Clementis was."

"That's what seems so dreadful to me," I said.

"It doesn't reflect on their education. For them this is liberation. They simply haven't admitted our world into their consciousness. They've refused it and everything it stands for."

"Blindness has given way to blindness."

"I wouldn't say so. They impress me. I like them *because* they're different. They love their bodies; we neglected them. They love travel; we stayed put. They love adventure; we sat our lives out at meetings. They love jazz; we produced an insipid imitation of folk music. They're selfishly devoted to themselves; we wanted to save the world. Yet with our messianic vision we almost destroyed it. Perhaps they with their selfishness will save it."

JAROSLAV

Can it be possible? The King! That mounted figure, veiled in bright colors! How many times have I seen him and imagined him! The most intimate of figures! And now it has changed into reality and all intimacy is gone. Suddenly it's just a colored chrysalis and I don't know what's inside. What intimacy can there be in this real world if it is not my King?

My son. The nearest person to me. I am standing in front of him and I don't know whether it's he or not. What do I know, if I don't even know this? What certainty can I have in this world if I cannot be certain about this?

*   *   *

LUDVIK

While Zemanek was eulogizing the younger generation, I was watching Miss Broz, finding her to my sorrow an attractive and friendly girl and experiencing an envious regret that she wasn't mine. She was walking at Zemanek's side, talking away, taking him by the hand every other moment, turning confidentially toward him, and I was reminded again that since Lucie I'd had no girl to love and respect. Life had mocked me by sending me, in the form of this man's lover, a reminder of the grotesque sexual contest in which only the day before I'd mistakenly thought I'd defeated him.

The more I liked Miss Broz, the more I realized how completely typical she was of her generation, for whom my contemporaries and I merged into a single amorphous mass, all deformed, as far as they were concerned, with the same incomprehensible jargon, the same ultrapolitical thinking, the same anxieties (that they considered cowardice), the same strange experiences from a dark and already distant era. In their view it's no longer even worth making the distinction between those of us who contributed to the oppression of that period and those who tried to defy it.

In that moment I suddenly became aware that the similarity between myself and Zemanek didn't rest merely in the fact that Zemanek had changed his views, bringing them more in line with my own. The way Miss Broz and her contemporaries regarded us, we resembled each other even when we were at each other's throats. I suddenly felt that if I were reluctantly forced to tell Miss Broz the story of my expulsion from the Party it would appear too remote, too much like *literature*, and that in the telling both Zemanek and myself would appear as equally unlikable—equally earnest, equally monstrous. I saw the healing waters of time closing over our dispute, which I'd felt to be still contemporary and alive. And time, as we all know, can smooth over the difference between entire epochs, let alone two unhappy individuals. But I fought desperately against accepting time's peacemaking. I am not living in eternity. I'm anchored to the trifling thirty-seven years of my own life, and I have no wish to be detached from them, in the way Zemanek detached himself when he was so quick to embrace the attitudes of his juniors.

And if Zemanek were to lean over to me confidentially and begin talking about what has been, and ask for reconciliation, I'd refuse him. Yes, I'd refuse reconciliation, even if it were mediated by Miss Broz, by all her contemporaries, by time itself.

JAROSLAV

Tired. Suddenly I wanted to say good-bye to the whole thing. To go away and stop worrying about it all. I no longer want to remain in this world of material things, which I don't understand and which deceive me. There exists another world. A world where I'm at home. There is the road, the briar bush, the deserter, the wandering minstrel, and Mother.

Then I attempted to control myself. I must. I must bring to its conclusion my quarrel with the world of material things. I must look into the very abyss of all error and deception.

Should I ask someone? The horsemen from the Ride? Should I make myself a laughingstock? I remembered this morning. The robing of the King. And at once I knew where I must go.

LUDVIK

"We have a pauper king, but greatly righteous," the horsemen were calling from a few houses ahead of us, and we followed them. The richly beribboned backsides of the horses bobbed up and down in front of us, blue, pink, green, and violet, and Zemanek suddenly pointed in their direction. "There's Helena." I looked, but all I could see was the colorful trappings of the horses. Zemanek pointed again. "There." Then I saw her half concealed behind a horse and felt myself blushing.

The way Zemanek had pointed her out—not as "my wife" but as "Helena"—showed he knew that I knew her.

Helena was standing on the edge of the pavement and holding a microphone in her outstretched hand. A wire ran from it to the tape recorder hanging over the shoulder of a young man in leather jacket and jeans, wearing large earphones. We stopped a short way away from them. Zemanek said, suddenly and out of the blue, that Helena was a marvelous woman, that she still looked fabulous and was very competent as well, and that he wasn't surprised we got on so well together.

I felt my cheeks hot. Zemanek hadn't intended his remark as an attack. On the contrary, he'd said it in a most affable tone, and I was also left in no doubt as to the real state of affairs by the way Miss Broz was looking at me, giving me significant, smiling glances, as if bent on showing that she was entirely sympathetic, if not directly in alliance.

Meanwhile Zemanek went on praising his wife, trying to make it plain, by hints and innuendos, that he knew everything but intended no trouble, since he was perfectly liberal as far as Helena's private life was concerned. To give his words an air of nonchalance he pointed out the young man carrying the tape recorder and told me that the boy ("Doesn't he look like a big beetle with those earphones on?") had already been dangerously in love with Helena for two years and that I ought to keep my eye on him. Miss Broz laughed and asked how old he would have been two years ago. Zemanek said seventeen— old enough for falling in love. Then he declared jokingly that of course Helena was not a cradle robber but a boy like that would get more and more furious the less successful he was and would be sure to put up a fight. Miss Broz, entering into the spirit of this charade, observed that I'd obviously know how to handle him.

"I'm not so sure about that," said Zemanek with a smile.

"Don't forget I've worked down in the mines. I've still got a few muscles from those days."

"Have you been down in the mines?" asked Miss Broz.

"These twenty-year-olds"—Zemanek stuck doggedly to his topic—"are really dangerous when they're in a gang. They can ruin anyone they take a dislike to."

"For how long?" asked Miss Broz.

"Five years."

"When was that?"

"I came out nine years ago."

"Oh, that's a long time. Your muscles will have gone all flabby by now," she said, wanting to add her own little joke to the friendly banter. As it happened, I was thinking at that moment of how my muscles had certainly not gone flabby, that I was still in condition, that I could have smashed this blond creature to smithereens, and—most important and most depressing—that my muscles were all I had in case I should decide to pay my old debt.

Again I imagined Zemanek turning jovially toward me and asking me to forget all that had happened between us, and I felt double-crossed; Zemanek's desire for forgiveness would be supported not only by his change of views, not only by time and its bird's-eye view of matters, not only by Broz and her contemporaries, but by Helena too (yes, now they were all on his side!). Because if Zemanek forgave me my adultery, then this was just a bribe for me to forgive him.

As I visualized his blackmailer's face, cocksure with the certainty of his powerful allies, I felt such a desire to hit him that I could actually visualize it: the shouting, whirling horsemen, the sun a splendid gold, Miss Broz making some inane comment, and before my furious eyes the blood pouring down Zemanek's self-satisfied face.

Yes, but this was all imagination. What would I really do if he were to ask me to forgive him?

I realized with a shock that I'd do nothing.

Meanwhile we'd come up to Helena and her technician, who was removing his earphones. "Have you met already?" Helena looked surprised to see me with Zemanek.

"We've known each other for a long time."

"We know each other from our student days," said Zemanek. "We were in the same college," said Zemanek, and I saw this as one of the last bridges across which he was leading me toward that ignominious calvary where he'd ask me for my forgiveness.

"Well, that's a remarkable coincidence," said Helena.

"That's the way it is in this world," said the technician, to demonstrate that he was equally worldly.

"I haven't introduced you," Helena realized and said, "This is Jindra, Jindra Kadlecka."

I shook hands with Jindra (an ungainly freckled young man), and Zemanek said to Helena, "Miss Broz and I had intended taking you back with us, but I can see now that this wouldn't suit you, that you'd rather go back with Ludvik . . ."

"Are you coming with us?" asked the young man in jeans, and he hardly sounded inviting.

"Is your car here?" Zemanek asked.

"I haven't got a car," I replied.

"Then come with us, and you'll be comfortable and in the best of company," he said.

"I can do eighty so don't worry," said the jeans.

"Jindra!" cried Helena.

"You *could* come with us," said Zemanek, "but I imagine your new girlfriend gets priority over your old friend." He called me his "friend" casually, and I was certain that the dishonorable truce was only a few steps away. Zemanek had grown silent, as if hesitating, and it looked as if any moment now he'd turn to me and ask to speak to me alone. I hung my head as if laying it on the block, but I was wrong. Zemanek looked at his watch and said, "I haven't much time—we've got to be in Prague by five. So I'd better say good-bye. Bye, Helena." He gave Helena his hand, then said good-bye to the technician and me and shook hands with us all. Miss Broz shook hands too, took Zemanek's arm, and they were gone.

They were gone. I couldn't tear my eyes from them. Zemanek was walking tall with his proud, victorious blond head

held high and his brunette floating at his side. She was beautiful from the back too. She walked lightly, I liked her—liked
her almost painfully, because her departing beauty was icily
indifferent to me, just as Zemanek had been indifferent (despite his affability and his friendly reminiscences), just as my
entire past was indifferent—the past I'd made a rendezvous
with in my own hometown in order to be revenged on it, but
which had simply strode past me unseeing, as if it didn't
know me.

I was stifled by humiliation and shame. I wanted nothing
more than to disappear, isolate myself, wipe out the whole
sordid incident, the stupid joke, wipe out Helena and Zemanek, wipe out the day before yesterday, yesterday, and today,
wipe it out so completely that not a trace remained. "Do you
mind if I speak to Mrs. Zemanek alone for a moment?" I asked
the technician.

I took Helena aside. She wanted to explain something, she
said something about Zemanek and his girl, she apologized
confusedly for having had to tell him everything. Nothing
touched me. I was consumed by a single desire, to be out of this
place, to be away from here and from the whole affair, to put
an end to it all. I knew I oughtn't to deceive Helena any
longer. She was quite innocent in the affair, and I'd acted des-
picably, for I'd turned her into a mere object, into a stone which
I'd tried—and failed—to throw at someone else. I was stifled
by the ridiculous failure of my revenge and the vileness of my
own behavior, and I was determined, even at this late hour, to
call a halt to it. However, it was no use trying to explain everything. Not only would I have hurt her bitterly with the truth,
but she would probably not even have been able to understand
it. So I resorted to the barest bones of the issue. I repeated to
her several times that this was our last time together, I wouldn't
be seeing her again, I didn't love her, and she must understand
this.

But it was far worse than I'd imagined. Helena turned pale

and started shaking, wouldn't believe me, wouldn't let me go. I went through a minor martyrdom before I could finally get rid of her and make my escape.

HELENA

All around me there were horses and streamers, and I stood there, just stood there for a long time, and then Jindra came over to me, took my hand, and squeezed it and asked me, "What's the matter?" and I let him hold my hand and said, "Nothing, Jindra, there's nothing the matter, why should there be?" and my voice was forced and high and I went on in a strange headlong way, "What else have we got to record? We've got the invocations, we've got two interviews, and I only have to do a commentary." So I went on talking mindlessly, and he stood there silent beside me, crushing my hand.

He'd never touched me before, he was always too shy, but everyone knew he was in love with me, and now he was standing beside me and squeezing my hand, and I was rambling obsessively on about the program. I was thinking about Jindra and how funny it was, then it occurred to me to wonder what I looked like to Jindra, whether the shock made me ugly. Maybe not. I wasn't crying, just upset, nothing more . . .

"Jindra, could you please leave me alone for a moment? I'll just go and write a commentary and then we'll record it." He held me a little longer and kept asking gently, "What's the matter, Helena, what's the matter?" but I twisted away from him and went over to the council offices where we'd borrowed a room. I went there and at last I was by myself, in an empty room. I collapsed on the chair, put my head on the table, and just stayed there for a while. My head ached painfully. I opened my bag to see if there was anything I could take. I don't know why I opened it because I knew I had nothing, but then I remembered that Jindra carries all sorts of pills around with him, and his lab coat was hanging on the hook. I put my hand in his pockets and, yes, there was a bottle of some sort, yes, it was for headaches, toothache, sciatica, and neuritis. It was no tranquilizer, but at least it would ease my head.

I went to the tap in the corner of the next room and poured some water in a shot glass and took two tablets. Two is enough, that should help, of course aspirin can't *really* help unless I were to take the whole bottle, because aspirin in large quantities is poisonous and Jindra's bottle was nearly full. It would be enough.

It was only an idea, a sudden flash, but it kept coming back to me and I couldn't help thinking, why was I alive at all, what was the sense in my going on, but it's not true really, I didn't really think anything of that sort, I was hardly thinking at all. I just imagined myself not living and I suddenly felt such bliss, such strange bliss that I wanted to laugh and I did in fact start laughing.

I put one more tablet on my tongue, I had no intention of poisoning myself, I just squeezed the bottle in my hand and told myself that I had my death within my grasp, and I was enthralled by the simplicity of it, I felt I was gradually approaching an abyss, not to jump into it, just to look down. I poured the glass full of water, took the tablet, and went back into our room. The window was open and the sound of *"Hear, oh, hear,"* still floated in the distance, but mingled with the racket of cars, of trucks and motorcycles—cycles deafening everything beautiful in this world, everything I believed in and lived for. The noise was unbearable and so was the pathetic feebleness of the voices, and so I closed the window and again I felt the long, lingering pain in my soul.

All his life Pavel never hurt me as much as you, Ludvik, hurt me in a single minute. Pavel I forgive, him I understand, his flame is quickly consumed and he has to seek fresh pastures, a new audience, a new public. He hurt me, but now through this fresh pain I see him without hatred, as his mother might— a showman, a comedian—and I smile at his attempts these last few years to dodge out of my arms. You can go, Pavel, you can go, you I understand, but you, Ludvik, I don't understand, you came to me in a mask, you came to resurrect me and, once resurrected, to destroy me. For you I have only curses, I curse you and I ask you to come, to come to me and have mercy.

God, can it just be some terrible misunderstanding? Maybe Pavel told you something when you were alone together, I just don't know. I asked you about it, I begged you to explain why you don't love me anymore, I didn't want to let you go, four times I held you back, but you wouldn't listen, you just said it was all over, finished, definitely, irrevocably. All right, so it's over. In the end I agreed and my voice went metallic, as if it was someone else talking, and I said in my metal voice, "Have a good trip then." It's silly, I don't know why I wanted you to have a good trip, but it just came out. "Have a good trip then, have a good trip then . . ."

Maybe you don't know the way I love you, you can't know how much I love you. Maybe you think I'm just another married woman looking for adventure, and you don't understand that you're my destiny, my life, my everything. Maybe you'll find me here lying under a white sheet and then you'll understand you've killed the most precious thing you ever had in your life . . . or you'll come, oh, my God, and I'll still be alive, and you'll be able to save me again and you'll be kneeling and crying, and I'll be stroking your hands, your hair, and I'll forgive you, I'll forgive you everything . . .

LUDVIK

There was nothing else to do. I'd had to undo that whole sorry episode—that bad joke—which, not content with itself, had gone on monstrously multiplying into greater and greater grotesquery. I wanted to erase the entire day, all the events that had only occurred because I'd overslept and been unable to get away. But I also wanted to erase everything leading up to it, the whole stupid, misconceived attempt on Helena.

I rushed away as though I could hear Helena's pursuing footsteps, and I thought: Even if I were able to cancel out these few useless days from my life, what good would that be, when the entire course of my life was conceived in error, through the bad joke of the postcard—that accident, that absurdity?

How glad I'd be to reverse the whole course of my life! Yet by what power could I do so, when the mistakes it grew from were not only my own? Who was at fault when my postcard was taken seriously? Who was to blame when Alexej's father—today, incidentally, long since rehabilitated, but nonetheless dead for that—was arrested and sentenced? The mistakes were so universal that they couldn't be regarded simply as exceptions or aberrations in the order of things. Who then *was* at fault? History? Divinely rational history? Why should it have been a mistake on her part? What if history plays jokes? Then I realized how feeble it was to want to annul my own joke when throughout my life I'd been involved in a monumental joke— all-embracing, unfathomable, and utterly irrevocable.

On the now deserted village green I saw a big placard announcing in red letters that today at four in the afternoon a cymbalo band would give a concert in the open-air restaurant. Next to the placard was a door into a tavern, and since it was lunchtime and I had almost two hours left before my bus was due to leave I went in.

HELENA

I wanted so much to move just an inch nearer the precipice, I wanted to bend under the railing and stare down into it, as if that could bring me solace and reconciliation, as if down there at least, if nowhere else, down there at the bottom of the pit, we might find each other and be together without misunderstandings, without malicious people, without old age, without sorrow, forever. I went into the other room again, and now I'd taken four tablets. That's nothing, I'm a long way from the edge yet, I can't even touch the railing. I poured the remaining tablets onto my palm. Then I heard someone opening the door, and I threw the tablets into my mouth and gulped them down. It was too much dry stuff at once, and I felt them grating painfully against my throat, even when I'd drunk as much as I could.

It was Jindra. He asked me how the commentary was coming. All of a sudden I was another person, the confusion had vanished, that metallic alien voice was gone, and I was purposeful and decisive. "Oh, Jindra, I'm glad you've come. I'd like you to do something for me." He blushed and said he'd do anything for me and he was glad I felt all right again. "Yes, I'm all right now. Wait just a minute. I want to jot something down," and I sat down and took some paper and started writing: *Ludvik, my dearest, I loved you body and soul, and now my body and soul have nothing left to live for. Farewell, I love you, good-bye, Helena.* I didn't even reread what I'd written. Jindra was sitting facing me, watching me, unaware of what I was doing. I quickly folded the paper and wanted to put it in an envelope, but there was none. "Jindra, do you by any chance have an envelope?"

He calmly went over to the cabinet by the table, opened it, and began rummaging around.

At any other time I'd have told him off for going through someone else's things, but at that moment I wanted an envelope, quickly. He gave me one with the local council stamp on it. I put the letter inside, sealed it, and wrote *Ludvik Jahn* on the envelope. "Jindra, do you remember that man who was with us when my husband and the young lady were there? Yes, that's right, the dark one. I can't go now and I'd like you to find him and give him this."

Again he took my hand, poor boy, I don't know what he was thinking, how he could have interpreted my excitement. He could never have guessed what it was about, he just sensed something bad happening to me. He held my hand tightly, and all of a sudden it seemed so dreadfully sad, and then he bent down and took me in his arms and pressed his lips against mine. I wanted to stop him, but he held me close and it occurred to me that this was the last man I'd ever kiss, and I suddenly felt reckless, returned his embrace, and opened my lips to feel his tongue on mine and his hands on my body. In that moment I had an intoxicating sense of absolute freedom, a sense that nothing mattered anymore, because I'd been deserted by everybody and my world had turned upside down and so I could do exactly as I wanted. I was free like the girl we'd fired from the institute. There was nothing to distinguish her from me; my world was shattered and I'd never put it together again, I no longer had anything to be true for, or anyone to be true to. Suddenly I was completely free like that little technician, that slut who was in a different bed every night. If I were to live on I, too, would be in a different bed every night. I felt Jindra's tongue in my mouth. I was free, I knew I could love him, I wanted to love him, love him anywhere, here on the table or on the bare floor, now, at once, without delay, to make love for the last time. But Jindra was already on his feet, smiling proudly, saying he was off and would hurry back.

LUDVIK

In the garden at the back, under a linden tree, there was an empty table; and here I sat down. A pathetic *"Hear, oh, hear,"* resounded now from such a distance that by the time it reached the tavern garden it sounded illusory. And this air of unreality made me think that everything around me was not of the present but of the past—a past fifteen, twenty years old, a past epitomized in the cries of *"Hear, oh, hear."* Lucie was the past, Zemanek was the past, and Helena was just a stone I'd wanted to throw at the past. I saw myself as a man on a moving staircase who runs against the movement. But the staircase was moving faster than I was and was slowly bearing me farther from my goal—away from the past of the political trials, the past of assembly halls where hands are raised, the past of fear, the past of black brigades and Lucie—the past that had bewitched me, that I was trying to unravel, and that prevented me from living as a man should live, with his face turned to the future.

And the main bond with which I'd tried to tie myself to the past was vengeance. But vengeance, as these three days had demonstrated, was just as useless as my running backward on time's moving staircase. Yes, it was when Zemanek was reading Fucik's *Notes from the Gallows* in the college lecture hall that I should have gone up to him and punched him in the face, then and only then. Today we were a different Jahn and a different Zemanek, so that if I struck out now, years later, my blow would be completely incomprehensible, would attain a completely different, unintentional and alien significance, and could be deflected in every conceivable direction, in a way I couldn't even control, let alone justify.

I cut into the large serving of veal on my plate, and again the *"Hear, oh, hear"* reached my ears, carrying faintly and mournfully across the village roofs. I imagined the veiled King and his cavalry, and my heart contracted at the incomprehensibility of human gestures.

For many centuries young men have been riding forth in Moravian villages just like today, with strange messages whose symbolic language they pronounce with a moving loyalty and a total lack of comprehension. Some long-dead people certainly had something important to say; and today they're revived in their descendants like deaf and dumb orators speaking to their audiences in fine but opaque gestures. Their message will never be decoded, not only because there is no key to it, but because people have no patience to listen in an age when the accumulation of messages old and new is so relentlessly unending. Thousands of deaf and dumb Rides of Kings will set out with their piteous and incomprehensible messages, and no one will have the time to hear them out.

I sat in the corner of the garden restaurant over my empty plate, having cleaned it without realizing, and I saw that I too had been submerged in the inescapable and boundless ocean of human forgetfulness. The waiter came and cleared away, stopping to brush a few crumbs off my tablecloth before hurrying to another table. I was seized with regret for the day, not only because it had been wasted, but because not even its futility would remain. It would be forgotten together with this table, with the fly buzzing around my head, the yellow pollen scattered on the tablecloth by the flowering linden, and the ill-natured service so characteristic of the society I live in. Even that society itself would be forgotten; but long before that its mistakes and errors and injustices would have been forgotten, the ones that had hypnotized me, on which I'd fed and which I'd vainly attempted to redress.

I took another careful glance around me because I knew that the linden tree would be forgotten, and the table, and the people at the table, and the waiter and this tavern, which uninviting enough from the street, was pleasantly overgrown with the vine on its garden side. I looked at the open door of the passage into which the waiter had just vanished, and from which there now emerged a youth in leather jacket and jeans. He stepped into the garden and looked around. Then he saw me and headed in my direction. It wasn't until several seconds had passed that I recognized him as Helena's technician.

It's a painful situation when a loving but unloved woman threatens to come back, and so when the boy gave me the envelope ("From Mrs. Zemanek"), my first thought was to postpone reading it. I told him to have a seat; he did, leaning his elbow on the table and yawning contentedly toward the sunbathed linden tree. And I put the envelope on the table and asked if he'd like a drink.

He shrugged his shoulders. I suggested vodka, but he refused, saying he was driving and adding that if I wanted one he'd be content to watch. I didn't, but since the envelope was lying on the table in front of me, and I didn't want to open it, any alternative seemed welcome. So I asked the waiter as he went past to bring me a vodka.

"You don't happen to know what Helena wants, do you?" I asked.

"How should I know? Read the letter."

"Anything urgent?"

"Do you think she made me memorize it in case I was attacked?"

I took the envelope between my fingers—it was office stationery with a printed heading: LOCAL NATIONAL COMMITTEE—then put it back on the table in front of me and, not knowing what to say, remarked: "Shame you don't drink."

"It's a case of your own safety," he said. I took this as a hint; obviously the boy wanted to clarify his return journey and his chances of being alone with Helena. He was a nice enough fellow; his redeemably childish face—abnormally small, pale, and freckled with a short turned-up nose—mirrored everything he was thinking. This boyish appearance could hardly be pleasing to a young man of twenty, because at that age it was a sort of disqualification which, like the boy officer in our camp, he felt obliged to disguise in every possible way: by his dress (his leather jacket was broad-shouldered, a good fit, and well sewn) and by his behavior (he acted self-assured, even arrogant, at times with exaggerated indifference). Unfortunately, in this disguise he was continually betraying himself: he blushed, he couldn't quite control his voice, which at the slightest excitement tended to break, he couldn't even control his eyes and his gestures (he'd wanted to indicate his unconcern about whether I was going to Prague with them or not, but when I now assured him I'd be staying here his eyes lighted up openly).

A moment later, when the waiter by mistake brought to our table two vodkas instead of one, the boy said there was no need for him to take it away again, as he'd drink it after all. "I wouldn't leave you to drink on your own," he said, and raised his glass, "Your health!"

"And yours!" I said, and we clinked glasses.

We started talking and I learned that the young man was expecting to leave in about two hours, as Helena wanted to go over the material they'd recorded, adding her own commentary where necessary, so that the whole thing could be broadcast tomorrow. I asked what it was like working with her. He blushed again gently and answered that Helena knew what she was doing but was too tough on her colleagues, as she was always ready to work overtime and disregarded the fact that others might be in a hurry to get home. I asked him if that applied to him. He said no—actually he was thoroughly enjoying himself here. Then, taking advantage of the fact that I'd started talking about Helena, he asked casually, "How do you know Helena?" I told him and he went on pumping me. "Helena's really nice, isn't she?"

Particularly when the conversation was about Helena he assumed a self-satisfied air, which I again put down to his wish for a disguise, since his hopeless adoration of Helena was evidently common knowledge and he had to fight constantly against being labeled the unrequited lover. Although I didn't take his confidence altogether seriously, nevertheless it did something to lighten the load of the letter lying in front of me, so that I finally picked it up and opened it: *My body and soul . . . have nothing to live for . . . Good-bye . . .*

I saw the waiter at the other end of the garden and shouted, "Check, please!" The waiter nodded but didn't allow himself to be deflected from his orbit and vanished into the passage again.

"Come on—there's no time to lose," I said to the boy. I got up and hurried across the garden, and he followed me. We went through the passage to the exit, so that the waiter had to run after us.

"Veal, soup, two vodkas," I dictated.

"What's going on?" asked the young man in a subdued voice.

I paid the waiter and asked the boy to take me quickly to Helena. We set out at a fast walk.

"What's happened?" he asked.

"How far is it?" I asked.

He pointed some way ahead of us, and I changed from a walk to a run; we were both running now and quickly arrived at the council building, a single-story structure, whitewashed, with a gate and two windows on the street. We went inside. From the dark hallway there was a door on the right, opening onto an uninviting sort of office. Under the window two desks were drawn up close together. The tape recorder lay on one of them, open, along with a pad of paper and a lady's handbag (yes, it was Helena's). There were chairs by both desks and in the corner of the room a metal coatrack. Two coats were hanging from it: Helena's blue trenchcoat and a man's dirty raincoat.

"This is it," said the young man.

"Is this where she gave you the letter?"

"Yes."

But the office was now hopelessly empty. I called out, "Helena!" and was alarmed to hear how uneasy I sounded. There was no reply. I called again, "Helena!" and the boy asked, "Has she done something to herself?"

"Looks that way," I said.

"Is that what the letter was about?"

"Yes," I said. "You weren't given any other room?"

"No."

"What about the hotel?"

"We checked out this morning."

"She must be here then," I said, and now I heard the boy's voice break as he called anxiously, "Helena!"

I opened the door into the adjoining room. It was another office: desk, wastebasket, three chairs, and a closet. There was no other door leading out; the two offices were evidently the only rooms in the building.

We went back to the first. I took the pad off the desk and thumbed through it. There were some nearly illegible notes concerning the Ride of the Kings, but no message, no further parting words. I opened the handbag: a handkerchief, wallet, lipstick, keys, powder, two leaking cigarettes, a lighter. There was no medicine or poison bottle. I tried feverishly to think what Helena could have done, and the most likely thing was poison; but in that case there should have been a bottle some-where. I went to the coatrack and rummaged in the pockets of her trenchcoat. They were empty.

"There must be somewhere else! A toilet! Or a cellar!" I said, and we went out into the hallway again. At the end was a door that the boy opened. The door led to a small backyard, with a cage of rabbits in one corner. Beyond the yard was an overgrown garden with fruit trees standing in the thick uncut grass. At the end of the garden in the shadow of an apple tree I saw an ancient wooden outhouse. I ran toward it.

There was no handle, so I inserted my fingers in the gap be-tween the door and the frame and determined by a slight pres-sure that the toilet was locked from the inside. This could mean only one thing: Helena must be inside. I said quietly, "Helena, Helena." There was no reply; only the apple tree, stirring in the gentle breeze, rustled its branches against the shack's wooden wall.

I knew that the silence from the locked latrine meant the worst and that the only course was to rip the door off. I inserted my fingers again in the gap between doorframe and door and pulled with all my might. The door, fastened as it was by a mere piece of string instead of a hook (as is often the case in the country), gave at once and swung wide open. Opposite me on a wooden seat in the stench of the latrine sat Helena. She was pale but alive. She looked at me with stunned eyes and in-stinctively pulled at her turned-up skirt, which even with the greatest effort hardly came halfway down her thigh; she gripped the hem with both hands and closed her legs. "Go away, for God's sake!" she implored.

"What's the matter?" I shouted at her. "What have you taken?"

"Go away! Leave me alone!" she screamed.

At this point the boy appeared behind my back and He-lena shouted, "Go away, Jindra, go away!" She lifted herself off the wooden seat and hurled herself at me with desperate strength. She gripped me with both hands by the lapels of my jacket and pushed me out. "You beast!" she shouted (if you could call the frantic efforts of an enfeebled voice a shout). She tried to shake me once or twice, then she suddenly let go and started to run across the grass toward the gate. But her panties, the same black lacy ones whose acquaintance I'd made yesterday, were still twisted around her knees, so that after covering scarcely three yards on her high-heeled shoes she fell heavily on the sun-washed lawn, under the branch of a tree near the tall gaudy sunflowers. I took her by the hand and tried to help her up, but she tore away from me, and when I made a second attempt she started flailing wildly and I caught several blows before I was able to seize her with all my might, pull her to me, pick her up, and imprison her, using my arms as a straitjacket. "Beast, beast, beast!" she gasped as she pummeled me in the back with her free hand. And when I said, as gently as possible, "Quiet, Helena," she spat in my face.

I still didn't relax my grip, and I said, "I'm not letting you go until you tell me what you took."

"Go away, go away," she repeated frantically, but then she suddenly went quiet, ceased all resistance, and said, "Let me go!" in such a different voice, quietly and in a tone of such utter weariness, that I set her down and looked at her. With horror I saw her face lined with some terrible effort, her jaws clamped shut, her eyes unseeing, and her body crouching slightly and bending forward.

"What's the matter?" I asked. But she turned without a word and made her way back to the outhouse. I'll never forget the way she walked. It was only three or four yards, but more than once she broke off her strange, erratic progress, and in those pauses you could sense from the cramping of her body the struggle raging inside her. Finally she reached the latrine and pulled the door shut.

A plaintive moan came from within, and I recoiled a step or two. Then I realized for the first time that the boy was standing beside me. "Stay here," I told him. "I've got to get a doctor."

I went into the office; the telephone was standing on the

desk. Finding the telephone book was harder. I couldn't see it
in either room. Finally I opened a closet. There on a pile of
documents was a green telephone book for the Brno district. I
took it over to the telephone and thumbed through for the
hospital. I'd already dialed and heard the ringing when the
boy rushed into the room.

"Don't phone anyone—there's no need," he shouted.

I didn't see why.

He tore the receiver from my hand and put it back on the
hook. "There's no need, I tell you!" I asked him to explain
what was going on. "It's not poison at all," he said and went
over to the coatrack. He rummaged in the pockets of the
man's raincoat and took out a bottle which he opened and
turned upside down. It was empty.

"Is that what she took?" I asked.

He nodded.

"How do you know?"

"She told me."

"Is it yours?"

He nodded. I took it from him. It was an empty aspirin
bottle.

"Do you think aspirin is harmless in a massive dose like
that?" I shouted at him.

"There wasn't any aspirin in it," he said.

"What was there then?" I shouted.

"Laxatives," he snapped.

I ordered him to stop trying to make a fool of me, that I
must know what had actually happened and I wouldn't put up
with his insolence. I ordered him to give me a straight answer
immediately.

When he heard me shouting he started shouting back. "I've
told you. There *were* laxatives in it! Has the whole world got
to know there's something wrong with my guts?" I saw then
that what I'd taken for a tasteless joke was the truth.

I looked at his boyish face and snub nose, small but sufficiently large to accommodate a flock of freckles, and the mean-

ing of the whole thing became clear to me. The aspirin bottle was a disguise for his ludicrous ailment, just as his jeans and leather jacket were a disguise for his ludicrous features. In that moment I liked him; with his boyish bashfulness he'd saved Helena's life and saved me from several years of sleepless nights. With imbecile gratitude I looked at his projecting ears. Yes, he'd saved Helena's life; but at the expense of one more humiliation, a further absurdity in a whole chain of deeds for which there could be no atonement. Suddenly I felt an urgent, if unformulated, need to run after her, raise her up out of her agony, humiliate myself before her, assume all the blame and all the responsibility for the whole senselessly cruel incident.

"What are you staring at?" barked the boy. I didn't answer and walked past him toward the door into the yard.

"What are you going out there for?" He caught me from behind by the shoulder of my jacket and tried to pull me toward him. For a second we looked into each other's eyes; then I grabbed his wrist and detached his hand from my shoulder. He pushed past me and stood blocking my way. I went up to him and he punched me in the chest.

It was a feeble blow, but the boy jumped back and stood in front of me again in an amateurish boxer's stance. His expression was a mixture of apprehension and rash courage.

"She doesn't need you out there!" he shouted. I stayed where I was. I thought that maybe he was right, that there was no way for me to redress the irredressable. And the boy, seeing me standing there and not putting up any defense, went on shouting, "She hates you! She hates your guts! She said so! She hates your guts!"

Nervous tension makes one defenseless against tears, and also against laughter. The absurd poetic justice of the boy's reference to guts made the corners of my mouth twitch. This maddened him. This time he punched me in the mouth. Then he stood back and again put his fists up in front of his face in boxing style, so only his pink ears were visible projecting behind them.

I said, "Stop that. I'm going."

He shouted after me, "You bastard! You bastard! I know you had something to do with this! I'll get you. You son of a bitch!"

I went out into the street. By now it was empty. Only a gentle breeze raised the dust, driving it over the flat ground that was as vacant as my own stunned head . . .

It was only later that I suddenly found I had the empty aspirin bottle in my hand. I looked at it. It was covered with scratches and had evidently seen long service as a permanent disguise for the boy's laxatives.

Later still the bottle reminded me of two other bottles, the ones full of Alexej's sleeping tablets. Then I began to think that the boy hadn't really saved Helena's life after all. Even if it had been aspirin in the bottle, it could hardly have caused Helena more harm than a certain discomfort in the stomach, with the boy and myself so nearby. Helena's desperation had settled its account with life at a safe distance from the jaws of death.

JAROSLAV

She was standing in the kitchen over the stove. Standing with her back to me. As if there was nothing wrong. "Vladimir?" she replied, without turning. "You saw him yourself, didn't you? Why ask?"

"No," I said. "Vladimir went off this morning with Koutecky's grandson on his motorcycle. I've come to tell you that I know all about it. I know why you were pleased that silly journalist came this morning. I know why I wasn't supposed to be there for the robing of the King. I know why the King kept silent even before the Ride. It was all very carefully planned."

My certainty confused Vlasta. But she soon regained her presence of mind and tried to defend herself by attacking. It was a strange attack. Strange, because the protagonists were not face to face. She was standing with her back to me, her face turned toward the gurgling soup. Her voice wasn't raised.

It was almost indifferent. It was as if what she was saying was some ancient self-evident truth which only my eccentricity and lack of understanding obliged her to repeat. If I had to hear it, then this was it. From the beginning Vladimir hadn't wanted to be King. Vlasta wasn't surprised. There was a time when the boys used to manage the Rides of the Kings by themselves. Now everything was arranged from above. Before, they used to elect the King themselves; now they had Vladimir "suggested" to them from above to gratify his father, and everyone had to obey. Vladimir was ashamed of these special privileges. No one likes the specially privileged.

"Do you mean Vladimir is ashamed of me?"

"He doesn't want to seem different from his friends," Vlasta repeated.

"Is that why he makes friends with the Kouteckys? Those bourgeois? Those pretentious fools?" I asked.

"Yes, that's why," said Vlasta. "Milos isn't allowed to study just because of his grandfather. Just because his grandfather ran a building firm. Vladimir had his way paved with roses. Just because you're his father. Vladimir finds it hard to take. Can't you see?"

For the first time in my life I felt angry with her. They'd tricked me. All the time they'd been coolly observing my anticipation of the Ride. My sentimental, emotional anticipation. They'd calmly deceived me and watched me being deceived. "Was there really any need to trick me like that?"

Vlasta poured salt into the water for the noodles and said I made things difficult. I was living in another world. I was a dreamer. They didn't want to take my ideals from me, but Vladimir was a different person. He had no time for my singing and yodeling. I'd just have to get used to that. Vladimir was a modern person. He took after her father. Her father was always a great one for progress. He was the first farmer in the village to have a tractor before the war. Then he had everything taken from him. But from the time the fields belonged to the cooperative they'd never yielded half as much.

"I'm not interested in your fields. I want to know where Vladimir went. He went to the motorcycle races at Brno, didn't he? Admit it."

She had her back to me, stirring the noodles, and calmly went on talking. Vladimir took after his grandfather. He had his chin and eyes. Vladimir wasn't interested in the Ride of the Kings. Yes, if I had to know, he did go to the races. He went to watch the races. Why shouldn't he? He was more interested in motorcycles than in streamered horses. What of it? Vladimir was a modern person.

Motorcycles, guitars. A stupid, alien world. I asked, "Just tell me how you define a modern person."

She had her back to me, stirring the noodles, and said that even our apartment wasn't allowed to be furnished in a modern way. What a fuss I'd made about that contemporary lamp! I hadn't even liked the modern chandelier. And yet anyone could see that the new lamp was attractive. Lamps like that were being bought everywhere these days.

"Shut up," I said. But there was no stopping her. She was in full swing. With her back turned to me. Her small, cross, bony back. That was what irritated me most of all. Her back. The back without eyes. The back so smugly sure of itself. The back I couldn't come to terms with. I wanted to shut her up. Turn her around to face me. But I felt such distaste for her that I didn't even want to touch her. I'll make her turn around. I opened the cupboard and took out a plate. I dropped it on the floor. She was silent for a moment. But she didn't turn. Another plate, another, and yet another. She still had her back to me. Huddled up within herself. I could see from her back that she was afraid. Yes, she was afraid, but she was defiant and wouldn't give in. She stopped stirring and stood motionless, gripping the wooden spoon in her hand. She was hanging on to it like a refuge. I hated her and she hated me. She didn't move and I didn't take my eyes off her even as I smashed more and more china. I hated her and her kitchen. Her modern kitchen with its modern kitchen cabinet, modern plates, and modern glassware.

I felt no excitement. I looked calmly, sadly, almost wearily at the floor covered with shards of china, with pots and pans strewn over it. I was throwing my home on the floor. The home I'd loved and to which I'd fled from Brno. The home in which I'd felt the gentle domination of my pauper girl. The home I'd peopled with folktales, songs, and good fairies. Over there on those three chairs we used to sit down to our dinner. Those delicious dinners in which the stupid trusting breadwinner was bamboozled. I took one chair after another in my hand and snapped the legs off. I set the crippled chairs down on the floor with the pots and broken china. I turned the kitchen table upside down. Vlasta was still standing motionless by the stove with her back turned.

I went out of the kitchen into my own room. My room had red globes on the ceiling, a contemporary lamp, and a hideous modern couch. My violin lay in a black case on the harmonium. I picked it up. At four we had to play in the garden restaurant. It was still only one. Where could I go?

I heard sobbing from the kitchen. Vlasta was crying. It was a wracking, heart-rending sobbing, and somewhere deep inside me I felt a painful regret. Why hadn't she started crying ten minutes ago? I could have let myself be taken in by the old self-delusion and seen her as the little pauper girl again. Now it was too late.

I left the house. The invocations could be heard across the village roofs. *We have a pauper but righteous king.* Where could I go? The streets belonged to the Ride, home belonged to Vlasta, the taverns belonged to the drunks. Where do I belong? I am an old, deserted, ousted king. A righteous and beggared king. A king without heirs. The last king.

Luckily there are some fields out there beyond the village. There is a road. And ten minutes away is the river Morava. I lay down on the bank. I put the violin case under my head. I lay there for a long time. An hour, maybe two. And I thought of how I'd come to the end of the road. I couldn't imagine any continuation. I'd always lived in two worlds at once. I'd believed in their mutual harmony. It had been a delusion. Now I'd been ousted from one of them. From the real world. Only the make-believe one was left. But I cannot live only in a make-believe world. Even though I am expected there. Even though the deserter is calling for me and has a free horse for me and a red veil to cover my face. Now I knew! Now I understood why he forbade me to take off the scarf and wanted me to know only what he narrated to me! Now I understood why the King must have his face veiled! Not that he should not be seen, but that he should not see!

I couldn't imagine myself getting up and going. I couldn't imagine myself taking a single step. I was expected at four. But I wouldn't have the strength to get up and go. I like it here. Here by the river. Here there is water flowing. It flows slowly and I will lie here long.

Then someone spoke to me. It was Ludvik. I expected another blow. But I wasn't afraid anymore. Nothing could shake me now.

He sat down and asked if I'd be at the performance that afternoon.

"You're not going?" I asked him.

"I am."

"Is that why you came?"

"No, that's not what I came for. But things turn out different from the way we expect."

"Yes," I said, "completely different."

"I've been wandering around the fields for an hour. I didn't expect to find you here."

"Nor did I."

"I've something to ask you," he said without looking me in the eye. Just like Vlasta. But I didn't mind it from him. I liked it from him when he didn't look me in the eye. I could see his

shiftiness was only reserve. And the shyness warmed and comforted me.

"I want to ask you," he said, "whether you might let me sit
in with the band this afternoon."

LUDVIK

There were still a few hours left before the next bus was due
to leave, so I set out, driven by the disquiet within me, from the
village and into the fields, trying as I went to drive from my
mind all thoughts of that miserable day. It was far from simple.
I felt my lip itch where it had been injured by the boy's fist,
and again the shadow of Lucie emerged to remind me that
every attempt to redress my wrongs had ended with my wrong-
ing others. I tried to keep my mind blank and to admit into it
only the distant calls of the horsemen that carried me away
somewhere beyond my own troubles and offered me relief.

I reached the bank of the Morava and set off along it downstream. Then in the distance ahead of me I saw a figure lying
on the grass. As I got nearer I recognized him; he was lying on
his back with his face turned to the heavens, and under his
head he had a violin case. Nothing would have been easier than
to avoid him. But on this occasion I didn't want to avoid him,
I preferred to avoid myself and the thoughts thrusting in on
me, and so I went up and spoke to him. He looked up at me,
and his eyes struck me as timid and apprehensive. This was the
first time I'd seen him at close range for a number of years,
and I noticed that only a sparse fringe remained of the thick
hair that had once added a good couple of inches to his lofty
stature, and that on the crown of his head there were only a
few sad strands covering the bare scalp. His lost hair reminded
me of the long years in which I hadn't seen him, and I suddenly regretted those years, when I'd avoided him (the calls of
the horsemen came, scarcely audible, from the distance) and
felt an overwhelming, guilty love for him. He lay before me,

resting on his elbow, and was big and clumsy while the violin case was small and black like a baby's coffin. I knew that his band—what was once *my* band—would be playing that afternoon in the village, and I asked him if I might be allowed to join them.

I made this request before I'd had time to think it out fully, but it was completely in accord with the way I felt. At that moment I was filled with a sorrowful love for this world I'd abandoned years ago, in which horsemen ride around the village with a masked king, in which people walk around in white frilled shirts and sing songs, a world that for me is merged with the images of my hometown and of my mother (my poor mother stolen and hidden from me) and of my youth. All day long that love had been quietly growing inside me, and now it had burst out almost tearfully; I loved that lost world and begged it to offer me sanctuary.

But how and with what justification? Hadn't I avoided Jaroslav two days ago precisely because his appearance evoked the hateful music of the folk song? Hadn't I that very morning regarded the folk festival with distaste? What had suddenly destroyed the old barriers which for fifteen years had stopped me from looking back with happy memories on my youth spent in the cymbalo band, stopped me from returning to my hometown with affection? Could it be because a few hours ago Zemanek had sneered at the Ride of the Kings? Was he perhaps the one who'd made me dislike folk song and had now cleansed me again of this dislike? Was I really in such degrading dependence on him? No, it was not just Zemanek's mockery that had made it possible for me to regain my love for the world of folk costumes, songs, and cymbalo bands. I could love it because this morning I'd witnessed it, unexpectedly, in its misery and abandonment—abandoned by the showmen and publicists, by the political propagandists, by the architects of social Utopias, by the swarms of cultural officials, abandoned even by Zemanek. Its abandonment had purified it, illuminated it with some irresistible ultimate beauty—its abandonment had given it back to me.

The performance was to take place in the same open-air restaurant in which I'd recently dined and where I'd read Helena's letter. When Jaroslav and I arrived there were already a few elderly people waiting patiently and almost an equal number of drunks tottering from table to table. At the back, around the wide-branching linden, were a few chairs. A double bass leaned against the tree trunk in its gray shroud, and not far from it a man in a white frilled shirt was sitting at the cymbalo, quietly running the hammers over the strings. The other members of the band stood a few feet away, and Jaroslav introduced them to me. The second fiddle, a tall, dark young man in folk costume, was a doctor from the local hospital; the bespectacled bass player was the educational inspector for the local district council; the clarinetist, who'd agreed to lend me his clarinet and to alternate with me, was a schoolmaster; the cymbalo player, the only one apart from Jaroslav whom I remembered, was a draftsman from the factory. Jaroslav ceremoniously presented me as a founding member of the group and a most presentable clarinet player, and we sat on the chairs around the linden tree and started playing.

I hadn't held a clarinet in my hands for a long time, but I knew the first song well and soon lost my initial reserve, especially when the others voiced their approval at the end of the song and wouldn't believe I hadn't played for such a long time. After one of the songs I nodded to the schoolmaster; he took the clarinet from me and said again that my playing was excellent. I was delighted and leaned up against the tree trunk, and while I watched the band, now playing without me, a long-forgotten feeling of warm companionship washed over me and I was thankful for its return at the end of this bitter day.

And now again Lucie emerged before my eyes, and I thought I finally knew why she'd appeared to me at the barbershop, and then next day in Kostka's account of her, which had been at once both truth and legend. Perhaps she'd wanted to tell me that her destiny—that of the corrupted young girl—was close to mine, that although we hadn't found understanding, our lifelines were linked, because they were both stories of *devastation:* just as physical love had been devastated for Lucie, depriving her life of its most elementary value, so my life had been robbed of values which were in origin pure and innocent —yes, innocent. Physical love, however much degraded in Lucie's bitter experience, is still an innocent thing, just as the songs of this region of mine were and are innocent, just as the cymbalo band is innocent, just as my home, which I'd despised, was innocent, just as the word *Comrade,* though it had a menacing ring for me, was as innocent as the word *you* and the word *future* and many other words. The blame lay elsewhere and was so great that its shadow had fallen far and wide on the whole world of innocent things (and words) and had devastated them. We lived, Lucie and I, in a blighted world; and because we didn't know how to show regret for things that had been blighted we turned away from them and in this way injured them and ourselves as well. Lucie, little girl who has known so much love, so much bad love, is this what you have come from across the years to tell me? Have you come to intercede for the world of devastation?

The song came to an end and the schoolmaster handed me the clarinet, saying he'd play no more today, as I played better than he did and deserved to play all the more since nobody knew when I'd come again. I caught Jaroslav's eye and said I'd be very glad for a chance to come back and see them as soon as I could. Jaroslav asked me if I really meant it. I said I did and we started playing. Jaroslav had long since abandoned his chair and was standing with his head bent, his violin leaning down his chest against all the rules, and walking around as he played. The second fiddle and I also stood up every now and then. In those moments when we plunged into adventurous improvisations—improvisations demanding inventiveness, precision, and total rapport—Jaroslav became the life and soul of us all, and I was amazed at what a good musician he was, belonging as he did (he especially) to the devastated region of my life. He had been taken from me, and I, to my detriment and shame, had allowed it to happen, although he'd been perhaps my most faithful, selfless, and innocent friend.

Meanwhile the character of the audience gathered in the garden was slowly being transformed. To the handful of mostly elderly people who had initially followed our playing with warm interest was now added a growing crowd of youngsters from the village or more probably the town, who occupied the remaining tables, ordered beer and wine, and very soon, as their alcohol level rose, began demonstrating their exuberant need to be seen, heard, and recognized. The atmosphere became noisier and more nervous—the youths were staggering from table to table, shouting at each other and at their girls—until I caught myself ceasing to concentrate on the music and watching the adolescent faces with an undisguised hatred. When I saw those long-haired, pimply kids strutting theatrically for their girls, my old resentment of adolescence flooded back until it seemed to me that all I could see was actors, masked to represent ostentatious virility, arrogant ruthlessness, and brutishness. I could see no mitigating circumstance in the existence under the masks of other, more human faces. Indeed, the real horror of the thing lay in the fact that the faces beneath were themselves fiercely devoted to the inhumanity and vulgarity of the masks.

Jaroslav evidently felt the same, for he suddenly put up his violin and said that he was in no mood to play for this kind of audience. He suggested, since it was a warm, star-lit evening, that we leave, make our way to a briar bush somewhere in the fields, and play just for ourselves—for our own pleasure—as we used to do. We'd got into the stupid habit of playing only on formal occasions, and Jaroslav had had enough of it.

At first the others all agreed enthusiastically, but then the bass player (the school inspector) reminded us that we'd agreed to play until nine, that we had to go through with it once we'd promised, and that we could play in the open air another time.

At that moment the lamps that were hanging on long wires stretched from tree to tree all came on. Since it was barely dusk, they spread no light around them but just hung there in the graying arena like big motionless tears, glimmering tears that cannot be checked and mustn't be allowed to fall. Jaroslav repeated almost imploringly that he didn't want to stay here, that he wanted to go out into the fields, to the briar bush, and just play there for his own pleasure. But then he made a gesture of resignation, pressed the violin to his chest, and began to play.

This time we didn't allow ourselves to be distracted by our audience but played with an even greater concentration than before. The more indifferent and rude the atmosphere and the more depressed we felt, the more we turned inward to each other, playing more for ourselves than for the audience, so that we managed to forget the noisy drunks and to create a magic circle of music, with us inside it.

"If the mountains were made of paper and the water of ink, if the stars were scribes, they could not write the whole testament of my love," sang Jaroslav without taking the violin from under his chin. And I felt myself happy inside these songs, in which sorrow isn't a jest, laughter isn't mocking, love isn't ridiculous, and hatred is unrestrained, where people love with body and soul (yes, Lucie, with body as well as soul!), where in hatred men reach for knife or sword, where in joy they dance, in despair leap into the Danube, where love is still love and pain is pain, where primal emotion has not yet been distorted and where values are not yet blighted. It seemed to me that among these songs I was at home, that this was where I came from, my home, a home I'd betrayed but which was more truly my home because of it—for the home we have wronged has all the more compelling a voice. But then I realized that my home was not of this world, that what we were singing and playing was only memories, recollections, a re-creation of something

that no longer was. And I felt the firm ground of this home of mine sinking under my feet, felt myself falling, my clarinet in my mouth, down into the depths of years, the depths of centuries, those peerless depths where love is love and pain is pain. I told myself with astonishment that my only home was this very falling, this searching, longing fall, and I abandoned myself to it and felt its delicious vertigo.

Then I looked at Jaroslav to see whether I was alone in my exaltation, and I noticed that he was very pale. He'd stopped singing, his lips were tightly clenched, his startled eyes had become more anxious still, he was playing wrong notes, and his violin hand was slowly slipping downward. Suddenly he stopped playing and sat down. I knelt beside him. "What's wrong?" I asked. Sweat streamed down his face and he was holding his left arm near the shoulder. "It hurts," he said. The others hadn't realized that Jaroslav was ill and were still caught up in the spell of their own music. The gaps left by the first violin and clarinet gave the cymbalo player a chance to cut loose, accompanied now only by second fiddle and bass. Remembering the second fiddle was a doctor, I called him over. He took Jaroslav's left wrist and held it for what seemed an age; then he lifted up his eyelids and looked at his eyes; then he touched his sweating forehead. "Heart?" he asked. "Arm and heart," said Jaroslav, who looked green. By now the bass player had noticed us; he leaned his bass against the linden tree and came over, so the cymbalo player was all on his own now, completely unaware of what was going on and thoroughly enjoying his solo.

"I'll phone the hospital," said the second fiddle.

"What is it?"

"Pulse very slight. Cold sweat. It must be a thrombosis."

"God," I said.

"Don't worry, he'll get over it," he consoled me and hurried toward the restaurant. He was held up by people who were by now quite drunk and had noticed nothing, being totally self-absorbed, intent on their beers, their boasts, and their insults, which in the far corner of the garden had even led to blows.

Now the cymbalo fell silent too, and we all stood around Jaroslav, who looked at me and said it was all because we'd stayed there, that he hadn't wanted to stay, he'd wanted to go out into the fields, especially when I came, especially when I came back to them, that we could have played beautifully out in the open. "Don't try to talk," I told him. "You need complete rest." I was thinking of how, although he probably would recover as the second fiddle had predicted, it would be a completely different life, a life without passionate devotion, without the ecstatic playing in the band, a life under the watchful eye of death. And I suddenly had the feeling that one's destiny is often completed long before death, and that Jaroslav's destiny was now fulfilled. Overwhelmed with grief, I gently rubbed the top of his bald head, where the sad long hairs covered the baldness, and I realized with a shock that my trip home, made in the hope of revenge on the hated Zemanek, had ended with my holding my stricken friend in my arms. Yes, in that moment I could see myself holding him in my arms, holding him and carrying him, big and heavy as he was—as if I were carrying my own heavy guilt—carrying him through the indifferent mob and weeping as I went.

We had stood around him like this for about ten minutes when the second fiddle reappeared and signaled us to help Jaroslav to his feet, and we slowly supported him through the noisy, drunken adolescents into the street where the ambulance was waiting with its headlights burning.